D1048398

Matteson:

Judas Owl

Scott Arnold

Matteson: The Judas Owl

Copyright © 2021 Scott Arnold

All rights reserved.

Farne Press

ISBN 978-1-7337524-7-3

Arnold, Scott.

Matteson: Judas Owl—1st edition

1. Fiction-Thrillers-Espionage 2. Fiction-Crime

United States of America

No parts of this publication may be reproduced, stored in a retrieval system, or transmitted in any form or by any means, electronic, mechanical, photocopying, recording, or otherwise, without the prior written permission of the copyright owner.

This book is sold subject to the condition that it shall not, by way of trade or otherwise, be lent, resold, hired out, or otherwise circulated without the publisher's prior consent in any form of binding or cover other than that in which it is published and without a similar condition including this condition being imposed on the subsequent purchaser. Under no circumstances may any part of this book be photocopied for resale.

This is a work of fiction. Any similarity between the characters and situations within its pages and places or persons, living or dead, is unintentional and co-incidental.

Cover: Warren Design
Interior Design: Jim Brown
Editor: Peggy J. Shaw

Dedicated to:

My brother Wayne, whose courage and tenacity have always been an inspiration.

Other Novels by Scott Arnold:

<u>Father Flenn Adventures:</u>
Uncommon Prayer
Rites of Revenge
The Poisoned Chalice
Shadow of the Saint

<u>Zack Matteson Adventures:</u>
Judas Owl
Matteson: The Backfire Effect

All titles published by Farne Press

Matteson:

Judas Owl

Pendo ni kitu cha hiari.

Love is out of choice.
—Swahili

Archer's Post, Kenya; Mid-Morning Yesterday

Clouds were sparse in the Kenyan sky but mourners even more so as three men lowered a simple wooden casket into the ground. Aside from the Anglican minister and the men with shovels at their feet, Zack Matteson was one of only two other men standing amongst a half-dozen women gathered on the lonely hill in the chill of the morning air. The women formed a choir of sorts, having arrived shortly after the pastor. They had sung only two songs, both off-key. As for the other man standing behind Zack—an old man, short of stature, and wearing a white suit—Zack had recognized him immediately, even after all these years.

It's not easy to forget someone who'd once tried to kill you.

"Even in the midst of life, we are in death…" the clergyman read from the pages of his worn prayer book. It sounded like the sardonic slogans trainees used to stick on the walls of the classrooms at Langley a quarter of a century ago, most of which had been removed and replaced by his CIA instructors many times before the instructors had given up and just let them remain.

The minister read a passage from Scripture and then concluded the brief service… "ashes to ashes, dust to dust…" Zack surveyed the small crowd on the hilltop and thought Samuel Kauxhohuena deserved more. He wondered about the women, whether they too had come from the local parish or if they'd had some other connection to his friend once upon a time. He doubted any of them knew the truth about the man in the box below, or if they had even called him by the same name; Samuel had used so many over the years.

Zack couldn't help but grin. He wondered what stories

Samuel might have amused himself with in talking to these women. Could they be anything like some of the whoppers Samuel had told his adversaries so long ago?

The service ended, and the women turned, each heading down the hill toward the road below. The minister also left leaving only the two white men and the men with the shovels. "It's hard to believe, isn't it, Sergei?" Zack said, without turning to address the man behind him.

"I am surprised he lived this long. You know, I could easily have been the one who killed him," answered the man, without the faintest hint of emotion in his voice. "Alas, the fates weren't obliging that day."

"You seem to have lost your accent. I suppose living abroad will do that to a person." Zack turned. "I've kept track."

"And you seem to have lost your insatiable curiosity, my old friend. You have yet to ask me why I am here."

Zack took stock of the small man with only a few wisps of thinning gray hair remaining atop his head. Sergei had once boasted a scalp of platinum blond. "I assume it was to find out if the rumors were true. Is the Judas Owl really dead? I trust it is not to try a second time to kill me?"

"The fates were unkind to us both that day, I think," the older man said, offering Zack a wan smile in return. "Do you remember?"

Unfortunately, Zack Matteson had never been able to forget. "Unkind? No, I never regretted what Sam and I did."

The Russian shrugged. "You look well, Matteson. Hardly a gray strand in that sea of black—and you appear even more muscular than you did two decades ago. How is that possible?"

Zack didn't allow himself to mirror Sergei's smile. Some courtesies didn't deserve to be returned. "Clean living. Maybe you should try it, Sergei."

"Ah, but I have little other choice these days. I am nearly

80 now. Life does not allow much joy to men my age. The women no longer flock to my side, and the vodka has left a hole in my stomach lining." He gestured to himself with both his hands in a sweeping motion. "I'm afraid that I am not the man you once knew."

"I suppose that's something to be thankful for."

The Russian shrugged. "You, on the other hand, have not changed that much since the last time we met. Still working tirelessly for the CIA, no?"

Zack didn't answer. There was no need. Sergei already knew the answer to any question he might ask. He, too, would have been keeping track. "And you? Who's pulling your strings now?"

The older man raised an eyebrow. "Always the same with you, eh, Mr. Matteson? I must admit that I am surprised they sent you."

"No one sent me. I simply came to honor a man who has helped the good guys out too many times to be counted."

"So, you are here to pay your respects to the Judas Owl?" Sergei's jaw tightened ever so slightly. "So pay them. I, on the other hand, must try and catch up with one of those beautiful women."

"I thought you said that those days were behind you?"

Sergei laughed. "Indeed. But one of them is my driver, and I do not wish to keep her waiting."

"Then you aren't here to try one last time to locate the object?"

"We both know where it is. I only hope generations from now no one will come across that damned thing."

Zack raised an eyebrow. "You surprise me, Sergei."

"I shouldn't. I told you before that my only goal was to prevent the genie from being unleashed from the bottle." The old man sighed. "I am the last one left in my organization. We disbanded after what happened in England. At least, after I told them it was hopeless. Only you and I and the Judas Owl knew the whole truth."

"So, you finally accepted it?"

"What else was there for me to do?" The Russian coughed long and hard. "The doctors give me six months, but I do not think it will be that long." He stared directly into Zack's eyes. "The responsibility now falls upon you. I trust you will let the knowledge of this matter die with you one day as I will." Sergei scratched his forehead with the tip of a wizened forefinger. "The Owl and his father were wise to guard their secret from us. Who knows what my superiors' actual motives were. And you… ha, you were too impulsive in those days. If it had been left up to you then you would have simply given the object to your people at Langley."

He sighed ever so slightly, as if the effort was painful. "You may not believe this, but I came only to ask you to take what you know to the grave." Sergei cocked his head to one side.

"So, you assumed that I would be here."

"Of course. Just as you assumed that I would be here, no? And that I would bring…it?"

Zack looked away.

The old man shook his head. "You are more like your younger self than you thought, Mr. Matteson." He sighed. "Still, I trust we will never see one another again. I doubt that either of us will find that disagreeable." With that, the Russian made his way down the path leading to the roadside and the parked cars.

Zack turned to the grave and watched as the earth was shoveled back into place. Samuel had owned this hill, and all the land around it, as far as the eye could see. He had picked this particular spot to be buried; it was a special place, a place he had brought Zack to once long ago. Not being a religious man, Zack hadn't come to participate in a ceremony, nor to reminisce about the man whose enemies had dubbed him "the Judas Owl." No, he'd come because he knew Sergei would come. Sergei would not leave the gates of hell open for another to stumble upon. He would not want the object to fall, as only cheap novels and Zack Matteson would say, "into the wrong hands." Zack reached into his pocket and pulled out a handful of loose jellybeans before walking over to where Sergei had been standing. He dusted the candy off before popping them into his mouth, dropping the licorice ones onto the ground. He looked down to find what he knew would be there. It was on the ground where Sergei had dropped the object and then covered it with his foot so no one would notice.

Zack bent down and scooped it up. Then he stared at the ancient key and sighed. The box it opened was safe—a relic of the past... a most dangerous relic. Sergei had kept the key all these years but Zack was glad that the Russian had never again searched for what this key had once opened. If he had, it might very well be a different world. The return of the key was symbolic mostly. Something only these two men would understand... now that Samuel was gone. Despite the Russian's arguments to the contrary, Zack never bought that Sergei was working independently from the Russian government.

He watched as the old man in the white suit ambled down the hill, never once looking back. Perhaps it was true that every man has a conscious. If so, in the end, Sergei had not betrayed his own.

Zack gazed down at the grave as the men shoveled the hole with dirt. He tossed the key on top of the casket. It was time to lay to rest the last dangerous remnant of the second world war... one that could have easily become the catalyst for a third.

CHAPTER One

10 miles south of Eritrea, East Africa; June 1941

Sturmbannführer Hans Kreps rarely donned a smile for anyone, much less his two manservants, Osmann and Kifo. But today was different, today the little man had something to smile about. His experiment had worked! Up until now, he had not told anyone what he'd been working on in his jungle laboratory. If the war had not interrupted a promising career, he would still be teaching chemistry at Munich's Technische Universität. Fortunately, the fates had better things in store. Now, with this discovery he would be destined for nothing short of greatness. Soon, he'd let Berlin know. It would be a turning point; the war would be over in months, not years, and his place in the annals of the Third Reich would be guaranteed. Only the Führer himself would be held in higher esteem.

The stench of death circled the white SS officer and his Black servants as they stepped over the bodies of dead villagers—men, women, children—all with the same look of surprise forever plastered on their faces. "Do you know what this means, Osmann? Kifo? Of course you don't. How could you? You're too stupid to know. I'll tell you what it means. It means that I will be

the Führer's favorite son. *Generalfeldmarschall* Kreps...
how does that sound to you?"

The mousy man with the short mustache didn't wait
for an answer as he thrust out his chest and stood as tall
as his miniscule frame would allow. "All the world will
one day sing my name!"

Although the nerve agent had dissipated within
hours, anyone who'd gotten even the slightest whiff of
Kreps poison gas would have died instantly. Still, Kreps
had worn a gas mask today just to be certain. No such
protection had been offered Osmann nor his younger
brother, Kifo.

Sturmbannführer Kreps held his Luger at the ready,
just in case the nerve agent had missed someone. It
hadn't. The three dozen residents of the remote village
had all died within seconds after someone had stepped
on the glass vial he had ordered Kifo to place next to the
village well three days ago. Kifo had been told to
carefully hide it under a straw mat next to where the
water bucket was kept. He hadn't been told the reason
why, nor had it been his place to ask. Other conscripts
had been shot for questioning Kreps.

For his part, Osmann stared in disbelief at the bodies
at his feet. Kifo had only this morning told him what
Kreps had ordered him to do.

Kreps had yet to name his discovery. He wouldn't
presume to do so, but neither would he allow some
bumbling general take credit for it either. Command had
stuck him in charge of an SS contingency here in the
middle of nowhere to prevent the Italians from gaining
all the glory in recruiting and training African troops in

the days leading up to the war. However, there had been little to do except swat mosquitoes and drink schnapps in this God-forsaken place. So, Kreps had established a laboratory for his own amusement, experimenting with a variety of unknown plants and barks from the region.

He had been told by a tribal chieftain to avoid the blossom of one particular plant. *Devil's Heart* the villagers called it.

At the height of the flower's maturation, a thick, brown, oily substance oozed from its pedals. Their ancestors had found that when they coated their arrows with the oil from the flower that their prey died almost instantly, even from what would have been a non-lethal shot. Even the aroma could make one severely nauseous.

The story of the flower intrigued him, so Kreps had spent the past year examining its properties and secretly experimenting with it on nearby children. Once he found a way to remove the odor, he'd discovered that even the slightest amount of the oil added to a bowl of rice could be lethal. But ingesting poison was not practical as a weapon of mass destruction, so, Kreps had worked for months to find a way to convert Devil's Heart into a gaseous state. He had told no one of what he was working on, allowing only his black servants to assist him. Four men had already died from exposure to the element. Only Osmann and Kifo had survived working so closely with Kreps.

"Here, hold this," Kreps told Osmann as he handed the Luger to his servant and bent down to examine the body of a teenaged boy. "Look at this, Kifo," he said. "Osmann, pay attention!" The older brother was holding back, sickened by the sight of so much death. "Notice how the flesh has turned red around the lips and the nose, but not the eyes. There is a reason for that. It's called…" he stopped explaining. *What was the use, these two were of an inferior race; they couldn't possibly understand.* "Never mind. We need to get back to our village and to my laboratory."

The lab was where he kept a metal box with the vials of deadly poison. Kreps had made certain the servants both knew that the box had been rigged with a tiny charge that would detonate should anyone ever attempt to open it without the key. "Let us hurry; I want to find out what a gram of this would do to a larger population." He thought for a second, still kneeling next to the boy's body. "No, a gram would be too large. Perhaps 250 milligrams would be sufficient," he thought aloud, stroking the stubble on his chin. "The children would all die immediately, of course," he mused to himself. "But how many in the adult population?"

He stood slowly, grunting as his knees complained. "Questions best suited for the lab, not for here."

He turned to see the Black, shirtless man pointing the pistol at him. Kreps rolled his eyes. "No, no, Osmann, that is not how you hold a weapon. Give it to me."

The look of shock on Krep's face surpassed even Kifo's as Osmann fired twice into the neck and chest of the Nazi monster.

CHAPTER Two

May in the Horn of Africa was hotter than hell. Zack Matteson kicked a rock against the skull of some poor animal who had also foolishly found itself out here in the blazing sun in the middle of nowhere. How his partner, Scott Flenn, had managed to get himself assigned to a cushy two months in Iceland while he was sweltering in this God-forsaken desert was beyond comprehension.

Zack wiped the sweat from his forehead as he peered into the sky. *Still no sign of that blasted helicopter!*

"Perhaps you should have remained at Camp Lemonnier, *eh* Matteson? You Americans have no tolerance for the desert."

"Where the hell is Captain Tomlinson? He was supposed to be here an hour ago."

"No tolerance *and* no patience."

Zack continued to search the sky. "Yeah right, Kwame. You were the one who said this was the spot… remember?"

The tall, dark-skinned man, who was all legs, frowned. "It is."

"What the hell are you talking about? Look around; nothing's been here for ages except for that unfortunate creature."

"It's a dog."

Zack shook his head. "Now, how do you know that? Oh yeah, I forgot, you're the man who knows *everything*." Zack had been working with his African equivalent for the past month, long enough for each to get a feel for the other. "The diamonds will be there, Matteson. Trust me."

Zack kicked the rock again. "Yeah, well look where that got us!"

"I'm telling you, they stopped here to camp during each run. If the CIA had moved faster, we could have been here two weeks ago and found the smugglers on their last trip to Addis Ababa. You would have gotten your photographs and we could have followed them to their contacts. Instead, you sat on your fat *vifungo* until they got away."

Zack didn't know what a vifungo was, although he had a good idea. *Only compared to this beanpole could he ever be considered fat.* "You told me that they were coming back today. You said that they always come here… that this is where they camp."

"It is."

Zack looked around. There was nothing but sand for miles. "We walked all night to find nothing. Look around you, there's not even the faintest tire tracks anywhere. You must have gotten the coordinates wrong. Probably why the captain is missing. Maybe Tomlinson is looking for us wherever the hell it is we are *supposed* to be."

Kwame shrugged. "I do not know where the helicopter is, but *this* is where the runners always spend the night. They may be out there somewhere even now, their truck covered in netting."

"And to think I left an uncomfortable cot in a Quonset hut to wander the desert with you," the muscular agent with jet-black hair groused. "This is nothing but a gigantic litter box. What a waste of time."

Kwame Muriuki lifted his binoculars and scanned the horizon. "Do you complain this much on every assignment, Matteson?"

Zack removed his hat and used it to wipe the sweat from his face and forearms. "It's the damned sun, Kwame; that's what it is. You've gone stark, raving mad. Just admit it, you're lost. Nothing other than that poor unfortunate mutt has been here for years."

Zack stared at the skull. "How the hell it got here is beyond me, but I suspect we may end up in the same boat if Tomlinson doesn't arrive soon."

Kwame shook his head. "I was told you understood the desert, that you and your partner were trained in the Middle East."

"We were, but Scott Flenn and I didn't just sit out in the middle of a sandbox and fry our brains into mush."

Kwame laughed. Zack shook his head. *The damn fool actually thinks this is funny!* Zack was a man of action and he hated following a dead end. "At least Flenn and I always knew where we were going. There's nothing I despise more than a wild goose chase."

Kwame looked up. "There are no geese here."

Zack, whose use of tired idioms was endless, rolled his eyes. "Come on Kwame, admit it. We're lost."

"I am telling you that this is the place."

The American gestured with both arms in frustration. "How can it be?"

"Matteson, you come from a land where everything stays the same. Trees, grass, shrubbery. Look around you—there is no shrubbery here."

"There's nothing here except that skull!"

"Precisely. That skull is what tells me that we are in the right spot. If you dig deeper, you will likely find the rest of the bones."

"Next you're going to tell me the diamond runners *ate* the damn thing the last time they were here."

Kwame nodded. "At last, you begin to understand."

Zack didn't conceal his disgust. "I've got a good mind to order Tomlinson to leave you out here... if he ever finds us, that is."

"Matteson, what is that under your feet?"

Startled, Zack looked down, relieved not to find a scorpion about to strike. "There's nothing there but sand."

"Precisely. Unlike your trees, grass and shrubbery, our sand is constantly moving. Nothing remains the same from one day to the next. Sometimes entire camps are buried or blown away by a sandstorm." He gazed into the distance. "This was indeed the place where they have been stopping to camp. I marked it on my GPS the last three times I accompanied them here. They say this spot has good juju. Smugglers are superstitious; what works for them once is considered to be lucky. They won't change from it."

"You could have saved us both a lot of trouble if you'd just gotten the photographs yourself."

Kwame made a sound that sounded like the grunts emitted by a retriever owned by Zack's father; the dog was a noisy sleeper. "What was I supposed to do, walk up to them and ask them to pose for the camera? My throat would have been slit in so many places it would look like a checkerboard. No, sometimes they do not even tell me their names, only hire me to drive the truck... to *this* spot."

"So, why didn't you drive them this time?"

Kwame shrugged. "They asked me."

"And you refused? Why?"

"Actually, I told them that I'm with Kenyan intelligence and presently working with the CIA." It was Kwame's turn to roll his eyes. "What do you think I did? I told them that I was sick in order to lead *you* here."

Zack reached in his pocket for what was left of the small bag of jellybeans he'd brought with him. He had given up smoking years ago and reached for a jellybean every time he wanted a cigarette.

"My stars, man, what the hell is that?"

They both stared at the melted multicolored concoction of gelatinous goo. Zack made a face before tossing the bag as far as he could. "Okay, if this *is* the spot, then we're obviously too late," he said, licking his lips from thirst. "When will there be another run?"

"Not for another month. We will just have to go back to Camp Lemonnier and wait."

Zack tugged at his collar. "You're kidding me, right?"

Kwame grinned. "Welcome to Africa."

Zack glared at him. "You mean this was all for nothing? First, we drop 10 feet out of a perfectly good helicopter because the pilot won't set down in this crap, then I walk six miles across the icy cold desert at night with only you for company and worrying about scorpions crawling into my boots…"

Kwame interrupted, squatting to conserve energy. "A month will go by quickly."

"I don't plan on being here a month! This is a temporary assignment. *Sheesh*, what a waste of time."

Kwame sighed. "I was told that your partner is much nicer. Why didn't the CIA send him instead of you?"

Zack looked up to search the sky. "That's exactly what I'd like to know. He's up there in Reykjavík taking steam baths with some Icelandic blonde, and I'm down here following a walking toothpick to God knows where."

The African cocked his head. "And so I ask again: Do you always complain this much?"

Zack sat down a few feet away. "Ask Flenn."

"Who?"

"My partner."

"*Ahh*, yes, the one in Iceland."

"If I didn't know better I'd swear he used some of his daddy's money to get him a vacation in paradise."

"Iceland is a paradise?"

"Compared to this oven it is."

Kwame scratched his chin as much for something to do as to cure an itch. "So, this Flenn… his father is a rich man?"

"Loaded. Owns a huge conglomerate in the States. Zack knew he could trust this man; after all, Kwame had worked for Kenyan intelligence, as well as the Djibouti

Armed Forces, gathering intel for years. From what Zack had discovered, Kwame was one of the best indigenous spies around. Still, he did not mention Flenn Industries by name. If Kwame was as good as Zack figured, he probably knew anyway. A good spy always checked things out before working with a new partner. For instance, Zack knew that Kwame was unmarried, possibly gay, was an excellent marksman, and had infiltrated over a dozen drug, diamond, and human-trafficking rings in the last year alone. No telling what Kwame knew about him. There really wasn't all that much to know outside his job. Zack was married with a young daughter and another on the way but seldom home long enough to become much more than a career spy.

Zack reached for his empty canteen to see if he could possibly coax a few drops out of it. *Nothing.*

"Here, take mine."

Zack looked away. "I told you before that I will not take another man's water."

Kwame shrugged again. "Suit yourself," he said before taking a tiny sip and replacing the cap. "You shouldn't have gone through your water so quickly."

"I was thirsty, okay? Is that *all* you're going to drink?"

"In the desert you must pace yourself, Matteson. I would think that you would know this. If you try and satisfy your thirst all at once, you will have nothing left." He glanced at Zack's canteen. "*Ahh*, but you have already discovered this, no?"

Zack stood and stomped off, at least as much as one

can stomp in a desert. "Do you always have this much trouble working with others," Kwame said, "or is it just with Africans?"

"Don't flatter yourself." The truth was that Zack Matteson seldom got along with anyone, except for Scott Flenn. His partner was his only real friend. If the truth were known, he felt closer to Flenn than to his own wife, Donna.

Zack found the skull again and kicked it in frustration. Instantly, the largest scorpion he'd ever seen emerged through its mouth and headed straight for him, intent on having revenge at losing its shade. It would have been comical to see the muscular American jump as fast as he did had Kwame not known that the creature was deadly.

Thwack!

The razor-sharp knife speared the scorpion through the middle, slicing it neatly in half. Zack stared at the scorpion and then at Kwame.

"A thank you would be appropriate."

"What?" said Zack. "For killing a bug?"

Kwame sighed. "You, my friend, are what we call a *kinuka mkundu.*"

"If that means someone who isn't afraid of bugs, then yeah, that's me."

Kwame chuckled. "I saw how you jumped like a little girl," he said. "Toss me my kisu."

"Your what?"

"My knife." Kwame shook his head. "You come thousands of miles to Africa and yet you do not speak the least bit of Swahili, how is this possible?"

Zack pulled the knife from out of the scorpion, checking first to make certain the creature wasn't moving. *Who knew if this scorpion had some juju of its own.* "I'm trained in Arabic mostly, some Farsi, Russian of course, and a bit of Polish... but Swahili? No." He sat down next to Kwame and returned the knife before glancing at the great expanse of white nothingness encompassing them. "Why would I? Nobody comes here."

"Yet here you are, along with 6,000 of your American soldiers."

"Yeah, well, chances are that most of them at the airfield in Djibouti don't speak Swahili either. They're here for eighteen months and then shipped off somewhere else. Here today, gone tomorrow."

The tall man stood and stretched. "Well, perhaps I will have to teach you since it looks as if you are going to be here for a long time."

"Like hell. My wife's pregnant. I'm going home in a... "

Kwame jumped to his feet. "Stand up!"

"What?"

"Stand up, unless you want to take a chance that the helicopter will miss us."

Zack searched the cloudless sky as the sun beat down on the two men. "I don't see anything."

"Neither do I, but I hear it."

The brawny American stood, black hair plastered to his forehead. He strained to hear the familiar *c-chuff, c-chuff* of the whirling blades, but it was another 10 seconds before he did. There in the distance, a little black dot was heading straight for them. Zack shook his head in disbelief. "I'm going to have to start calling you Radar O'Reilly."

"Who?"

Zack grinned for the first time since leaving Camp Lemonnier. "It's from an American television show. They called this guy Radar because he could hear choppers long before anyone else... oh, never mind." They watched as the helicopter began to descend. Tomlinson would not land on the shifting sand, but would get within a few yards and toss down a rope ladder. Zack could almost taste the bourbon waiting for him back at camp. "Better late than never," he said waving at the copter.

No sooner than he said it, however, the sky appeared to catch fire and the whirling bird came crashing down hard into the ocean of sand.

CHAPTER Three

Zack and Kwame ran toward the crashed helicopter with hopes of finding Clive Tomlinson alive. Although, as they got closer it was clear that no one could have survived this. Shards of metal and plastic were everywhere; the airframe was torn to bits, and the blades were bent beyond recognition. The cabin had been ripped almost in half, and the captain's spine severed in such a way that neither could bear looking at him.

Zack surveyed the sky and then looked back at the wreck. "Surface to air missile," he said, matter-of-factly. He searched in every direction. "But from where?" As if in answer to his question, a brown dot appeared on the hazy horizon, rapidly becoming bigger and bigger. A vehicle was heading their way! "Quick, see if the copter's .50 cal. machine gun is operational!" he shouted to Kwame.

Kwame did but the machine gun was nothing but scrap, totally useless. "Not a chance!" he shouted as a Jeep with two men bore down on them. Zack darted behind the fuselage with Kwame close behind him.

"Are those our guys?"

Kwame nodded. "I think so. Two of them, at least."

Zack frowned. "What a time for them to show up. I thought you said they had a truck."

"They sometimes use a support vehicle, in case something goes wrong."

"I bloody well think something has gone wrong!" Zack straightened to his full height before reaching behind his back for his pistol. Zack was getting ready to fire when he felt the barrel in his back. "Kwame, what the hell are you…"

"Give me your pistol, Matteson. Now!"

"Kwame?"

"I am serious; give it to me!"

Damn.

"You traitorous son of a…" He was interrupted by a spray of gunfire.

"Do not shoot!" yelled Kwame in English. "It is me, James. I have found something for you!"

"I not know one named James," shouted one of the men, his English not as good as Kwame's, though passable.

"Be quiet, you idiot," barked the other. "James? Our driver?"

"Yes! And I have a prize for you… an American!"

A bald man with arms to rival those of a heavy-weight champion climbed out of the Jeep, holding an AK-47 assault rifle. "Show yourself!"

Without another word, Kwame shoved Zack out from behind the copter, still pressing the pistol into his spine. The big man with no hair smiled. "It *is* you! How did you get here?"

Kwame nodded toward his prisoner. "This fool thought I was helping him to capture diamond runners. The joke is on him, *eh*?"

Both men stopped in front of the Jeep, although neither lowered his guard. "How did you get here? I see no vehicle."

"By helicopter last night. We were coming to find you."

The smaller man, about 5-foot-nothing, gestured with his weapon. "To find us? You have betrayed us!"

"I had no idea you would still be here," Kwame answered. "Why *are* you here? The truck should be miles away by now."

The big, bald man stepped forward and looked inside the helicopter to make certain the pilot was dead. "The truck is gone, but there was a change of plans. There is another shipment coming in three days, which is why we turned around. We were told to head to Ali Sabieh to meet some Frenchman at the makahaba there." The big man scowled. "It is reckless; too soon, I told them…" he sighed. "But we must do as we are ordered, no?"

The behemoth eyed the white man before saying to Kwame: "Why did you bring him here?"

"What else was I supposed to do? He kept insisting. Better to bring one man alone to the desert where I can kill him than a whole regiment, is it not?"

The bald man nodded, then told the shorter one to frisk the American. When he was satisfied that the white man carried no weapons, he stepped up so that they were nearly nose-to-nose. Four eyes narrowed, each man poised as a cobra about to strike. The African stepped back and then punched Zack in the chin, sending him sprawling into the sand. Zack grabbed a fistful of sand ready to throw it into the bald man's eyes when Kwame kicked him hard in the side, pointing his .45 straight at Zack's midsection.

The big man grinned from ear-to-ear. "I have always wanted to do that to an American."

Kwame nodded. "I must admit, I've been wanting to do that to *this* American ever since I met him."

The three men laughed heartily, which was the break Zack was looking for; his plan was simply to dive into the gut of the smaller man and grab his gun to shoot the other two. But it was the break Kwame had been hoping for, as well. He fired twice into the big man's chest before shooting the shorter one through the left eye. An experienced marksman, Kwame had no problem neutralizing both thugs at this range.

"I knew it!" shouted Zack, grinning as he got up to dust himself off. "I knew you were just pretending."

"Oh, did you now? Is that why you were about to get yourself blown to pieces? I saw how you were about to jump at that human tank. I would have preferred you to wait until I found out where their truck had gone."

Zack took a canteen off the tank, nearly draining it dry before relieving both of the dead men of their weapons. "Well, at least we don't have to wait for a ride," he said, gesturing toward the Jeep.

He and Kwame climbed in, but not before inspecting the rocket launcher in the back. "These things are a dime a dozen down here," Zack muttered angrily. "There's no telling how many of our choppers they could've managed to take down with one of these. Zack pressed the canteen to his lips a second time. His thirst finally assuaged, he pointed to the fuel gauge. "Do we have enough petrol to make it back to the base?"

Kwame checked. "Yes."

Zack reconsidered. "Enough to get to Ali Sabieh?"

"Ali Sabieh?"

Zack nodded. "You heard Muscles. That's where he said they were heading to meet some Frenchman. Sounded like they've never met." He gestured to the motionless bodies in the sand. "We'll just take their place. All we gotta do is find this *makahaba* place he mentioned."

Kwame cocked his head to one side. "You think it is that simple, *eh*?"

"Sure, why not. What is a *makahaba* anyway, a market?"

Kwame grinned. "Of sorts."

"Good. Maybe I can find some jellybeans while we're waiting to meet this goon."

Kwame shook his head as he set the GPS in the Jeep for Ali Sabieh.

CHAPTER Four

"Elinah, hurry, they will be here any minute!" The slight woman scooped their little girl off the floor and ran with their eldest daughter, Durah, onto the front porch of the simple wooden house. Neighbors were hurrying down the road, in advance of the rebels.

"I cannot find Samuel!" she shouted, tears flowing down both cheeks. "I told him not to go far!"

"Take Durah and the baby and join the neighbors, I will find him," Osmann shouted.

Osmann's wife of 11 years shook her head, a look of utter desperation in her eyes. "No, I will not leave without you!"

He wrapped his hand around the back of Elinah's neck and pulled her to him, kissing her reassuringly. "Do not worry, *Bundi*,—his pet name for her—once I find him we will catch up with you... now go!"

The Mau Mau rebellion in Kenya had been quashed by British overlords, but what remained of the insurgents were burning and pillaging neighborhoods suspected of being supportive toward the whites. The rebel leader, Dedan Kimathi, had been captured two weeks ago, signaling the end of the rebellion; not even the help of the Maasai and Kamban guerillas could turn the tide back to the Mau Mau's earlier victories. In fear and rage, many of the rebels were storming through unprotected villages and neighborhoods south of Kenya, such as the one in which Osmann and Elinah lived.

Osmann smiled as he rubbed little Durah's head. "You and mama go, now. I will be with you soon." He playfully swatted his wife's backside. "Fly, Bundi, fly. I will catch up with you."

Reluctantly, Elinah turned to join the throng of fleeing neighbors. Osmann stood on the porch, making certain that she did not turn back before dashing inside to the loose floorboard next to their bed. Quickly he popped the board so that it opened, revealing the two objects he'd come for. One was the Luger the evil SS officer had foolishly handed him 15 years ago. The other, was much smaller and attached to a silver chain. He threw the chain over his neck and clutched the pistol before running out the back door to find his son. He knew just where Samuel would be.

Osmann ran through the tall grass behind the house to a grouping of three large boulders. In the distance, he could hear gunfire and people screaming. He made it to a small stream and turned to the right. Sure enough, there was his 10-year-old son, with the baby owls he kept as pets in a small wire cage. "Samuel! What are you doing?! Your mother has been looking all over for you. Come, child; come with me!"

The small boy did as he was told. He could sometimes find ways to work around his mother's demands, but never his father. "Coming, Baba!" He ran to his father's side in fear of a spanking, but instead his father fell to one knee and clutched him to his breast. "What were you thinking, Samuel? Did you not hear the gunfire?"

"Yes, Baba, that is why I came to feed my birds. I did not know when they would be able to eat again."

Osmann shook his head but offered a gentle smile. "You are a good boy, Samuel; kind and compassionate. But these men are not like you. They will kill all of us if we do not leave now. Your mother and sisters have already fled. Come, we must join them."

At just that moment, a bullet ricocheted off a nearby fever tree. Osmann saw a single gunman in the distance. The man was reloading an ancient musket-type rifle, the kind of poor weaponry that had cost the Mau Mau the rebellion. Osmann went for the Luger and fired twice, catching the man full-on in the chest and knocking him backward. "Baba!" the frightened boy cried.

"Come, Samuel, let's go!"

Osmann grabbed his son by the wrist and yanked him hard as they ran toward the boulders. Ahead, the gunfire intensified. His father forced him to crouch low in the grass. "It is too late now, Samuel. There will be others. You must stay and hide here. I will lead them away from you. Tonight, make your way for the main road, turn left and follow it to Archer's Post where Auntie Gemma lives. It is a long way, but you can make it. Archer's Post is where your mother is taking your sisters; you will be safe there. The Samburu people are well armed and the Mau Mau fear them almost as much as they fear the British."

"No, Baba, I want to stay with you!" the terrified child cried.

Gripping the Luger tightly with one hand, Osmann reached around his neck with the other and removed the object he'd kept hidden away for so long. "Samuel, do you remember me telling you the story of what this is?"

The 10-year-old nodded, trying to fight back tears.

"And do you remember what I said it could do?" Again, Samuel nodded. Osmann placed the chain around his son's neck. "You are its keeper now. You must never tell anyone about the power that it possesses. I have kept it a secret for many years; only my brother knows what this key unlocks." Osmann's eyes narrowed. "I was a fool to ever have trusted Kifo."

He gazed imploringly into his son's eyes. "But you, Samuel, you are the only one who knows exactly where the box lies hidden. Never tell anyone, understand?" The boy swallowed but said that he did. "Perhaps when you are older, God will guide you into knowing what you must do." He swallowed hard. "For now, you must take care of your mother and sisters. Always be brave, and always stand against wrong." They were familiar words which Samuel had heard his father utter many times. He grasped the key on the end of the chain. "And never let that out of your sight. Now, hide here and do not make a sound."

"Baba?"

"*Shh*, my son." Osmann stroked the back of Samuel's head as he stared lovingly into his son's eyes. "Always remember that I loved you with all of my heart." He snatched the boy to his breast and hugged him tightly before pushing Samuel closer toward the boulders. In an instant, he was gone, running toward the house, praying that no one saw the direction he'd come from.

From his vantage point, Samuel could see his father duck behind their house and then make his way round to the left. A moment later he heard a fury of pops and bangs. He pushed his small fingers into his ears as tears fell on the stony ground below. He did not need to be told; he knew that his father had perished.

That night, long after the screams and the gunfire had subsided, Samuel crawled out of his hiding place and made his way to the coop. He quietly opened each cage, grateful that the rebels had not spotted the young owls and eaten his tiny friends. He stroked the iron key that his father had guarded for so long and turned toward a path he knew ran parallel with the main road. He knew that the rebels would not go anywhere near Archer's Post, but they might be camping at the crossroads. He would wait in the brush near the main road to make certain that they were gone before going to find his mother and sister.

He turned one last time to see what was left of his home. The rebels had burned it, along with all the other houses in Saint Alban's township. Slowly, he turned his gaze to the little owls who had trusted him since their mother had abandoned them. Hopping from the cages to the ground they spread their wings and flopped left and right. Samuel had known they were ready to fly; he had just been delaying it. "Goodbye," he whispered, knowing that they, like him, must forever flee from this place.

As hard as he tried, he could not stop the tears. In his mind he kept hearing his baba's voice. "Always be brave, and always stand against wrong."

CHAPTER Five

"Why didn't you tell me a 'makahaba' is a brothel?"

Kwame chuckled. "You didn't ask. Besides, from what I hear, it is your kind of place."

Zack wiped his chin after finishing off what passed for a hamburger at the open-air diner across from a mud-brick building painted red. A sign outside simply read Madame Tulame's. "My kind of place, hell. I told you, I'm a married man. Besides, there's no telling what ancient pox is circulating inside there. Are you sure *this* is the place?"

Kwame nodded after taking a sip of tea from an ancient porcelain cup. "You heard the man as well as I did. He said a Frenchie was coming here." He nodded toward the red building. "This is the only makahaba in Ali Sabieh."

"So, what's the plan, Tonto? Are we just going to sit here and wait?"

"Unless you want to go inside and sample the local fare," Kwame said sardonically. "And what is a Tonto?"

"I'm guessing you don't watch much old American television, do you?"

Kwame raised the cup of scalding liquid to his lips. "The smuggler said that the Frenchman is supposed to come here today. Do they not teach you how to be patient in the CIA?"

"It wasn't on my curriculum list, no."

Kwame rolled his eyes. "Just as well; I assume you would have failed anyway."

Zack glared at his African counterpart, opening a bag of some sort of candy he'd managed to find earlier in the market. He broke off a piece and popped it into his mouth. *Damn. It tasted like licorice.* "Tell you what, I'll go back to that thing they call a hotel and wait for you to call me. I might as well take a nap; we've been here all morning and nothing has happened."

"What is it you Americans say? 'It's your funeral.'"

"What's that supposed to mean?"

"With your white skin and your... um... *unique*... attitude, you probably won't make it to the hotel if you go alone."

"I haven't had any problems in Africa, I'll have you know."

"Yes, but that was in Djibouti. Here, things are different."

Zack pointed down the long street to a group of buildings. "There's a white guy down there. Nobody's bothering him."

"Look closely. Do you see the two men standing behind him? Those are his bodyguards. He is here on business. No doubt it is a business neither you nor I would approve of. Whites come here only to make deals."

"Deals?"

"Diamonds, weapons, counterfeit money... here in

Ali Sabieh it is said one can find anything—for a price."

"You spend much time here, do you?"

Kwame blew across the rim of his cup. "Not if I can help it. Whites are not the only ones who can find themselves on the wrong end of a machete in Ali Sabieh."

Zack threw up his hands. "Fine, fine, I'll stay here and keep *you* safe. Why don't we go over our plan again?"

"*Our* plan?"

"Okay, whatever. *Your* plan. Satisfied?"

"I doubt I ever will be as long as you and I have to continue to work together."

"God, if I had wanted this kind of abuse I could have just stuck with Scott Flenn."

"Your partner? I thought your partner was the nice one."

"Maybe to the rest of the world. He's a lot like you, otherwise."

Kwame grinned. "Must be a grand fellow. Too bad they didn't send *him*; I think Iceland would have suited you much better."

"I wish I were there now," Zack sighed, asking Kwame to request the waitress for a dessert menu. The woman laughed. They had only one sweet concoction which was nothing more than a bland muffin with frosting. Zack ordered it anyway.

"You eat too much sugar."

Zack gestured to his muscular torso. "Do I look like I'm out of shape? Maybe you should try some once in a while; maybe then you wouldn't look like a spider on stilts." Before Kwame could respond, a large, shiny Toyota barreled down the street, escorted by a Jeep painted in desert camouflage. Zack nodded to Kwame. "You thinking what I'm thinking?"

Kwame nodded. "It must be our guy."

"Don't stare at them; you'll draw attention."

"This is not Paris or Lisbon. *Not* staring is what will draw attention. How many cars like that do you think the people in this neighborhood see on a given day?"

Zack didn't answer, instead he sat eating his muffin in silence as they watched the Toyota pull up to the bordello across the street. "Guess there's no time to go over our plan after all." He took a breath. "Showtime."

Kwame didn't budge. "Not yet. Remember, we're supposed to be the runners. Let's wait to see who gets out. If there is anyone I recognize, we'll have to abandon this whole idea and call in a drone."

"Drones are so boring," Zack complained. "I went through a two-week operational familiarity course on those things back at Langley. They make everything so… dull."

"Still, I'm not going in there unless the men who get out of that car are total strangers. From what little those two runners said back in the desert, I gather this is a small operation. The Frenchman will tell us what the job is. If it is like most, he'll want to pass along the diamonds to us and we take them across the desert to someone."

"That's insane. What's to prevent a runner from keeping the diamonds for himself?"

Kwame stared at him in disbelief. "Do you know what happens to runners who take more than their payment? They are tortured for days and then left in the middle of the desert with a canteen full of petrol. The few who have been found later all had empty canteens."

"They drank gasoline?"

"The desert is not kind." Kwame stared at the men getting out of the vehicles. "Nor are the people the runners work for. There is no mercy for a thief."

"I thought they were all thieves."

"You do not understand. This is not like organized crime in most countries. There are rival factions, yes, but they all insist on absolute loyalty from the runners. It doesn't matter who you steal from, even if you steal from a rival you will be dealt the same sentence."

Zack frowned. "So why would anyone be a blasted runner?"

"Money. The runners are paid extremely well. They are the ones risking their lives in the desert. Interpol has drones too, you know."

Zack scratched his head. "I still don't get it. If this dude is wanting diamonds, why doesn't he go to the source, to the mines? Why do the runners bring them across the desert?"

"You wouldn't ask that if you had been to a mine." Kwame's chin hardened. "Slave camps. Men, women, even children, forced to dig until they drop. The barbarians who run the camps only feed the laborers if they find diamonds." He looked away. "God help them if they try to run away."

"Sounds a lot like North Korea." Zack glared at the white man getting out of the Toyota and strolling inside the brothel with four armed guards on either side. "And they say slavery is dead," Zack added, finishing the simple dessert. "So, explain to me what is happening inside. Is Frenchie buying or selling?"

Kwame shrugged. "I suspect selling but it could be either. Deals go both ways. Sometimes diamonds are brought here to sell to European middle-men, who purchase them for a fraction of the cost and then sell them to legitimate dealers. They're cleaned, cut and catalogued without a trace of where they actually came from."

"The dealers don't ask?"

"Why would they? The dealers suspect, of course, but if someone like the Frenchman tells them that they are legitimate, they're not going to argue. They don't want to know. It's too easy to pretend that the diamonds aren't soaked in blood."

Zack nodded across the street toward the house of ill repute. "But if those two in the desert were meeting up with Frenchie…"

Kwame finished the sentence: "Then he may indeed have diamonds to sell and wanted the runners to take them to a fence. There is a rumor that a team of Israeli diamond-cutters are set up in Berbera."

"Berbera? Isn't that where the Somali pirates hang out?"

"At times. But the Israelis would be well guarded by their own mercenaries. And trust me, no one wants to play games with those guys. Most of them are former Mossad. You must understand that here diamond smuggling is unique. It is different than drug smuggling."

"Nah. I don't see much difference. It just attracts a different kind of criminal."

Kwame raised an eyebrow. "Why, because he is white?"

"No, I mean…"

Kwame sighed. "I know what you meant." Across the street, two of the heavily armed guards positioned themselves at the entrance to Madame Tulame's. "The Frenchman probably has the diamonds. Otherwise, there would be someone else here for him to negotiate with, and theirs are the only vehicles around. He is here to meet with the runners that we disposed of in the desert. He will want to size us up to evaluate whether it is worth the risk of running them across the sand."

"You sound certain."

Kwame shook his head. "Not as certain as I'd prefer. There are so many ways that these deals go down. Diamond smuggling is like the shifting sand; it is never the same. The only thing that remains constant is the job of the runners. They transport, nothing more."

Zack shook his head. "I can't believe anyone would trust a runner to that degree. It would never go down like that in the drug trade."

"Yes. That's what I told you. There are too many places for a smuggler to hide in your world." Kwame made a sweeping motion with his hands. "Here, there is no place to hide. You will be found, and so will your family. Diamond runners are especially careful to do the job right the first time, for they will not be offered a second."

Kwame stood to pay the waitress, who hurried to

their table. Nodding toward the painted house across the street, he said, "Keep your pistol close. If you end up having to go for it, shoot everything that moves... and I mean *everything*. Do not hesitate; they certainly won't."

CHAPTER Six

The familiar *glug-glug* of a nearby bottlebird awoke the boy sleeping in the brush. Samuel raised his head cautiously in search of any Mau Mau rebels. When he didn't see any, he stood to look for villagers on the road or those who might have camped nearby—he saw no one. The usually well-traveled road was eerily quiet. *Perhaps it was too early*, he thought… *or perhaps there is no one left and the rebels have killed them all.* The thought caused a lump to rise in his chest, but it also drove him to approach the road and begin the 40-kilometer trek to Archer's Post. Auntie Gemma would be there; she would know if his mother and sisters were safe.

Samuel's stomach ached. He thought of the waakye and bits of fish his mother had served for breakfast yesterday. *What he would give now for just a small bowl of the rice-and-bean dish.*

His neighborhood had been the farthest from the town of Kianji. His father had chosen to be close enough from the small city to enjoy some of its benefits, without having to live amongst a crowd of people. Samuel fingered the key under his brown shirt. This had something to do with that decision, something about his father not trusting his uncle Kifo who had long ago left for the North. Samuel didn't know what their rift had been about, only that his father had warned him that Kifo was never to be trusted.

The road ahead was long. Samuel could see for several kilometers. Other than two giraffes lumbering across the plain in the distance, the boy and the birds seemed to be the only things stirring. *Was that because the Mau Maus had killed everything else?* He had heard his father telling his mother how fierce the rebels were, and how merciless. Samuel chased the thought from his mind. *He would not allow fear to overcome him.* He had a mission to accomplish—to make it to Archer's Post.

He had cried himself to sleep last night at the memory of his father disappearing behind their house just before it had been set ablaze. The men had not bothered to search behind the boulders or venture into the brush behind the house. There had been enough to keep them busy as they had chased after Samuel's fleeing neighbors. Some of the men, like his father, had pistols and had likely put up a fight, although brief and useless. As for the women, even at 10, Samuel knew what had probably happened to them. The boys they had not killed would be taken to special camps and trained for a future insurrection, one that his father had assured him would be futile. The Brits were well armed and had plenty of reinforcements; and they were not going to leave Kenya anytime soon.

His father had become a friend to the British during the war, eventually joining General Montgomery's troops and fighting the Italians and Germans in the West. His uncle Kifo had joined with him for a time. The British had even taken his father and uncle back to England for training.

His father had told him that he had taken the box full of Nazi poison with him to a place called Durham and had hidden it there when he had been given orders that he was to accompany the British recruits on a secret mission into Nigeria. It was during that mission that his father and uncle had parted ways. All Samuel knew was that, the argument had something to do with the box and the key around his neck.

Osmann told Samuel that the Nazi scientist had placed the vials of poison inside two airtight glass containers and sealed them in wax before packing them inside a simple metal box. His baba had then taken them to England in the hopes of turning them over to the Allies, but had changed his mind, convinced that no military power should ever possess such a thing. When Samuel had asked whether his father had ever opened the box, his baba told him that that inside was a booby-trap. If one tried to force it open, or used the wrong key, the box would explode, unleashing hell itself. When Samuel had asked about the wisdom of having such a volatile substance blow up, his father had simply shaken his head and said something about how evil men do not care about the people they hurt. It had been his father's hope to one day have enough money to return to England, find the box, and sink it in the depths of the North Sea. A hope that now rested fully upon Samuel… but first he must make it to Archer's Post.

A crane flew silently overhead and Samuel began to wonder about his pet owls. He knew they would be even now trying out their wings near the cage he had so lovingly constructed. If a hungry cobra did not find them, they would all be flying by the end of the day. He also knew that once they could take to the air, they would be safe. He brushed a tear aside and prayed that his mother and sisters would also be. As he walked along the dusty road, his thoughts returned to his father. *He had been a good man; everyone who knew him thought as much. People in their neighborhood had come to him often, trusting that with his connections as a low-level clerk for a British official, he could help them with their interactions with the English. Of course, that wasn't the only time the neighbors had come seeking his father's advice. He was a wise man, and a man of faith. He had helped counsel many people when life had turned difficult. God, Baba, why did you leave me?*

Samuel wiped the tears from his cheek. He could only hope that he would be as brave and true as his baba had told him to be. *But one thing was sure*, he told himself, *if he lived long enough, he would one day go to England and finish what his father had been unable to do*. In that way he would be honoring his baba's pledge to himself—and not just to himself, but to the entire world.

CHAPTER Seven

Ali Sabieh; 2005

The inside of Madame Tulame's smelled of incense and musk. Carpeted tapestries hung from the walls of the main sitting room, where Zack assumed young women would greet their customers before escorting them down one of three dim hallways.

"So, you must be Yazid," a short man in a white suit said in an accent that was definitely not French.

Kwame nodded. "I am. And this is my partner."

The man raised an eyebrow. "A white man?" His eyes narrowed slightly as he stared at Zack Matteson. "Where are *you* from?"

Zack answered truthfully. "Delaware, originally."

The man's eyes widened in surprise. "An American?"

"Of sorts. I'm a traveler. I owe allegiance to no one."

Kwame studied the man in front of him who was much shorter than he. In his 60s, blond hair and grayish-blue eyes. He had a small scar underneath his chin and close to the jugular, suggesting a tougher man than his stature and pristine white suit suggested—seasoned no doubt by more than one close call. "Sir, Tilly has proven himself useful to me on more than one occasion. He can circulate among the whites without drawing any attention. The scouting parties from Djibouti never question him. Nor me, when I am with him." Kwame laughed. "They mistakenly think that he is the one in charge."

Zack shot Kwame a look.

"Well, Yazid and Tilly, shall we sit?" Zack may not have been as good as Scott Flenn at identifying accents, but this one was definitely Russian, not French. They sat on large colorful cushions arranged closely together with two of the Russian's brawny guards standing over them. The man in the white suit dismissed them with a nod of his head as scantily clad women brought trays of a steaming hot liquid and bits of melon wrapped in thin slices of pork. Kwame reached for a cup, as did both of the white men. Zack waited for Kwame and their host to drink first. It was neither tea nor coffee, but it tasted sweet and strong. No doubt Flenn, with his penchant for caffeine, would have found whatever the hell this was quite acceptable. Zack took two of the melon sticks and winked at the pretty girl serving them.

"Gentlemen," the man in the white suit said, raising his porcelain cup, "where I come from it is customary to toast a new adventure."

"And just where is that?" Zack asked.

Kwame shot him a warning glance. "Tilly, it is not our place to question our employers."

Zack bit into a bite of the meat and melon. "Sorry, but we were told that you were French. That is not a French accent."

Kwame started to say something but the man's disarming smile stopped him.

"Your compatriot is wise to be cautious, my friend.

In our business, one cannot be too careful, *eh*?" He stared at Zack. "You are correct. I am not from France. I came here from Paris, which is where I have spent a lot of my time lately. But, like you, I am a traveler. Pick somewhere, and I've probably been there."

"America?"

"Many times. Although I am not welcome anymore."

Zack nodded. "Neither am I. A federal prison cell is all that waits for me back there."

The man smiled appreciatively. "I have friends in your prisons. They were not so lucky as you, no?"

Zack flashed an arrogant grin.

Placing his cup on the floor next to him, the man rubbed his hands together briskly. "Forgive me. I have as yet to tell you my name. Although, I'm sure your superiors gave it to you."

Zack smelled a trap. "Are you kidding? All they told us was that you were white and were a Frenchman. I guess one out of two ain't bad."

Test passed.

"It is just as well; I do not believe I told them my name anyway. I am Sergei. I see no reason for surnames. Our relationship shall be relatively brief. How much have you been told about my present needs?"

This time it was Kwame who spoke. "Very little. Our boss likes it that way. Only that our services would be required to cross the desert."

"Indeed."

"I am assuming diamonds?" Zack said, trying to look bored by another tedious assignment.

"You would be incorrect, my friend."

This time Kwame raised an eyebrow. "You do wish us to take you across the desert?" Kwame asked.

"That is exactly what I wish. I have paid your boss handsomely for just such an experience. I assume he has paid you?"

"The standard fee," Zack offered, continuing the ruse. "Although tips at the end of the journey are welcomed."

Kwame bristled. "Forgive my friend, Bwana Sergei. He is like most Americans, impudent and rude. But he is good at his job. There will not be any additional fees for our service."

Sergei smiled warmly. "*Ah*, but I have plenty to spare, gentlemen. I will not mind leaving you with a generous gratuity once we arrive in Addis Ababa."

So that's where we are heading. Zack shook his head. "Yazid hates it when I ask questions, but if you do not have something to smuggle into the city, why not just fly there?" Indeed, Yazid looked as if he wanted to punch him.

"Diamonds and drugs are not the only items that would catch the attention of the authorities." He turned to face Kwame. "I hear it would take only hours by car along the road, but two days across the desert. Obviously, we do not want to risk being pulled over by border patrols, which is why we are traveling through the desert and I am using your services. But, before my friend in Addis Ababa and I agree to hire your boss permanently, we must be convinced of the safety of your route. Therefore, I am going with you on a trial run."

Kwame spoke before Zack could. "Certainly, sir. When is it you wish to leave?"

"Well, I *was* prepared to go immediately." He leered at the woman who was busy refilling their cups. "However, I see no reason to rush. An hour from now will make no difference. Wait for me outside." He smiled at the woman, who did the same in return. "Perhaps we should make that two hours from now."

CHAPTER Eight

Kenya, the middle of nowhere; 1956

A hazy yellow sun was disappearing on the western horizon, illuminating the plains with an eerie golden glow. A grove of water-pear trees stood silently, unmoving in the breezeless heat of early evening. Samuel knew better than to make his bed for the night amongst them; venomous snakes often lurked beneath the branches. There was even a legend about a secretary-bird and a cobra locked throughout eternity in mortal combat. At the end of time, a neighboring old woman had once told him, whichever proved to be the victor would spell out the destination of humanity—whether to be with the gods or the demons. His mother had shooed the woman away and had reassured him that it was only a fairy tale.

Samuel's mother was a devout Christian; as had his father been. His family had begun and ended each day at the family table with a prayer. He longed for the comfort of those prayers right now, almost as much as he did the food she'd served—though neither as much as he missed his family.

Were his mother and sisters dead? Could his father have possibly escaped and merely been taken prisoner? Or, although it was unthinkable, what if his father were lying wounded in the ditch across from their house... *had he abandoned his baba to suffer alone?* More than once he had thought of turning back, but the occasional sound of artillery and small-arms fire in the distance had dissuaded him. Three times he had taken refuge in the brush as army trucks loaded with British soldiers and Kenyan loyalist forces had passed him on their way east to eliminate whatever was left of the resistance. Samuel trusted no one right now, but in his heart, he fantasized that they might find his father still alive, and kill the butchers who had destroyed his home. As he passed the water-pear grove, he saw two huge secretary-birds searching through the grass for dinner. He wondered about the old woman's tale and why it had frightened him so. Not even a cobra could win against such a clever and powerful hunter.

Samuel continued to walk until the stars appeared when he began searching for Venus, the Evening Star, just as his father had taught him. He made a wish, as his baba had insisted they do every night, though his mother usually rolled her eyes at the gesture. Tonight, Samuel gazed into the night sky and wished his mother and sisters to be alive. He couldn't bring himself to do the same for his father, for that would have meant that he had abandoned him. Samuel took a breath. *Be brave*, his father had told him. He would try.

As darkness slowly claimed the landscape, Samuel walked for another hour before finding a kapok tree and deciding to spend the night in its branches. Yes, a leopard might spot him there, but sleeping on the ground a second night seemed to him more dangerous. Plus, he had spent the day scratching his limbs raw from whatever insect had feasted on him the night before. His mother had taught him to spit into the dirt and make mud to roll over an insect bite, but as dehydrated as he was, he could no longer make enough saliva. Fortunately, he was able to find a spot in the tree where several sturdy limbs grew together, just right for a small boy to nestle himself against the bark.

Samuel was asleep within minutes, never noticing the cheetah that passed through the grove an hour later. The big cat stopped and sniffed before staring up into the tree—but just before it jumped to the lowest branch to make its ascent toward the child, two enormous owls swooped down from the sky and drove it away. The owls remained in the tree throughout the night, although Samuel was unaware of their presence. They were both gone when he awoke in the morning to the sound of a truck heading his way.

Hoping to evade detection, Samuel struggled to dislodge himself from the limbs of the kapok tree but both legs were numb. He ended up half-climbing, half-falling to the ground where he crumbled in a heap at the base of the tree.

The driver must have seen him fall; he was slowing down… now, he was stopping! Samuel tried to stand and run, but to no avail. His legs simply wouldn't allow it.

"Mwana, uko salama?"

The words stung. *This man was not his father; why should he refer to him as son? And, no, he was not okay.* His legs were the least of his problem. He was hungry, sore, and so very thirsty.

"Come here, boy; I will not hurt you." The man was

middle-aged, balding, and wore loose-fitting khaki pants and a floral shirt. He had a salt-and-pepper beard, but no mustache. And he spoke gently. "You are running from the rebels, are you not? Have no fear. There was a battle last night; those the British did not kill, ran away. We are safe."

He gestured to the child. "Come. I have water; I have figs."

Although the feeling was beginning to work its way back up his spindly legs, Samuel neither moved toward the man nor ran away. Instead he found the courage to ask, "Unaenda wapi?"

"Where am I heading?" The man smiled. "To Archer's Post. I am Samburu."

The Samburu people had a peculiar history with the British, but their hatred for the Mau Mau was well known, even by Samuel. "Why are you so far from home then?"

"I have many cattle farms. I was tending one near Isiolo when the rebels came. Come, child. I have no intention of staying here all morning. Do you want my water and figs or no?"

Samuel did. Desperately.

He stepped cautiously toward the truck. The man with the beard reached into the cab and brought out a paper bag and a large thermos, which Samuel reached for first.

"Slow down, mwana, you will make yourself vomit," the man said.

Even as he drank, Samuel never took his eyes off the man's hands, in case he were to reach under his shirt for a weapon. Instead he reached into the sack and offered Samuel a fig. "Eat slowly, mwana, you do not wish to make yourself sick, *eh*?"

Samuel snatched the fruit and devoured it, paying more attention to his hunger than the man's warnings. "You are really going to Archer's Post?"

"Yes."

"So am I," Samuel said, eyeing the bed of the Ford pickup. The truck was not new, but it was not rusty and worn-out the way so many of the work trucks were in Kenya.

"It is a long walk," the man said before offering a kindly smile. "Why don't you ride with me?"

Samuel shook his head, although half-heartedly. "I can walk. I am strong."

"I have no doubt; but there are cheetahs about. Hyenas too. And they are hungrier than you are, child."

Samuel stuck out his chest. "I am brave, like my father."

The man nodded. "I have little doubt. Tell me, where is your father?"

Samuel looked away. The man understood.

"Your mother the same?"

Samuel shrugged. "I do not know. She was taking my sisters to Archer's Post."

The stranger cocked his head to one side. "But not you, little one?"

Samuel's voice trailed off. "I was tending my owls. My father came to find me. He…" Samuel choked back the tears.

The man looked off into the distance as silence fell

over them. At last, he said: "War is a terrible thing, child. May this be the last one that you ever see." He got down on one knee and stared into Samuel's eyes. The man's face was kind, not unlike the parish priest. "Your mother and father taught you not to take rides with strange men, no?" He didn't wait for the answer. "Ordinarily, that is good advice. But the Brits have forbidden traffic on this road, and this may be your only chance for days."

Samuel stepped back. "If the Brits are stopping people, how did you get here?"

"Let's just say they know me. I have worked for them in the past." He patted a folded piece of paper in his shirt pocket. "They gave me permission for today." Samuel felt his shoulders relax. *His father had also worked for the British.*

"The plains are dangerous, child, especially at night. If you do not trust me then you can ride in the back of the truck." Samuel took another drink and handed the Thermos back, eyeing the sack of fruit. "Here," the man said, handing him the paper bag. "I am driving away now. I do not wish to leave you here alone. But it is your choice."

Samuel slowly nodded.

"Good. Good!" The man smiled as he got to his feet. "My name is Osuroo. What is yours?"

Samuel almost gave him is real name before deciding it might be better to offer a false one. "Osmann," he said, using his father's name.

"Well, Osmann, will you be riding in the cab with me or in the back?"

"In the back," Samuel answered as he waited for

Osuroo to lower the tailgate. Osuroo moved a box of tools and a wooden ladder to one side of the truck bed and then stepped back as Samuel climbed in.

"If you see a military vehicle, tap on the window to make certain that I pull over. The Brits do not like anyone in their way."

"I thought you said you worked with them?"

"The soldiers will still demand our identification. If we get stopped, I will tell them that you are my son." The look on Samuel's face caused Osuroo to change his mind. "Perhaps I should tell them you are my nephew instead, *eh*?"

Samuel's response was simply to look away. No more was said as Osuroo Bankole closed the tailgate and inserted the metal pins on either side. Samuel gazed into the azure sky where only a single cloud floated above. A crowned hornbill flew toward the top of the tree that had been his bed. In the distance, he thought he heard the sound of rifle fire. Some of the rebels would have undoubtedly slipped away.

He was glad to be heading in the opposite direction.

CHAPTER Nine

Ali Sabieh

Zack tried not to appear impatient as he leaned against the Jeep, waiting for the man in the white suit to exit Madame Tulame's. Kwame sat instead in the passenger seat with his knees pressed against the dashboard and his eyes closed. Behind him was the launcher that had been used against the helicopter, along with two small missiles.

"Don't you think you should move those to the back before our passenger arrives?"

Kwame opened one eye. "*Um*, are you forgetting yourself, Tilly? You work for me, remember?"

Zack rolled his eyes. "How long are you going to milk this?"

Kwame leaned back into the seat and smiled. "As long as I can, my brother, as long as I can." Zack got out and opened the rear door and carefully picked up the launcher and moved it into the back of the vehicle. No one around seemed to notice, as if brandishing a surface-to-air rocket launcher was commonplace. *Perhaps it was*, thought Zack.

"So," he said moving one of the missiles as gingerly as possible, "what is boss-man's big plan? We shake the Russian's bodyguards and take him to Camp Lemonnier for interrogation?"

Kwame grunted. "Do you want to know the problem with you, Zack Matteson? You have no imagination. None whatsoever."

"If by that you mean that I would have thought twice about going unarmed into a disheveled whorehouse in the middle of nowhere to chance getting shot by a Russian smuggler and his bodyguards, then, yes, you are right, I have no imagination."

"That surprises me," Kwame said. "Your superiors told me that you are one to take chances. That is why I agreed to work with you. Anyone who goes after diamond smugglers has to be willing to take chances. Perhaps I misjudged you."

Zack placed the second missile in the back of the Jeep and wiped his hands on his trousers. "Taking a chance is one thing; being reckless is another."

"I'm not being reckless. I plan on taking this guy into the desert and interrogating him myself—once we get rid of his guards, that is."

"And just how do you propose to do that?" said Zack.

The door of the brothel opened wide as the man in the white suit sauntered outside, followed closely by his men. "That, I will leave up to you, Tilly."

"Where the hell did that name come from anyway?" Zack groused.

Kwame climbed out of the Jeep. "My wife has a dog named Tilly," he answered. "An ill-tempered, impatient, unruly mutt. You remind me of him."

"I swear, Kwame…"

"Yazid."

"What?"

"The name is Yazid," he whispered. "*Ah!* Bwana Sergei, are you ready for our journey together?"

The Russian whispered something to one of the guards and then smiled appreciatively toward the black runner and his white underling. "I am, indeed, gentlemen," he said as he climbed into the passenger seat of the Jeep. "Which one of you is driving?"

"That would be me, Bwana. Tilly is terrible with directions." He glanced at Zack who was more than willing to climb into the backseat behind the Russian. *Should trouble arise, it would be easy enough to shove the eight-inch knife he had strapped to his ankle through the car seat.*

"Two of my men will be following us to Addis Ababa, said the Russian. "Do not worry. They will not get in your way. I know your people do not like surprises."

One thug was manageable, three was a different story. Still, at least two of the guards were staying behind.

Kwame nodded. "I do hope that they have plenty of petrol and water in their vehicle. Where we are going, it is fatal to have a shortage of either."

"We came well supplied, my friend. Have no fear."

Zack wondered what else they might have with them. A global positioning device, no doubt; perhaps a satellite radio, as well. For the first time, he began to wonder if someone else might be watching from a distance. He glanced up at the sky. Drones, satellites… technology was developing faster than he could keep up with it. And as luck would have it, he and Kwame were without either. Everything had been stored on the helicopter with Captain Tomlinson.

If the bodyguards had connections elsewhere, he and Kwame would be at a disadvantage in some sort of firefight. Hopefully, he would find a way to have Sergei dismiss his guards long before they veered off to interrogate the Russian. Zack scratched his head. Was he even certain that Sergei was Russian? Could he not be Ukrainian or even a Chechen? Too bad Scott Flenn wasn't here. Flenn was the master at languages and dialects, not him. Still, until he knew otherwise, he'd figure Sergei for a Russkie.

"Shall we be off then?" Sergei said, ready to begin the journey.

Kwame placed the Jeep in gear. "As you wish, Bwana. I do hope you are not looking forward to a scenic drive. I'm afraid that all we shall see is sand." He shrugged. "And, perhaps a jackal or two." Zack nodded, thinking of the two human jackals pulling out behind them.

"I am not here as a tourist, Yazid. You need not treat me as one." The Russian turned toward Zack, as if interpreting his thoughts. "And you need not worry about my guards, Tilly." *There was something about the way he smiled at him.* "They are completely harmless… as long as *I* am safe."

Zack pretended to scratch his leg, feeling for the knife instead. He looked behind him and frowned. *It would take a lot more than a knife to take care of those two Sherman tanks.*

CHAPTER Ten

Grand Bara Desert

Zack had seen movies about people stranded in the desert, and after seven hours of driving through the sand, with little to look at save the back of two heads, he found that he was almost grateful for the two thugs in the camouflaged Toyota Land Cruiser behind them. At some point, though, they were going to become a problem. Kwame would stop soon and make camp for the night. Hopefully, he'd be able to get his partner alone to probe his thoughts on getting rid of the guards. Until then, he was glad that they were a close distance behind should something happen to the Jeep in the middle of this great white nothing.

Sergei, had talked quietly with Kwame for the first half-hour or so but had fallen asleep, apparently comfortable to let down his guard with these two strangers. *And why shouldn't he be?* Zack told himself. The Russian was convinced they were simply paid runners who would deliver him to his contact safely or face severe repercussions. If even half of what Kwame had told him happened to runners who betrayed their mission, no one in their right mind would stray from their given task.

Of course, having not one but two gigantic goons

armed to the teeth was Sergei's extra insurance. If push came to shove, Zack could take them both out in their sleep tonight, but he hoped it wouldn't come to that. Zack had killed plenty of times before, but mostly as a last resort. *Of course*, he reasoned, *the world would be a better place without Twiddle-Dum and Twiddle-Dee.*

He glanced behind him and saw the Toyota easily keeping up with them. Like the Jeep, it no doubt had an extra gasoline tank bolted underneath and carried a five-gallon drum of extra petrol. He looked at the yellow gasoline canister in the back next to the missile launcher. Next to them were several canteens, which he and Kwame had filled to the brim.

He didn't know who Sergei was, but wanted to, desperately. The Russian could be one of a hundred different international criminals the CIA had a dossier on in this part of the world. Drugs, diamonds, slaves… Africa had them all, and some of the world's worst thugs were taking advantage of the opportunity before the Chinese finally took control of the eastern half of the continent. China had been working for decades, wresting the French and British influence out from underneath them. The Chinese had lost several recent opportunities though, and as a result, other influential players were also taking advantage of the turmoil throughout the continent.

Egypt, Botswana, South Africa all remained relatively stable in comparison to many of the other nations. As European influence diminished, others had stepped up to the plate: Russia, Turkey, Vietnam were at the forefront. As the sub-Saharan world struggled for its very existence, and foreign powers largely ignored the plight of refugees, a cruel twist of luck had fallen upon the most disenfranchised of Africa's citizenry. Religious militias began a campaign of recruitment and terror, the likes of which had not been seen since the days of the Ottoman Empire. Massacres were brazenly conducted by ruthless guerillas in remote villages. Kidnapping child brides and boy soldiers had become commonplace, and human trafficking was happening on a scale that had not been seen in centuries. This, on top of a runaway AIDS epidemic, rampant malnutrition, and an uncaring world ignoring the needs of the continent, allowed criminal elements to take advantage and bring further despair.

Zack had become familiar with some of the chaos in Africa since being assigned to relieve one of the CIA operatives at the airbase in Djibouti a month ago. The airmen regularly shared horror stories of things they had either seen or heard about during their tours through Camp Lemonnier. Sure, Zack and Scott Flenn were no strangers to the worst of human behavior, and he'd figured that he had become immune to the evils of what people do, but little of what he and Flenn had seen rivaled stories of the crucifixion of children or the mutilation of women that the airmen had told him about.

Weary of the ride, Zack shifted his weight to relieve the pressure on his thighs. The man sitting in front of him was an unknown. *Was he a middle-man, a freelancer, or possibly someone connected to Bratva, the Russian mafia?* The way Sergei carried himself said that he was a man used to being in charge. Bratva had very few of those; at least ones who were as old as Sergei.

Zack thought the Russian to be in his late 50s or early 60s. He had an air of authority about him—someone used to having his way. It was an attitude that had been bred and not learned. Sergei was small in stature but lean and muscular, although he walked with a slight limp. His hair was blond and thick with just a trace of gray at the temples. And while he had no wrinkles on his brow, tiny ones were beginning to form around his dark eyes and several on the back of his neck. The man wasn't exactly pale, but he wasn't tan either. It was obvious that he'd not spent much time in the African sun. It didn't take long here before a Caucasian's skin displayed the harsh effects of the sun's rays. Zack had developed a rich tan within a week of first landing at Camp Lemonnier. This guy, Zack reasoned, had only just arrived. *But from where? He had said Paris, but that could simply be part of his cover.*

"Let me know if you get tired of driving," Zack offered, growing more and more uncomfortable in the cramped backseat, which had been pushed forward to allow room for the stuff they were carrying in the back.

"I'm fine, Tilly."

Zack was glad that their guest couldn't see him staring holes through the back of Kwame's head. *Tilly—it sounded like something one ordered from the back of a Guatemalan ice cream truck. "Chilly-Tilly." He could just hear Scott Flenn now.*

"Well, *I'm* not. I need to get out and stretch," Zack grumbled.

"I wouldn't mind stopping myself," Sergei announced, obviously not asleep after all. Perhaps he had only been feigning sleep but really listening should the two runners say something of particular interest. Zack told himself that was exactly what he would have done.

"Yes, Bwana. Perhaps it would do us all some good," Kwame said, keeping up the subservient act. He slowed down, as did the vehicle behind them, and they both came to a stop, though neither turned off their engine. No sense in taking unnecessary risks. Should a battery die out in the middle of nowhere, it would mean certain death. "Mind your step, Bwana. There are scorpions about."

Oh great! Zack thought. *Just what I need.*

The two guards climbed out of their vehicle, both with .45s tucked visibly inside their waistbands—as well as a look which left no doubt that they'd be able to draw them at a moment's notice. Zack could feel the men staring at him as he went off to make a puddle in the sand. If the time came to neutralize Tom and Jerry—the names he'd just now given the guards—it wouldn't be an easy matter. He'd have to catch them unawares, and, so far, he had seen no sign that was even a remote possibility.

No, the best option would be if Sergei let them turn back once they'd gotten within a few miles of Addis Ababa. Then, once free of Tom and Jerry, he and Kwame would be able to question Sergei all they liked. Of course, the Russian was no doubt also armed. They'd have to get the drop on him. *Shouldn't be too hard,* Zack told himself as he zipped his fly. *A simple chokehold from the backseat and the barrel of his Glock pressed firmly against Sergei's temple should do the trick.*

Zack smiled. He looked forward to discovering the truth about this Russian. Then, once they had delivered him over to the flyboys back at Camp Lemonnier, he'd be free from his assignment to Kwame and could go back to sitting behind a desk in an air-conditioned Quonset hut and wait for the regular guy to return.

CHAPTER Eleven

Archer's Post, Kenya; 1960

Standing next to his uncle's aging pickup truck, Samuel could smell the early evening wind before he felt its caress. Each night for the past two weeks, the wind would bring with it the pleasant scent of the fountain-tree blossoms. It was difficult to believe that nearly four years had passed since he had come here with Osuroo. Tall and spindly now, the 14-year-old—still calling himself by his father's name to everyone save his auntie—heaved the last of the straw bales into the truck.

It was the same truck Osuroo Bankole had picked him up in so long ago. The kind man had helped him find his Auntie Gemma and had checked on the two of them every day for weeks, and then months after that, as much to see Gemma as to see about him. Samuel sighed at the memory. His mother and sisters had never arrived.

Leaning against the truck bed and looking across the expansive farm, just one of many owned by Osuroo, Samuel wondered again what might have happened to them without their friend. "Osmann," he heard Osuroo call, "the cows will not feed themselves! Finish and you can be done early. Gemma reminded me that today is your birthday."

"On my way, Mjomba." Samuel had taken to calling

the kindly man "uncle" years ago, not long before Osuroo and Gemma had gotten married and she and Samuel had moved in with him.

Mjomba Osuroo had worked as a liaison for agricultural affairs between the British and the Kenyan farming institution before the rebellion. Samuel wasn't exactly sure what Osuroo had done during the Mau Mau rebellion but apparently the Brits had rewarded him handsomely for it. Samuel looked up to Osuroo and knew him to be a good man; whatever it was that he had done for the British would have only been in the best interest of the local people.

"You say that you are going, but I do not see any movement," Osuroo scolded, though he wore a smile. "Go, Osmann, or I will send your auntie to bring me a switch. You are not too old for me to whip, you know." Of course, he was teasing. Empty threats, just like all the others. Osuroo had never laid a hand on the boy. Nor had he called him by the name Gemma did. If Samuel wished to retain his father's name, then so be it.

Samuel climbed behind the wheel to turn the keys which Osuroo always left in the ignition. Today however, there was a gigantic wooden keychain with the name *Samuel* burned into it. A note had been taped to the side.

Happy Birthday. The truck is yours!
We love you,
Osuroo and Gemma

Samuel leaped from the cab and ran to Osuroo, throwing his arms and legs around him like a little boy.

"Thank you Mjomba! Thank you; thank you so very much!"

An attractive woman with slightly graying hair and dressed in yellow gingham came from around the side of the barn where she had been feeding the chickens. "What, you don't have any hugs for your favorite auntie?"

The 14-year-old peeled away from the man who'd become like a father to him and ran to his aunt to give her a bearhug. "I cannot thank you enough," he said.

She grabbed his shoulders and pushed him back so that he could see her face. "Do not drive that on the road, Samuel." Her eyes narrowed. "Only on the farm until you are 16."

"Or, when I am with you," added Osuroo as he came up and gathered them both in his arms.

"Husband, he is not ready to drive on the road. We have had this discussion," argued Gemma.

"Yes, and I did not agree."

"You *did* agree," she said, trying to look stern, although her eyes were sparkling. The two of them seldom argued in earnest.

"If I had agreed with you then we would have both been wrong," he teased. It was just one of his many favorite sayings. "Osmann may drive the car for a bit when I go to check on my other properties." Gemma frowned. "You worry too much, woman; I will be right beside him. Besides, how else will he learn? Now go inside and start my supper," he said, swatting her on the backside. "And as for you, Osmann, my cattle are hungry. Go!"

"There will be no supper for you, if you do not watch out," she teased. "I will give it all to our birthday-boy instead."

Samuel gave them both a gigantic grin before running for the truck and then driving to the other side of the pasture where a dozen head of cattle were still waiting for their dinner.

"He is a good boy," Osuroo said as they watched Samuel drive to the other side of the farm.

"Yes, but you spoil him too much," chastised Gemma.

Osuroo shrugged. "He is the closest thing you and I have to a son, woman; I think he can be spoiled from time to time. Besides, I can afford it."

"You can afford lots of things, my husband, but Samuel needs to know the value of money and the importance of work. My sister and brother-in-law would have wanted it that way."

"What do you mean? He works hard every day. He comes home from school and feeds the cattle, he rebuilds my fences, he takes care of his pet owls, he…"

"Alright, alright… enough." She watched the truck disappear over a hill and into a cloud of dust. "I just want what is best for him. He is all I have left of my sister's family."

Osuroo looked down at the ground below his feet and then kicked at the dirt. "So…?"

"So what, husband?"

"You know very well what. When are you going to tell him?"

"Every day, the same question."

"And every day you fail to answer. When are you going to tell him what happened to his mother and sisters?"

She looked away. "Certainly not today. It is his birthday."

"I agree, but he is old enough to know. When will you tell him?"

She looked back toward the barn. Two of the chickens had emerged from the coolness of the shade and were pecking the ground nearby.

"I will answer that only when you answer my question."

"Not that again, Gemma."

"Yes, that again. Things are becoming tense in the village. You need to hire guards for our home. There is trouble brewing; I can feel it. People know that you are a rich man."

"There is always trouble. The tribal elders have their hands full with the younger ones. It has always been that way. You know that I do not want guards on my property."

"Why not? You have them at your other properties."

He shook his head. "That is because I am not there. Here, I am enough to keep you and Osmann safe."

"You're an old fool is what you are."

He shrugged, tired of the endless request. "Okay, okay." He had been planning to tell her anyway. " I will hire one guard, but only for nighttime." Her eyes brightened. "And only if you promise me that you will tell the boy… *soon*."

She glanced back at the chickens, her eyes moist.

"How do you tell a child that his mother was raped and murdered and his baby sisters thrown to a pack of hyenas?"

"You don't. You only tell him what the other refugees told you that day, *that* they were killed… not *how* they were killed."

"It will crush him. You see how he still looks down the road as if he expects them to magically appear one day."

"Which is why he must know." Osuroo reached to gently stroke his wife's cheek. When he is older and finds out for himself, he will hate us for not telling him. Tomorrow, sit him down after school and tell him that he is old enough to finally know what happened to his family."

She looked into his eyes. "Why cannot you tell him, husband?"

Osuroo shook his head. "You are blood. It must be you."

She nodded, reluctantly. "You promise a guard here by the end of the week?"

He hadn't liked the idea, but he nodded his agreement. "Yes, yes, you win. I will have a night-guard here by the end of the week."

She smiled. "And one for the day?"

"Don't press your luck, woman."

She smiled, sheepishly. "I just want *both* of our children to be safe."

Osuroo's eyes grew large. "*Both*?"

She placed her hand on her mid-section and started to laugh as he swept her up into his arms.

CHAPTER Twelve

The incessant squeak of a Jacobin cuckoo somewhere in the brush was almost enough to drive Samuel up a wall as he and Osuroo finished the picnic lunch Auntie Gemma had packed for them.

"Why are you letting it bother you, Osmann? It merely wishes to share a bite of your bread."

"Bread is not good for birds," Samuel answered. "Besides, the bloody thing would only beg for more."

His uncle frowned. "Watch your language, Osmann."

Samuel looked away. "Why? There are no women present."

"Ach, teenagers." Osuroo rolled his eyes. "Did I teach you that cursing is *ever* okay?"

"No, but…"

"A cistern is known by the taste of its water," Osuroo said, trying to appear serious. Actually, he was amused, but he wouldn't let the boy know that. Like all the other times Osuroo quoted old African proverbs, Samuel had no idea what his uncle was talking about; still, he would obey and try to watch his language from now on—at least he would around his uncle.

Squeak.

Uncle Osuroo broke off a piece of crust from his brawn and onion sandwich and tossed it toward the bird, which flew down and caught it before it even touched the ground. The pair watched the bird as he went back to the brush with his prize. Uncle Osuroo smiled. "There, you see. That was all he wanted."

Squeak.

"Oh, bloody hell," cried Osuroo.

Samuel fell to the ground laughing, holding both his sides to keep them from hurting. Soon, Osuroo joined in the laughter. "Come now," he said a moment later. "Finish your sandwich. We have work to do before we go home."

It had been three months since Gemma had told the boy what had happened to his family. He'd wept, of course, and kept to himself for a time, but gradually he'd started to accept the awful truth. The weekends helped. Samuel enjoyed Saturdays most of all. It was when he was allowed to accompany his uncle to one of the family's other cattle farms to check on things. Each week they would go to a different one. Sometimes they would sleep in the truck overnight, or his uncle might bring along a tent and sleeping bags if they went as far as the cattle farm in Magado. Today, however, they were just outside Meru, only a couple of hours from home. They would be back tonight in time for a late dinner.

The two finished lunch, leaving the scraps for their obnoxious new friend before greeting the guard at the other end of the pasture. The three of them then walked amongst dozens of cows, his uncle showing Samuel how to vaccinate cattle—without getting kicked—before turning the job over to him. Osuroo and the guard laughed as they watched the boy nervously approach a skittish white cow and then end up chasing it across the pasture, waving the syringe and yelling at the top of his lungs: "But it's good for you!"

****

The drive home was often the best part of each Saturday as he and Uncle Osuroo, tired from the day's work, talked and laughed and teased one another. Samuel had learned a lot about his uncle on those drives—how Osuroo's mother had died delivering him and how Osuroo's great grandfather had been a Samburu chief. Osuroo's grandfather, had left their homeland for Nairobi where he'd managed to make a small fortune before returning to Kenya. He'd used the money to buy a number of small farms. Osuroo's father had turned them into lucrative meat producers, amassing capital until heeding the British call for Kenyan leaders to resist an industrial and political movement among the country's large Indian population. Osuroo's father had been murdered one night by a band of disgruntled Indian workers.

Osuroo was still quite young when he was made the sole heir of the family's great fortune. He could still recall how he had cried for days when the British official pinned a medal on him and told him that his father had died defending their country. As his uncle had grown and learned of the way the Indian population had been discriminated against, he no longer treasured the medal as he once had.

Samuel had learned much about his uncle's deep sense of right and wrong. Like Samuel's own father and mother, Osuroo was a devout Christian. They attended services at the village Anglican church every Sunday, often packing enough food to share with others for the days in which the priest's sermon went on too long. Although steeped in the Christian faith, Osuroo had passed on his convictions that all religions had much in common and that people needed to find ways to work together despite their differences.

"The Nile has many tributaries," his uncle would say, "but the great river ends up flowing only in one direction." Samuel didn't always understand his uncle's pithy proverbs, but deep down he enjoyed hearing them… *well, most of them.*

Osuroo checked his watch. "We are late," he said. "Your fried chicken will be cold."

"Yes, Mjomba, but you are the one Auntie will be angry with, not me."

Osuroo laughed. "Unless of course I tell her we spent half the afternoon waiting for you to catch a single cow."

Samuel's eyes widened. "You wouldn't… would you?"

Osuroo just laughed again. *Another empty threat…* at least Samuel hoped so. He thought it best to change the subject. "Mjomba, why did you hire a new security guard? What was wrong with the last one?"

"Nothing, Osmann. His brother wanted him to join him in Nigeria. There is much unrest there; he is going to help his brother relocate his family to Kenya. He will come back to work for us in the spring." He shook his head. "But I do not think that I am going to keep this new man, Chega. He drinks at night. I do not like that."

"But *you* drink beer?"

"Yes, but I do not drink when I am working, Osmann. There is nothing wrong with alcohol as long as you are in charge of it and it is not in charge of you."

"So, you will fire him?"

Osuroo chuckled. "Yes. I just hope that I do it before Gemma does. She is very angry about his attitude."

"And the drinking?"

The older man shook his head. "Osmann, do you think me a fool? If I were to tell Gemma the man is a drunk, she would have bounced him out on his head that very day."

They were within 15 minutes of home when Osuroo had Samuel pull the truck to the side of the road. "You had best let me drive from here," he said. "You know how your auntie gets about my letting you drive on the road."

Samuel made a face. "She still thinks I am a child."

"Only because she loves you. One day you will be in charge of all my property, but even then, you will still be as a little boy to her, I think."

The news came as a jolt to Samuel. "I will be in charge? I thought that would go to your son."

"We do not yet know if it is a boy. It could be a girl, you know."

"Still," Samuel persisted, "Samburu law says land falls along blood... boy or girl."

Osuroo didn't say a word. He got out of the truck to

swap seats with his nephew, but when they met behind the truck, he placed his hands on the boy's lean shoulders. "Do you know why I still call you Osmann?"

"No, sir."

"Because you told me that was your name so long ago. When I discovered that it was your father's name, and not yours, I continued to call you Osmann, yes?" Samuel nodded his head. "I do this because you have never asked me to change it. Osmann is a good name; a strong name. And so is Samuel, but until you tell me that you wish to be called by the name your mother gave you, then I will honor your words to me." He looked deeply into the boy's brown eyes.

"I want you to do the same for me. I want you to honor my words. What I am going to tell you is important; you must believe me when I say them, for I do not say them lightly. Do you understand?"

Samuel nodded solemnly.

"*You*, Osmann-Samuel, *are* my son."

The boy blinked, fighting back tears.

"I understand that from your standpoint I cannot be your father the way that Osmann was, just as Gemma cannot be your mother in the same way. But to us, you are *our* son. We will treat you no differently after the baby gets here. You will *both* be our children. We will not differentiate between the two of you. You are older, so when we are gone, despite my tribe's custom, *you* will be in charge. Your brother or sister will own the land with you and you must always include him… or her… in your decisions, but *your* word will be final."

Samuel could not hold back his tears. He locked his

arms around his uncle and wept. He had always known love within Osuroo's house, but *this*—this was beyond all expectations. It wasn't duty or familial obligation that had made Osuroo say those words… it was love.

Osuroo gazed over the boy's shoulders at a round hill in the distance. There were no trees on the hill, only tall grass that waved in the breeze like a blanket drying on a clothesline. "Osmann, turn around; do you see that hill?" Samuel was grateful for the moment to dry his eyes, embarrassed now that he had let his uncle see him cry, even if they had been joyful tears.

"Yes, Mjomba, what about it?"

"I have always thought that to be the most beautiful piece of land around. The Twanga family has owned it for generations. They are good people. Matthew Twanga's father died fighting the Italians. Matthew was nineteen and I was ten years his senior. We would help each other keeping the land. Matthew had four younger brothers. Together, we managed to take care of the land our fathers had loved." Osuroo smiled. "I would do anything for Matthew and he for me to this very day. Yet the one thing I have wanted most from him was the one thing which I could not ask."

"What is that, Mjomba?"

Osuroo pointed to the hill. "I have always envied him this land, particularly that hill. Do you not agree that it is beautiful?"

Samuel nodded. He did indeed.

"Why have you not offered to buy it?"

Osuroo smiled ever so slightly. "It is true. I have often wanted to purchase it."

"Mr. Twanga would not sell it to you?"

Osuroo shrugged. "I suppose he would, if the price were right."

"Then why haven't you? You certainly can afford it."

"But I have no *need* of it, you see, and I would be denying Matthew and his family the pleasure that I seek for myself."

Samuel shook his head. It was times like these that he did not understand his uncle. But, it was not his place to argue. Instead, they both leaned against the truck and stared at the faraway hill—Osuroo, enjoying the beautiful view, and Samuel simply being with the man who had just called him his son.

CHAPTER Thirteen

Grand Bara Desert; 2005

There are few places left on earth that are as dark as a starless night in the desert. Kwame and Zack had managed to build a small fire to ward off the chill and cook a meager meal from the supplies Kwame had purchased back in Ali Sabieh, knowing their journey would include a night on the sand. Kwame had gone to sleep in the Jeep while Sergei seemed content to lean against the grill of the Land Cruiser and stare into the nothingness. Both Tom and Jerry kept a watchful eye— how and for what, Zack could only guess.

Zack sat cross-legged in front of the fire, deliberately not looking at the others as he warmed his hands. As Tilly the runner, he would be a man accustomed to the desert and would think little of having men with machine guns studying him. As Zack the spy, strangers with guns who could easily have the upper hand were more than a bit disconcerting. Not to mention the jackals, and whatever the hell else it was out there that Tom and Jerry were guarding against. As much as he'd complained about being assigned to Djibouti, he'd much rather be back there than in this God-forsaken place.

"How long have you been a runner?" Zack hadn't heard the Russian come up from behind him. He glanced into the man's face as he stood over him and then back into the fire.

"Not long. Maybe six months."

"I must say I was surprised to see another white man out here. I wonder just how you got involved with such a dark trade."

Zack didn't know if Sergei was serious or making some sort of a racist joke. "We all gotta' do something," Zack said, reaching to toss another stick into the fire.

Sergei grunted slightly as he sat down next to him. "I suppose that is true. Still, I am curious. How did you get mixed in with Yazid?"

Zack knew it was a test. Sergei would no doubt be asking the same question of Kwame when he wasn't around. If the two stories didn't match, it would end up very badly for the both of them. He and Kwame had already rehearsed an answer. He kept his explanation simple.

"I was a mercenary without a cause. No one was hiring until I met up with Yazid in a bar in Ras Dashen."

"And that's it?"

Zack stared into the fire trying to look bored. "That's it."

"He said that you met in Addis Ababa." It was nothing more than a trick. Zack knew that Kwame hadn't had a moment alone with Sergei since they'd left Madame Tulame's.

"Nope. It was Ras Dashen. Addis Ababa is not as welcoming to mercenaries, at least not white ones.

Sergei smiled. "Da, I must have been mistaken, no?"

Zack shrugged.

"So, tell me, what wars have you fought as a soldier for hire?"

"The Congo mostly, then Sierra Leone, then in Kenya as bit of private work for a man there."

"What kind of work?"

"Like I said, private work."

"And do you miss your former work… I mean, compared to the life of a runner?"

"The pay is better and I don't get shot at as much, if that's what you mean."

Sergei continued to probe. "And just how much will you be paid from this job?"

"Yazid handles all of that." He glanced over at him, the Russian's face reflected an amber glow from the fire but his eyes seemed not to reflect any light at all. "You ask a lot of questions."

Sergei offered a practiced laugh. "What else are we going to do tonight? We can't even count the stars. It's your turn. Ask me a question?"

It was another test. A runner would never probe into the dealings of the people who used them. "Okay. What's up with Manchester United? I haven't heard a game in weeks."

Sergei shook his head. "I'm afraid that I don't follow football, European or American."

"That's too bad," Zack said. "It's the one thing I miss about the old days. Over here, though, you don't hear about American sports, so I got into the whole soccer thing. It's not as dull as I thought it would be."

Sergei reached into his jacket and pulled out a small

flask which he offered to Zack, who refused. "What, an American mercenary that doesn't drink?"

Zack snorted. "Used to," he lied. In truth he'd love a bourbon right now but wasn't about to risk liquor loosening his guard or his tongue. "Developed a problem."

"Come now, a sip won't hurt you."

"That's what I kept telling myself. In fact, I was telling myself just that the night Yazid found me." He took a stick and stirred the fire. "Besides, I'm not allowed when I'm with a client."

Sergei nodded, seeming satisfied and then put the flask away without taking a drink. *Just what was in that flask*, Zack wondered.

"Get some rest," Sergei said. "You do not have to stand guard; my men will watch over us throughout the night."

Zack looked behind him at one of the guards and then to his left where the other one stood. Both were peering into the darkness. "What, all night?"

"They are like cats those two, they see best at night."

"Yeah, but both? Why don't they take shifts?" Zack didn't like the thought of Tom and Jerry awake while he slept. Flenn used to say that Zack could sleep through an avalanche. What was to keep them from slicing his throat in the middle of the night?

"They will take turns sleeping in their vehicle tomorrow. It is okay, Tilly," the Russian continued as if intuiting his concern. "They will not harm you unless I am in danger. They are sworn to protect me with their lives." The Russian looked away quickly, as if he had just given away something.

Zack didn't respond, but filed it away. No doubt, there were others involved with this Russian. Maybe he and Kwame could get to the truth once they had managed to get Sergei to Camp Lemonnier. "They look able enough," was all he said.

"As do you, my friend. I suspect with those muscles you could rip a man in half if you chose to do so."

Zack pretended to be flattered, but he didn't relish the thought of having to find out against those two.

"So, if you do not mind my asking one more question," Sergei added, "I would just like to know…" He stopped short, seeing both of his guards move quickly out of the firelight.

"Tonanza, what is it?" Sergei called out. Zack didn't wait for an invitation; instinctively he rolled to the side, out of the way of whatever was out there, just as something whizzed past him. He heard a *thwang* and then a hiss as something punctured the tire of the Jeep. *Who the hell has a bow and arrow in the middle of the desert?*

Both guards began firing into the night, spraying bullets in a wide pattern. A second later and the guards disappeared into the blackness. Zack peered into the dark but couldn't see anything moving. He looked behind him and saw that Sergei had disappeared as well. The door to the Jeep was open, but Kwame was nowhere in sight. He rolled again, hoping that whoever was out there would see the movement and give away their position. Glock in hand, he waited for his pupils to dilate enough to return fire. Tonanza, whichever of the behemoths that was, and the other guard had stopped firing.

Either they'd been hit or were waiting for whomever was out there to make their move.

Zack strained to hear anything at all, other than the crackle of the campfire, but was met with silence, until at last he heard someone whispering behind him. He whipped around, ready to fire at one of the attackers who'd flanked them but saw only Kwame, a couple of meters behind him, crouching low and staring off to the left. "Sandsifters," he thought he heard Kwame whisper.

"Stay down." That he was sure he'd heard. As if in affirmation, an arrow landed not a foot away from Kwame's knee, sending him rolling to the left. Zack thought he saw movement 20 meters in front of him and fired twice before rolling to the right. He was certain he'd hit whatever it was. Several more arrows flew into the camp as if fired at once by a dozen men, none finding their mark. Suddenly the night burst into the God-awfullest sound he'd ever heard. It was made by several human voices crying out simultaneously. A shrill, horrible cacophony that sent a shiver down his spine; the only good thing about it was that it was fading into the distance. *They were running away!* A few seconds later and he heard the sound of machine gun fire chasing after them.

Kwame crawled up beside Zack, holstering his weapon. "Definitely Sandsifters. They live out here. Not particularly fond of visitors."

"Obviously. Just who are these people; how can they possibly live out here?"

"Like the scorpions, the Sandsifters know how to survive. They were probably after our water."

"Not our cargo?"

"Diamonds and such aren't useful to them. Out here, water is the most precious thing there is. They're primitive; they deliberately shun the use of technology. They'd kill us, take our water and possibly our carcasses."

Zack's nose wrinkled in disgust. "Don't tell me they're cannibals too?"

"Okay, I won't tell you."

Sergei called to them from behind the Jeep.

"Whatever you do, don't act surprised," Kwame warned. "Just follow my lead."

"Got it," Zack said. "We don't want the Russian to think this is my first rodeo." Kwame raised a puzzled eyebrow but ignored the remark.

"Have they gone?" Sergei called.

Kwame peered into the night. "Only to regroup, I'm afraid. They will be back."

Zack shuddered at the thought.

Sergei stood and crossed over to them. *Courageous or crazy,* Zack thought, still keeping his eyes peeled toward where the attack had come. After a moment, he and Kwame also rose to their feet. "Any idea who they were?" Sergei said. It was more of a command than a question.

"Sandsifters, I'd say. What about you, Yazid?"

Kwame nodded, refusing to smile at Zack's total ignorance of what he was talking about. "Mchanga-sita. That's what my people call them. They are nomads; primitive but vicious toward outsiders."

"They likely wanted our water." Yazid nodded, as Zack tried to upstage him.

"Yes. And since we have no animals, perhaps our flesh, as well."

Sergei didn't respond the way Zack thought he would. He merely sighed and walked toward the back of the Toyota where he retrieved an AK-74. It appeared brand new. Zack admired the 74 series over the 47 for its sheer power. It could cut a man in half in the blink of an eye. It was now the standard-bearer for the Russian Army. He gazed down at his Glock .45—deadly, but nothing in comparison to the AK.

One of the guards appeared from out of the darkness, soaked with sweat. He strode up to his boss, leaned in and whispered something, then waited to make certain whatever he had said had sunk in.

"Gentlemen," Sergei addressed Zack and Kwame, his eyes betraying alarm. He nodded in the direction of the Toyota. "In the back of our vehicle you will find two more assault rifles. "I suggest you replace your tire swiftly and we put as much distance between us and these… these sand people as we can."

As dangerous as it was to drive in the desert at night with no idea about what was beyond the beam of the headlights, Kwame quickly decided it was the lesser of two evils. The bandits would return and they would likely have reinforcements. He motioned to Zack to change the tire. As the perceived low man on the totem pole, all the menial jobs would naturally fall to him.

"Where is your other man, Bwana?" Kwame asked. "I hope he is not pursuing the Sandsifters; they can be most cruel to those they capture."

Sergei's jaw tightened. "I'm afraid they cannot do him any more harm."

Kwame understood. So did Zack. He had the tire changed in no time flat.

CHAPTER Fourteen

1960

The guard was not at the gate. Osuroo checked his watch; it was an hour past when the man was to have started duty. *Drunk again, no doubt*, he told himself. *He would definitely fire the man tomorrow. Perhaps Matthew Twanga would allow him to hire one of his sons until he could find someone to take the guard's place. Gemma would insist that there be someone.* As rumors of another rebellion filtered through the countryside, he no longer blamed her for feeling insecure. Truth be told, he felt better having someone to watch over her while he was tending cattle, especially with her four months pregnant.

They made their way up the long drive to the house in silence; Osuroo did not want to burden the boy with his mounting anger. As he parked the truck, Osuroo told him: "Osmann, would you go out back and check on the chickens, I want to speak with your auntie alone." Samuel walked toward the barn as he was instructed. He, too, had noticed the guard's absence.

Even from the barn he could hear his uncle's anguished cry. He ran for the door, through the kitchen and into the bedroom. As long as he would live, he would never forget what he saw there. His uncle was cradling his auntie, holding her to his chest and making sounds that Samuel had not heard since the day the Mau Maus had swept through his neighborhood. Auntie Gemma was motionless, her tattered and torn clothes thrown beside the bed. The quilt that she told him that she and his mother had made when he was small was soaked in blood. He turned and ran to the toilet where he vomited twice. He couldn't bring himself to go back to the bedroom so he ran into the kitchen. Few houses this far out had telephones, but he knew the Twanga family had one. He picked up the receiver and dialed the number that Auntie Gemma kept in a small box with some pencils and paperclips.

He was waiting outside minutes later when Matthew Twanga and his two oldest boys drove up in their Jeep; all three were carrying rifles.

"Samuel, are you all right?" Mr. Twanga shouted. Samuel nodded, then pointed into the house. "Jimiyu," Mr. Twanga called to his youngest boy, "stay with Samuel." Mr. Twanga and Gichinga, the eldest son, sped into the kitchen and didn't come back out for a long time. Samuel wanted to go in as well, but could only make it as far as the threshold. Only a year Samuel's senior, Jimiyu, usually a talkative boy, was silent.

The sun was setting over the far pasture and Samuel felt sick again. *Someone had killed Auntie Gemma, and perhaps the guard, as well.* An idea struck him. "Jimiyu, did you see our guard on the side of the road? Shot perhaps?"

Jimiyu shook his head.

"If your father comes out, tell him I am going to the end of our drive and see if he might be in the ditch.

Whoever k…, whoever did this, must have attacked Mr. Chega first."

"Unless Chega…" Jimiyu didn't finish the thought. From the look on Samuel's face, he could tell that he didn't have to. Samuel climbed into the truck and turned the vehicle in the short grass, sending clods of dirt and loose gravel spraying as he sped down the long drive to search for evidence that Chega had been attacked and was lying in a nearby ditch.

He found nothing.

****

The funeral for Auntie Gemma was attended by nearly 600 well-wishers and members of the Samburu people. The normally sunny sky had been overcast, as if the sun itself was too grieved to watch. Samuel stood next to his uncle, both in black, as the drums fell silent and the Anglican priest opened his prayer book.

Funerals here were a mixture of customs. Many of the Samburu had converted to Christianity generations ago. Some held to the old ways, and still others practiced ancient rituals that Osuroo and Gemma had not embraced. Even as remote as their home was, Samuel had heard of barbaric practices in some Samburu homes, particularly on young females. But today, as he stood by the open grave in the churchyard, he paid no attention to the brightly colored clothing or the beaded necklaces worn by the tribesmen and women. Instead, he stared at the open hole in the earth. It was the perfect metaphor for his soul right now… first, his father, then his mother and sisters, and now this. It was too much for him to bear. He wanted to jump in the hole with his auntie and have them cover him with dirt so that he would never again know such pain.

For his part, Osuroo stood straight and tall, somber but distinguished. His choice of European black for the funeral instead of the ancient colors of his people, was less about culture than it was expectation. Wealthy land-owners, Kenyan or English, normally wore black to fu-nerals. Samuel thought it appropriate— how could there be color left in the world without any other member of his family left alive. He felt the key which he still wore underneath his clothing, and remembered something he had long forgotten: *He had an uncle.* The man had been despised by his father, but somehow, even for a fleeting moment, it was reassuring to know that there was at least one living soul who shared his bloodline.

"In the midst of life we are in death," read the priest. "To whom may we look for help, but from you, Lord, who for our sins are justly displeased."

Justly displeased? What sin had Auntie Gemma possibly committed that deserved this? Samuel nearly bit through his bottom lip.

So far, Chega had denied everything to the police. Only two policemen serviced this area, and they had nearly 60 kilometers to cover. Neither was known for his intelligence or efficiency. Samuel exhaled, not realizing that he had been holding his breath. His eyes scanned the crowd for any sign of the man he thought might have killed his auntie. What was it he had read in the American spy novel? Something about a criminal always returns to the scene of the crime.

Samuel had wondered aloud in front of Osuroo how they might force Chega to confess. His uncle hadn't responded, which in itself was evidence that the same thought was going through his head. "The council will investigate," his uncle had finally said after Samuel had pressed. "We must leave it to them." The Samburu council meted out justice after most offenses committed in Archer's Post. Actual crime was rare, but property squabbles were commonplace, as were decisions of marriage, and sometimes patrimony. However, in rare cases when a crime was committed, the police weren't necessarily the first to be called in to investigate. The council would meet with the victim—always a man, even when the true victim was a woman—and ask appropriate, and sometimes inappropriate, questions. If warranted, they would select two of their own to question others. Then, there would be some sort of day-long, mystical consultation which involved the tossing of bones and the rolling of dice and a lot of smoking of leaves from the jujari tree. Pronouncement would be made by the head of the council at daybreak; and punishment, when it was called for, was to be executed by nightfall.

Osuroo and Gemma had exhibited little faith in the old ways, so it was surprising to hear his uncle tell him that they must wait upon the council. Samuel had wanted his uncle to confront Chega. Instead, his uncle had insisted upon patience. "You want revenge, Osmann," his uncle had said. "That is understandable, but you are too young to realize that revenge never satisfies a grieving heart. Wait instead for justice. It will come. If not from the council then from God."

The words had infuriated Samuel. He had stormed out of the house that day, slamming the door behind him. It was then that he devised a plan. *He would force Chega to confess!* His uncle kept a hunting rifle, but it was locked away. His friend, Jimiyu Twanga, however, had a .22 with him the day that his family had come. He would speak to Jimiyu after the service. Samuel would not involve his friend, only have him leave the .22 by the back door one night.

Samuel knew the shack where Chega lived. Out of respect for his uncle's wishes, he would give the council the remainder of the week, but if they had not moved to settle the matter by midnight Friday then he would take matters into his own hands on Saturday.

The priest was concluding now. "Grant to us who are still in our earthly pilgrimage, and who walk as yet by faith, that thy Holy Spirit may lead us in holiness and righteousness all our days." Everyone joined in the *Amen*; everyone, that is, except for Samuel. It was not a prayer he wanted to affirm.

Revenge, not righteousness, was the only thing on his mind. And, unless the council acted soon, he would make certain to have it.

CHAPTER Fifteen

Grand Bara Desert; 2005

Each man was wide awake as the two vehicles made their way through the pitch black of the starless night. Zack and Kwame took the lead, with Sergei and Tonanza following a safe distance behind. Kwame had warned Tonanza that he wouldn't be driving faster than 20 kilometers an hour. It would be equally calamitous to fall into the hands of the Sandsifters, plummet into a pit, or get caught in a sudden sandstorm.

Zack spent the first half-hour going over both of the AK-74s Sergei had lent them. He had been correct—they were new, seemingly fresh from the factory. *How had Sergei gotten hold of such pristine weapons? More importantly, why was he packing such an arsenal?* The Russian hadn't shown much surprise at the attack; nor had he asked them a plethora of questions about the Sandsifters. *Perhaps he knew of them and that such a danger existed. Was that why the guards had chosen to stay alert back at the camp?* There was definitely more to this Russian than being a smuggler. *But what?*

Personally, Zack couldn't wait to get him back to Djibouti. While he hadn't planned on losing someone, he knew it would be easier to deal with one guard than two when the time came. Kwame's scheme was to separate them on the outskirts of Addis Ababa, capture Sergei and get him to a CIA safehouse that Kwame knew about. From there, they should have no trouble ordering a military flight back to Camp Lemonnier.

"So, who do you think he really is, Tilly?"

Zack grunted. "Would you cut it out with the *Tilly* crap when they're not with us."

Kwame grinned. "Got to keep in practice," he retorted.

"I mean of all the names you could have come up with, you gave me a dog's name. God, I hope Flenn never hears about this."

Kwame laughed. "I suspect you are wishing more than ever that your partner had been assigned to this job instead of you, no?"

"Ugh."

"I understand. Sergei is—what do you Americans say—a tough customer."

"Sergei doesn't scare me; he's just a puzzle that's all."

"*He* may not scare you, but I saw the look on your face when the Sandsifters came."

Zack leaned back in his seat. "Just surprised, that's all. I wasn't expecting Geronimo to start shooting arrows at me."

"Gerono-who?"

"Never mind. When do you plan to stop for the night? We're both going to need some sleep before we arrive tomorrow."

"Another hour should do it. If they are following, they shouldn't be able to catch us sleeping."

Zack glanced in the side mirror. "They're on foot, right?" Kwame nodded. "Then what's the problem, we've already put ten kilos behind us."

Kwame shook his head. "Do not underestimate them, my friend. The Sandsifters are called that because they can run swiftly through the sand as if it were as smooth as glass. At least the young ones can."

"What about the old ones?"

Kwame's jaw tightened. "I do not know. No one has ever met one."

"Good Lord, they don't eat their own people... do they?"

"Do not your Eskimos place their elderly on ice floes and set them adrift?"

"That's just a fairy tale."

Kwame nodded his head slightly. "But are not most fairy tales grounded somewhere in the truth?"

Zack checked the mirror again. "Perhaps we should just keep driving then."

"No. You are right, we need some rest. Plus, we will need the morning light to be able to finish our journey. I will stop in an hour and we will take turns guarding the camp."

Zack thought it was a sound idea. "No fire though; we don't want to attract any more bad guys."

Kwame shrugged. "They won't need a fire. If they want us, they will know how to find us."

"Geez, Kwame, you're just a barrel full of fun, aren't you?"

"The desert is not a place for fun, my friend."

Zack tightened his gripped on the AK-74. "Between you, the Sandsifters, and Sergei, I'm beginning to believe you."

CHAPTER Sixteen

Darkness entombed the usually bright kitchen as Samuel half-stumbled, half-dragged himself to the table before collapsing into the chair where his Auntie Gemma used to sit at meal time. He stared into the dark, grateful that he could not see anything more than silhouettes of the objects around him. By far his favorite room in the house, the familiarity of Auntie Gemma's kitchen brought him little comfort this night.

The kitchen table had been where he used to sit for hours and talk with his auntie after dinner. This was where she'd helped him with his homework, talked to him about family long gone, and even advised him on how to make an impression on the girls at the parochial school he attended. *Chega had stolen all of that from him!*

His rage hadn't been satisfied by what he'd done tonight the way he thought it would be. It had simply broadened, encompassing his every action until at last, when it was all said and done, left him feeling totally spent. *Uncle Osuroo was right, he should have left it to the council.* His impatience and distrust of the ancient ways would only made things worse. How would he be able to live with himself now that the deed was done?

"Be brave," his father had told him. *Had he? Or had it*

been an act of ultimate cowardice, facing an unarmed man? Would he have pulled the trigger if Chega hadn't charged him? Unfortunately, he'd never know. He realized now that he had only deluded himself into thinking that he was doing this for the good. Samuel sat alone in the terrible silence, feeling as if everything he had once known, had once trusted and relied upon, all his inner grounding, had suddenly and irrevocably been ripped to shreds by an act of revenge. The tears began as a slow trickle and soon turned into gut-wrenching sobs.

His uncle stood in the shadows of the doorway for several minutes before announcing his presence.

"Your auntie used to say that 'tears may wash the heart from pain, but that the mind will always remember.'"

Uncle Osuroo sighed heavily. "What you have done you cannot undo," he said, understanding what had transpired tonight. "You must learn to live with it."

Samuel searched through the tears and the darkness for his uncle's face. Would disapproval be found there? Rejection? Relief? Oddly, he found none of those. Instead he saw only empathy, as if his uncle knew everything that he was feeling, and what he would go on feeling for the rest of his life.

"How did you know?"

Osuroo ignored the question. "You feel now that your world has changed forever. You are correct; it has. I wish I could tell you otherwise." He sighed again, and then warned: "The terrible thing about life is that once you have done a thing, it becomes that much easier to do it again."

Samuel stuttered, "I can't... I won't... I swear." His head fell into his arms on the table, his body jerked violently as he wept.

After a time, his uncle said, "If you keep those words, Os... *Samuel*, then in *them*, and not in what you did tonight, will you truly honor Gemma. *Huba inaondoa unyonge*, Samuel. Love will always remove misery."

Osuroo turned and left as silently as he had appeared. It was the only conversation they would have about the matter that night, or ever again.

In the morning, Osuroo found Samuel still at the table, asleep but fitfully so. Half boy, half man; Samuel was on the threshold of a changed life that neither his father nor his uncle would have ever wished for him, but one which would have made them both proud of the man *their* son would later become.

CHAPTER Seventeen

Once they'd finally stopped for a rest, Zack chose to remain in the Jeep and sleep while Kwame and Tonanza kept a lookout for Sandsifters. Kwame had insisted that the mysterious desert raiders were opposed to all forms of modern technology and, as such, would not have access to a vehicle. Common sense told him that there was no way the bandits could cover the 35 or so miles and catch up with them here. Still, his sleep was fitful, marred with dreams of flying arrows.

Kwame, for his part checked multiple times on Zack, and once on Sergei, who was sleeping in the Toyota. He and Sergei's remaining guard, Tonanza, said little to one another and kept their eyes peeled for any sign of movement in the desert. Tonanza, no doubt, had heard many of the same stories Kwame had about the sand people and their remarkable abilities. *Sure*, Kwame told himself, *Zack was probably right, they would have no reason to follow them all this way; the little water they carried was not worth the effort, and the rumors about their gruesome diet were probably nothing more than that, just rumors.*

Kwame however knew otherwise. The Sandsifters had a reputation for being tenacious, never giving up, and often following their emotions rather than reason. If they were determined to put an end to these intruders who had trespassed into their world, they would stop at nothing. Fortunately, the clouds were beginning to break and while there was no moon tonight, the stars were casting some light one-by-one upon the desert floor. Kwame would give it another hour and then suggest that they drive another 10 or 15 kilometers before resting again and letting Zack take watch for the rest of the night. He glanced at his counterpart. This was not Tonanza's "first rodeo," Matteson would probably say. Kwame promised himself that he would find out just what a rodeo was once they got back to civilization. For his part, Tonanza kept methodically moving his head left to right, slowly scanning the landscape. The dissipating clouds were allowing them to see better than before—of course, that worked both ways. Their enemies could see them too. Kwame was tall, lean, and fast. This guy was built like a brick wall with limbs, and likely he could crush an opponent with one arm. The Sandsifters were tall, like him, and fast, but Tonanza could take several out in hand-to-hand combat if it came to that. *Why was he doing this to himself? The sand people would never catch up to them. They were safe here.*

The sound of an engine in the distance changed his mind. Tonanza heard it, too. *No, it couldn't be the sifters; unless they hadn't been Sandsifters after all, but then why shoot an arrow into a tire? If it were anyone else, they would have used bullets. Could they have a vehicle after all? What the hell was he doing wasting time asking himself stupid questions?!* Kwame crossed quickly to the Jeep to awaken Zack. Tonanza had already alerted Sergei.

Zack wiped the sleep from his eyes. "What's going on?"

"We've got company," answered Kwame. Zack grabbed the AK and stepped out of the Jeep. By now Sergei and Tonanza had joined them and the four men strained to hear the sound of the distant motor.

"I thought you said Sandsifters don't drive," Zack complained.

"They don't," Tonanza said. "Whoever it is, they're not Sandsifters."

"Runners?" Zack said.

"Is that good?" Sergei asked.

Not for them, Zack thought, *not if they all knew each other, which they probably did. At the very least, they'd be curious about these strangers, and that would not bode well.*

Tonanza motioned for everyone to keep quiet. "No. Not runners. There is more than one engine. Sounds like heavy trucks or armored vehicles."

"Patrols?" Sergei asked.

Tonanza and Kwame both nodded. "Militia," Tonanza said, his eyes narrowing.

"Whose?" asked Zack.

"Does it matter?" Kwame countered.

Zack tightened his grip on the AK. "What are they looking for?"

"Us." Kwame answered.

"But how?"

"Not us exactly. Runners. Every now and again some of the military go out in search of runners to confiscate their money or their diamonds."

"And then what?" Sergei demanded.

Kwame walked to the back to the Jeep. "It doesn't end well."

"They're no more than assassins," Tonanza said. "Raised in war, and the blood of their kin; they will think nothing of killing us."

"If they can find us," Zack offered.

Tonanza's jaw became like stone. "They will find us."

Sergei, who'd shown little fear of the Sandsifters earlier, looked first to Tonanza and then to Zack, more concerned about well-armed militia than he had been about bandits with bows and arrows. "We should try and outrun them, no?"

Zack certainly thought it was a good idea.

"No," came a voice behind him.

The three men turned to see Kwame holding a rocket launcher loaded with a surface-to-air missile ready to fire. "We will stand and fight."

CHAPTER Eighteen

The retiring dean of Kenya's former Royal College, now the University of Nairobi, gazed at the young and eager faces of the 1973 graduating class and felt a wave of pride sweep over him. His 35 years of teaching was coming to a close but the satisfaction he felt at having helped channel some of Africa's greatest minds was deeply gratifying.

He called the names of the doctoral students first. When, at last, his favorite student, stood before him, Dean Muthoni smiled broadly. "Samuel," he whispered to the young man as he handed him his diploma, "you are indeed destined for greatness. I will miss you most of all." Not many of Dean Muthoni's engineering students remained to earn their master's, much less a Ph.D. Samuel was one of only five in the past three years.

At the conclusion of the ceremony, Samuel refrained from joining the other students who had thrust their hands up in a victory sign—or peace symbol as the American hippies had turned it into of late—Uncle Osuroo did not approve of calling attention to one's own accomplishments. Still, Samuel knew that his uncle had been extremely proud as he sat in the audience watching his nephew cross the stage.

This was a bittersweet day. Already, the truck Osuroo had given him so long ago was packed with his belongings for the long drive to Rhodesia. It would take Samuel nine days to drive the 3,000-plus kilometers to Harare, and another couple of days to settle into his new apartment. He would begin teaching the summer course at the Rhodesian Royal College in a little over two weeks; it was all so hard to imagine. Uncle Osuroo had been saddened, of course, to see him take a job so far away, especially with the troubles currently going on in Rhodesia. *But this was Africa, where was there not trouble?*

"With times of great stress come great opportunities," his uncle had said at last, giving his blessing to Samuel's decision. "Just write me every week, and call once a month." Samuel had promised.

The ceremony completed, some of the graduates playfully whipped their graduation stoles over their head as they headed outside for a grand banquet. Friends embraced one another for the last time, and individual professors were presented with small gifts and tokens of appreciation by their former students. It was an exciting, sad, joyful, scary, wonderous moment… made more poignant by the gift Uncle Osuroo handed his nephew. Samuel held the hand-carved wooden box in his hands. "What is it?" he asked turning the box from side to side.

His uncle smiled. "A memento of the past and a promise for the future."

"Another one of your riddles, Mjomba?"

Osuroo smiled. "Not at all, Samuel." He had not called his nephew Osmann since that night at the dinner table a decade ago. "There is no mystery contained in this box... only my great respect for the man you have become and the love I will always have for you."

Samuel raised an eyebrow. "I thought you said that it is not a mystery," Samuel said. "What greater mystery is there than love?"

"You quote *me*, now, do you?" Uncle Osuroo smiled as Samuel carefully opened the box to find copies of the deed to all his uncle's properties. "What is this, Mjomba?"

"Notice whose name is at the top of each deed." Samuel couldn't believe it; it was his own.

He stared at the papers, then his uncle, then the papers again. "I do not understand."

"You are my heir and would inherit all that I have when I die, but this way there can be no mistake, no legal battles, no corrupt politicians to bribe. You own all my land now. I will be your steward and care for it while you are teaching in that big city college, no?" He touched the box lightly. "But these papers mean that you have roots here in Kenya, deep roots. They will draw you back to me from time to time." He smiled through the tears. "This is always your home, Samuel. The land of my fathers is now your land, for that is a father's right: to pass what is his down to his son."

The words brought tears to Samuel's eyes. Osuroo was every bit his father just as Osmann had once been. Mjomba, he had always called him, *uncle*, but looking into the dear man's face he knew that this was—now and for all time—his *Baba*, his dad.

Osuroo brushed back his own tears with the back of his still strong hand and nodded toward the box. "There is one thing more… something from long ago. When you were little you wore it around your neck every day. I found it amongst some of your auntie's things and kept it. You gave it to her for safekeeping and told her that it had belonged to your father. You were wearing it the day that I found you on the road."

A lump formed in Samuel's throat. He had all but forgotten the iron key and the story behind it. Yet now, here it was, in the bottom of the box, still on the same chain he had once worn. His uncle appeared perplexed as Samuel's lips tightened and his eyes narrowed. "I am sorry; I have presented you with a sorrowful gift, perhaps?"

Samuel shook his head. "No. Only a memory. Neither bad nor good." He forced a grin. "Thank you. Your gifts are beyond my words. I do not know what to say."

Osuroo took him by both shoulders. "Only say that you will return to me in two-years-time and spend the summer at Archer's Post, just as we agreed. I can occupy myself with many things taking care of your land until then." Samuel nearly dropped the box as he reached around his uncle and hugged him tightly.

The walk to the truck was a somber one, neither man ashamed to display emotion before the other. The final hugs and goodbyes were said and Samuel opened the door to climb in. His uncle stepped back and straightened himself to his full stature as best he could. "*Mungu akupe kheri daima*, Samuel."

Samuel nodded his head slowly at the blessing. "God has blessed me many times over… he always has, from the moment my first father hid me amongst the boulders to the day he led me to you, and to this very moment. And... **Baba**... I know that God will lead me back to you, my second father." He started the ignition and drove away, not wanting Osuroo to be burdened with his ensuing sobs, lest it remind him of that horrible night so long ago at the kitchen table.

Osuroo waved until the truck was out of sight before his body could no longer support him. He half-sat, half-fell to the ground. But it was not just from the weight of a decade of grief and worry, it was also the knowledge that he could no longer protect Samuel from whatever was out there. *Africa*, he knew, *could be like a pack of hyenas hiding in the brush*. These days there were terrible things lying in wait for the innocent and unprepared.

Wiping his eyes, Osuroo managed to get to his feet a few moments later. *Samuel is neither innocent nor unprepared,* he reminded himself. *He is a good man, with a quick mind and a strong back*. "You old fool," he said aloud, not caring if others heard. "He will be fine. God will take care of him." He turned his eyes heavenward in more of a demand than a prayer. "Just watch over him and let me see him again before I die is all I ask."

As Osuroo turned to head back to his own truck, he thought about what Samuel had called him for the first time. He stretched himself once again to his full height. The word filled his heart with renewed pride and satisfaction. At length, he smiled. *"Baba!"*

CHAPTER Nineteen

2005

"Tilly, quick get a second rocket!" Zack hesitated a second before doing as Kwame instructed. The sound of the approaching vehicles—Zack could distinguish two, possibly a third—was getting closer. Zack wasn't happy about this at all. *Were they really going to fire on an unsuspecting convoy of who-knows-who-the-hell-they-are?*

Sergei's momentary trepidation had been just that, momentary. He quickly retrieved two more AK-74s from the back of the Toyota—*just how many of those things did these guys have?*—and handed one of them to Tonanza, who slung it across his shoulder as a backup. He stared at the rocket launcher. "You guys know how to handle that thing?"

"Yes, Bwana," Kwame said. "It has already taken down an American helicopter. We know what we are doing." Kwame lowered his voice then so only Zack could hear: "Do we?"

"I know how to fire it, if that's what you mean." Zack said, hoping it wouldn't come down to that.

Sergei turned and stared in the night toward the sound of the engines. "Damn these stars! There is too much light. From the direction they are coming, they'll be sure to see us."

"Doesn't necessarily mean that they'll take an interest." Even Zack didn't believe what he'd just said.

"They'll take more than an interest. They'll take our vehicles and leave us face down in the sand." Sergei almost spat the words. "Not to mention the shipment of AK-74s."

Zack cocked his head. "I've been wondering about that, Sergei."

"What?"

Oh well, in for a penny, in for a pound. "Just why do you have so many of these shiny tinker toys?"

Sergei placed his left hand around the foregrip of his assault rifle. "Not everything in Africa has to do with diamonds."

Sergei wasn't a diamond smuggler after all; he was a Russian gun-runner! At the moment however, it didn't matter what type of criminal he was; they were all in danger.

"Yazid, you and Tilly hide behind the vehicles and be ready to fire on my order." Sergei gestured to his guard. "Flank them from the left; wait for them to fire and then pick your targets. Don't waste ammunition. We don't know how many soldiers they have." Zack stared at Sergei. *This man wasn't an ordinary gun-runner. He'd had military experience. Command experience.* For the hundredth time, Zack asked himself, *Who the hell is this guy?*

Zack and Kwame made for the Toyota and crouched behind it. "You know, if they hit this truck it's going to go up in one big bang."

"Know it? I'm counting on it. I don't know about

you but I don't want to fall into their hands. Do you know what the militia do to their captives?"

"What?"

Kwame shook his head. "Never mind. Best that you do not know."

"So, let me get this straight. You are just going to blow them to smithereens without knowing who they are first."

"I know who they are."

Zack was getting angry. "You can't possibly know. Maybe they're the good guys."

"Matteson, don't you get it yet? There are no good guys out here." He handed the heavy launcher to Zack. "Here, finish getting this thing ready to fire."

Zack armed the weapon, even though it was making his stomach turn. *Killing those who deserved to be killed was one thing, but this... this was something else. This was murder.* He still wasn't convinced they were the enemy as he got his first glimpse of two lightly armored pickup trucks coming over a sand bank. He watched as they slowed and then turned toward their direction. So much for hoping to go unseen.

"Yazid, you and Tilly get ready to fire! Take out the lead truck first, on my order."

"Who does this guy think he is?" griped Zack.

"Our boss," answered Kwame.

"Maybe it's time to show him otherwise. I mean, if you think I am going to murder innocent..." A volley of machine-gun fire stopped him mid-sentence. "What the hell? They don't even know who we are!"

"They don't care who we are, just what we might

have that they can take." Another volley. "They're testing us, trying to get us to reveal our positions. Get that damn thing ready to fire."

Suddenly, protecting the rights of the innocent was no longer at play. Kwame was right. Whether they were wearing uniforms or not, these were nothing but bandits. He flipped off the safety switch and got ready to fire.

"What's the range of that thing?"

"I can take either one of them out right now."

"Don't. Let Sergei give the order and think that he is in command. If we live through this, we still have a job to accomplish."

Kwame couldn't see Zack's face turning red. "Oh, I'm going to live through this, all right. And, first chance I get I'm going to find out who that Russian son of a bitch is, I promise you."

Kwame raised his AK toward the attackers. "First things first, brother."

CHAPTER Twenty

Rhodesia; 1975

Gunfire erupted somewhere on the campus, causing the students in the classroom to duck for cover. Yet the professor refused to hide behind his desk. He knew from repeated experience that it would be over soon. The military, ordered to guard the Royal College by President Dupont, had met resistance from both students and the occasional guerillas. And the military did not hesitate to use lethal force in response.

Violence had become increasingly commonplace both at the school and throughout the city of Harare in recent months. Professor Kauxhohuena was glad to be taking the next semester off.

Samuel stood motionless and waited for the commotion to end. *It would be good to be back in Archer's Post with his uncle.* Kenya was relatively calm compared to Rhodesia. While Samuel refused to allow his classmates to see him react at the sound of machinegun fire, inwardly he was concerned that the soldiers were taking things too far. Across the world, even in America, there were reports of student unrest and soldiers firing on unarmed students. Here, the rumor was that some students were armed, but Samuel had his doubts.

The military had proven it was not above firing upon

the innocent. Of course, the soldiers had been genuinely provoked for nearly a year, which was why they were on the campus in the first place. There had been several guerilla groups in Harare who'd thought nothing of posing as scholars in the hopes of turning young people against the government. If rumors were true, President Clifford Dupont would be resigning soon. Not that it mattered all that much in the grand scheme of things. The presidency was ceremonial; the real power lay in the hands of Rhodesia's Prime Minister, Ian Smith. Both men were white, appointed by the Queen of England, and as out of touch with the needs of the people as the British had been in Kenya before leaving in 1963.

Sure enough, just as Samuel had predicted, the shooting stopped. After a few eerie moments of silence, the students emerged from underneath their desks. Although he had nearly completed the lesson plan for the day, Samuel didn't dismiss the class until he was certain that they'd be safe leaving the building. He continued to teach, using chalk against blackboard, outlining how to accurately measure the amount of pressure on a bridge truss. Some of the students resumed taking notes, while others watched the door or nervously glanced toward the windows—one of which had still to be replaced after having been shattered by a stray bullet two weeks ago.

After class, as Samuel was gathering up his books, a young man who always sat in the back approached him. "Professor, how is it that you are always so calm when the shooting starts?"

Samuel glanced up but continued to fill his briefcase. "Emmanuel, isn't it?"

The young man nodded. "Yes, sir."

"Emmanuel, what good does it do to be afraid?" He quoted his uncle Osuroo. "If we spend our lives fearing what is in the shadows, we will never be able to enjoy the sunshine."

The aspiring engineer scratched his head. "You believe there can be sunshine when a foreign power tells us what we can do, whom we can do it with, and how we must do it?"

"I believe we can find peace in almost any situation."

"How can we find peace when there is no justice in the land?"

Samuel tilted his head downward, keeping his eyes fixed on the student and giving the same impression of disapproval that the older professors did when they stared over their spectacles after a student blurted something absurd. "Tell me, Emmanuel, if Rhodesia throws off the Brits, then what? Will not the people find fault in whatever forces come to power? I am not saying that Rhodesia must accept foreign rule, but what I am saying is do not delude yourself into thinking that salvation comes from the other side of the same coin. First be at peace within yourself, then you will find your voice, a much stronger voice than the one which simply spouts the rhetoric of others."

Samuel had long heard the Rhodesian version of the American civil rights movement: 'No justice, no peace.' While he agreed that justice and peace must go hand in hand, he knew that many who wielded such clever sayings had no appetite for either and were simply seeking ways to justify their violent actions.

"Changes are coming, professor."

"Yes, indeed. Only the foolish believe that things stay the same. Change is the only constant—outside the world of engineering—that I am aware of. But not all changes are for the better," he cautioned. "Dedicate yourself to your studies. You can affect the biggest change in your world, simply by doing that. Bloom where you are planted, Emmanuel, and you will, as Ghandi once said, become the thing that you wish to see happen." *God, he was sounding more and more like Uncle Osuroo every day.*

"So, you do not believe a man can do more than one thing?" the student argued, not willing to stand down,

"I believe," Samuel said, perhaps a bit too sharply, "that a student's main purpose is to *study*. If you truly wish to change Rhodesia for the better, immerse yourselves in your books. An educated engineer will build bridges on land and between minds. *Education*, not reckless emotion, is the key to a better Rhodesia. Now," he said, eager to go home to start his weekend, "if you will excuse me. I will see you in class on Monday."

Samuel carried his briefcase outside, checking first for signs of military or student activists. Seeing none, he made his way to his truck. The ancient truck had finally bitten the dust, but the Toyota he drove now was in remarkably good shape to be eight years old. No one in Rhodesia drove a late model vehicle without an armed escort. *New* was synonymous with *money*, and *money* was synonymous with *bait* for kidnappers.

Too many people had become targets lately—politicians, business leaders, even foreign missionaries. Most were released after ransoms had been paid, although a few had never been seen again, even after money had changed hands. Police were overwhelmed by the sheer numbers of people being taken, and unlike the police in the movies from America and Britain, Rhodesian police simply advised paying the money. It made their job simpler, and kept most of the kidnappers from resorting to violence.

Samuel had only known one person at the university who'd been kidnapped. It had been the dean of athletics. Apparently, the dean's wife was from a wealthy family. After the man had been returned to campus, Samuel had asked him about the experience. "Safer than being here," the dean had told him. "They never threatened to hurt me; they fed me well and we even played basketball every evening. Only one of them had a gun. I don't know if he would have used it if I had tried to escape, but I wasn't about to find out. They weren't asking that much money from my wife's parents, and God knows they could afford it."

Samuel opened the door to the Toyota and climbed behind the steering wheel. His apartment was only minutes from the campus but he needed to run some errands first. The last errand was a stop at the market for some lamb. He was planning on making pilau, a kind of spicy curry, for his dinner. He could never make it as good as his Auntie Gemma, but then neither could his uncle.

Samuel smiled. He was looking forward to going

home. It had been three years—a promise broken to his uncle. His old truck had not able to make the journey and the airport had been under siege by rebels last year, making flights out impossible. His uncle had said he'd understood, but Samuel still remembered the disappointment in Osuroo's voice. Thankfully, he had a road-worthy vehicle this year, and if the airport was attacked again, he at least had a Plan B. Only one more month, and then he would be off to spend an entire summer at home.

At that thought, Samuel's smile grew bigger. He had a surprise planned for his baba. He had talked with Jimiyu's father and had managed to purchase the hill that Osuroo had admired for so long. Samuel planned on presenting it on July 18, his uncle's birthday, but first he was going to build a wooden bench atop the hill along with a small shelter for shade. He liked picturing how he'd surprise his uncle with the gift.

The market was unusually quiet this afternoon. There weren't the usual evangelical preachers shouting damnation through megaphones, or even a single would-be politician making a speech in the courtyard. The few people that were shopping for their evening meal seemed tense, and in a rush to make their selections before hurrying off. It felt odd. There were no groups of women in colorful dresses swapping stories or old men sitting under the cassia trees whittling pieces of bark. Several of the fruit and vegetable sellers had already left for the day while others were busily closing shop.

Fortunately, one butcher stand was still open; Samuel made his way to the burly man in the red stained apron. "One pound of chopped lamb," he requested, "and if you still have any ground beef, I could use a couple of pounds of that, as well."

The butcher filled the order quickly, although he kept glancing across Samuel's shoulder toward the street. "What is it?" Samuel asked. "Why does everyone seem on edge this afternoon?"

"Rumors."

Samuel knew what that meant. "Police or rebels?" he asked, waiting as his meat was wrapped in brown paper.

"Who knows." the butcher answered. "But tension is high. Something is definitely blowing in the breeze, man. If I were you, I'd take this and go straight home. If I didn't have this much fresh meat left to sell, I'd be home myself right now."

"Won't it keep?" Samuel asked as he paid the butcher for his dinner.

"The ice man didn't come today. Too afraid. Is there anything else you need? I'll make you a good price."

Samuel's freezer was getting low; perhaps he should take advantage of the offer. "I could get some extra lamb," he said. Just then he heard someone gasp and saw a mother carrying an infant drop her bag and scurry past him. Both Samuel and the butcher turned to see more than a dozen heavily armed men march into the square in desert camouflage, with the familiar crisscross ammunition belts strapped across their chests. Samuel turned to say something to the butcher, but the man had disappeared out the back of his stand.

A huge man in the center of the guerillas carried a megaphone which he used to order everyone not to move. An old woman screamed, threw up her hands and ran past them as a few younger rebels laughed at the sight. The man with the megaphone shouted: "The next person who runs will be shot. Stand perfectly still." The rebels all raised their weapons to the ready as their leader made his way to the center of the courtyard where evangelists and politicians usually stood. Though the big man was doing his best to intimidate, Samuel was unimpressed when the man whipped off his dark sunglasses and turned in a slow circle, glaring at the women and shopkeepers. He had met bullies before; most weren't carrying Chinese assault rifles or had hand grenades strapped on their chest... but a bully was a bully, and his uncle had taught him never to cower before such a person.

"Today is your lucky day," said the big man through the megaphone. "Today you have the good fortune of being able to contribute to the rising nation of *Uhuru*!" Samuel's eyes narrowed. The bully had called Rhodesia *Uhuru*—freedom. Only one group was known to do that. These weren't ordinary rebels. They were *Mpiganaji*, the most ruthless of all those fighting the government. Their beef wasn't just with the Brits; they hated all whites, British... Russians... French... Poles... it didn't matter. White skin was, to them, synonymous with evil. Ironic, since the Mpiganaji were also known for their ruthlessness to anyone, white or black, who crossed them.

"You do not need to worry about your safety... as long as you do what I tell you." The bully kept turning in a slow circle, making eye contact with quivering women and children in the small crowd. "I am not here to hurt you, and I am not one of those sniveling cowards who like to kidnap the rich." He beat his megaphone to his chest twice before continuing. "No, if I take you it is for one of two purposes: either to accept your allegiance to me… or to *kill* you." The big man waited for the words to take their effect. The bully knew how to frighten, Samuel had to give him that.

"But as I look around this cowering group of sheep, I see no one here worth taking under my tutelage, or wasting a bullet upon… so… I will make you a deal. You all will be allowed to leave here this evening and go back to your puny little lives." Some in the crowd wiped their eyes while others waited for what they knew was coming. For his part, Samuel simply stood, waiting for the spectacle to be over.

"My men will now come among you and receive your tributes to the cause. Wallets, money, jewelry, watches… we will gladly accept them as your contribution to the freedom of our homeland. With your generosity, we will purchase more weapons to fight off the colonialists." He turned his attention to a frail little man in the crowd who'd dared glare at the big man. "Do not hold back, old man, lest you wish to be made an example of by one of my new recruits."

The bully glanced at his men and made a jerking motion with his head toward the crowd. Some of the armed thugs began to move through the crowd with cloth bags, while people stripped themselves of their jewelry and reached into their pockets. Others ransacked the open stalls and booths for cash.

Samuel sized up the young recruit heading his way. He could take the kid easily, seize his weapon, even take out four or five of the henchmen, including the bastard with the megaphone. It wasn't the fact that he knew he'd be killed in the process which stopped him... it was the promise he had made to his uncle... *no, never again would he kill another human being.*

The young criminal lowered his head and went inside the butcher's stand instead of coming to relieve Samuel of what little money he had in his pockets. He turned to watch the thief as he went through the butcher's cash drawer and couldn't believe his own eyes. "Emmanuel?"

His student refused to meet the professor's stare. "*Shh,*" he whispered. "They think my name is Mpenda."

"What in God's name are you doing with these people?"

"I am not *with* them. Please don't draw attention to yourself; Mukami is a dangerous man."

Confused and disgusted, Samuel turned to face the man in the middle of the courtyard. The bully's vile sneer was one Samuel wished more than anything he could wipe from the man's face. Unfortunately, there were too many armed men preventing that at the moment. *Nothing but common thieves*, he told himself, *using the political unrest sweeping Rhodesia as an excuse to rob poor people of what little they had. And one of his own students was helping them!*

"You!" The bully was staring at Samuel now. "Empty your pockets." He called to Emmanuel. "Mpenda, this man wishes to contribute to the cause. Finish what you are doing and make certain he shares everything that he has." The man Emmanuel had referred to as Mukami glared at Samuel, challenging him to defy his order. Samuel was no coward, but his uncle used to say that "when the odds were against you, comply for the moment so that you might turn the tables on your aggressor another day." *Not for revenge,* Uncle Osuroo had insisted, *only for justice.*

Samuel lowered his gaze in faux submission and pulled his wallet from his back pocket. *What was 33 dollars anyway? Certainly nothing worth dying for.*

Emmanuel stood before him with an open bag. "I am sorry, professor," he whispered. "I really am. Please, just be silent and we will be gone in a few minutes before the soldiers arrive. Mukami won't risk a battle with the police. Half of the men here don't even know how to fire their weapons."

Why was Emmanuel telling him this? He bit his bottom lip, refusing to speak the words that sought permission to spring from his lips.

"Please, your watch also."

Samuel glared into Emmanuel's eyes, but what he saw there was more than embarrassment, it was something else, something he couldn't put his finger on. *What did it matter now?* Reluctantly, he pulled the wristwatch from his arm and dropped it into the bag.

"On behalf of our glorious and soon to be land of freedom, I wish to thank you all for your generous contributions," bellowed the big man. "My men and I will leave you now. Please," he said mockingly, "have a good day." With that, Mukami handed the megaphone to one of his men and signaled the others to line up behind him. Less than a minute later, they were gone.

Samuel looked down at the bag of meat still in his hand. He felt guilty for some unknown reason, as if holding the meat when the butcher had just been robbed of a day's income was adding insult to injury. Still, the man *had* left him standing here... and he *was* hungry. He took the beef and lamb and walked across the street to his truck, grateful that he'd been able to conceal the keys from Emmanuel—else, they'd have likely taken his Toyota, as well. As he climbed behind the wheel, he wondered about the man who'd seduced a bright mind such as Emmanuel's. Most of the Mpiganaji were either criminals or unemployed herdsmen. Even the name Mukami meant one who milks cows. Samuel wondered how the son of a farmer had turned to such a life. *Probably nothing more than an opportunist with a gun,* he told himself. *Someone who enjoyed frightening old women and little children.*

Samuel knew he should just leave the matter alone, but no matter how hard he tried, he kept thinking of the people in the marketplace and all the others Mukami had robbed. There had to be a way to stop such a man and people like him. He spent his entire weekend ruminating over the incident... until, at last, an idea came to mind.

CHAPTER Twenty-One

Three speckled mousebirds sat on the kitchen windowsill of Samuel's apartment as he finished washing the dinner dishes. The pilau had been filling, but he'd hardly been able to enjoy his supper, thinking of Emmanuel and his involvement with a band of gangsters masquerading as patriots. *What could have possibly drawn such a capable young student to those people?* Sure, he had expressed sentiment for the underground rebellion, but the Mpiganaji were nothing but punks dressed up as warriors. They had seldom braved facing the army or the police for that matter. Locals feared them but considered them to be nothing more than hoodlums with heavy weapons.

The rhetoric of the Mpiganaji might have been similar to that of other groups in Rhodesia, but their modus operandi was always the same: attack the weak and the vulnerable, steal as much as you can, and then retreat into the shadows. Other rebel organizations condemned the Mpiganaji for their blatant thievery and violence against their own people. The only thing that they seemed to agree on was their mutual disdain for white-rule in Rhodesia. The Mpiganaji, however, were on the extreme, insisting that whites be forced to leave the country… *one way or another*. Already, whites were hiring body guards and erecting razor wire around their homes, further increasing tensions.

Samuel watched the three visitors on his windowsill as he sipped his evening coffee. "What would Emmanuel be doing with such a hate-filled group of bandits?" he asked the mousebirds. "I thought he was a nice kid; hot-headed maybe, but he's not like the others." From what he'd heard about the Mpiganaji, unlike the Mau Maus in Kenya, they were small bands of loosely connected young men headed by local criminal elements. With the exception of their camouflage fatigues and the crisscross ammunition belts, the Mpiganaji cells had little in common with one another. There had even been reports of clashes between some of the individual groups.

Two of the birds flew away while the third remained, content to watch Samuel drinking his coffee. "Birds of a feather flock together." The words of Auntie Gemma popped into his head. She'd used them when explaining to Samuel why some of the kids in school looked askance at him because of his family's wealth and position. "They think that you consider yourself to be better than them," she had said. "That is why they will not play with you."

"But I do not think I'm better," Samuel had protested one autumn afternoon, fighting back tears at having been shunned by his teammates at football.

"It is what they think, nonetheless," she had said. "In order to understand someone else, you must put yourself in their place. Ask yourself: What would you think if you were them?"

"How can I do that, Auntie?"

He still remembered her patient smile. "*Ahh*, that my dearie, is what you must discover for yourself. Empathy must come from within. When you learn how to understand your *friends*, you will find a way to get along. But," she had added in a more serious tone, "such knowledge can also allow you to outmaneuver your *enemies*. Your father had not wanted to serve the Nazis, but it had been the only way to ensure his family's safety. He learned to understand them, and thus was able to outthink them."

Samuel placed his coffee mug on the counter and went into his bedroom where he got down on his hands and knees to reach the box underneath his bed. It no longer contained the deeds to his uncle's property; those were stored safely in a British bank. At least he assumed that they were safe. *Perhaps, he should take them back to Kenya with him when he visited his uncle. But then, again, his uncle would have a certified copy registered with his attorney back home.*

Setting the box on the bed, he opened it to reveal its only content—a single key. He ran his thumb and index finger across the length of it. His father had carried the weight of this key for decades. He had no idea what his father had wanted him to do with this knowledge, or with this key. Had he given it to him that day simply for safekeeping, or did his father expect Samuel to do go to England one day and do *something*… something to save the world from itself? Whatever had possessed his father to share the story with him at such a young age, Samuel could only guess. Had his father foreseen the day when he would no longer be around, or had the Mau Mau rebellion caused him to fear for the future should something happen to him?

Samuel closed the box and returned it underneath his bed. He wasn't worried that someone would steal it; in fact, he would be relieved if they did. As long as the key was his, there was an implied responsibility… a responsibility that was too grave for one person to bear.

These days, there were too many people like that bully in the marketplace. *Perhaps he should tell someone the story his father had told him… but who?* That had been his father's dilemma. As he knelt beside his bed, he tried to imagine his father's dilemma so long ago. It had been far too big a risk to hand the key over to the police or some other low-level agency. The Kenyan government had been under duress for years, and even if they had believed him and found the poison, they couldn't be trusted to destroy it. It would have been too great a temptation to use it as leverage for power.

Samuel winced. Even if he went to England now, who could he give it to? *Who could be trusted to destroy the contents of the box his father had secretly buried?* He sighed. The foreign superpowers would have the ability, *but would they have the will?*

Not much had changed in the world as far as Samuel was concerned. He remembered where his father had told him the doomsday box was, and just how to find it. Samuel drew a deep breath and then exhaled slowly—releasing the tension from his body. The Nazi poison was hidden away. At least it was safe…

…for now.

CHAPTER Twenty-Two

2005

Ping…

So much for a peaceful greeting. Whoever was shooting at them left no doubt about their attentions as bullets ricocheted off the fender near Zack and Kwame.

"They're in range, Kwame, fire the damn thing!"

Kwame steadied the rocket launcher on his shoulder but his finger was nowhere near the trigger. "Boss-man said not to fire until he gave the order."

"I'm the bloody boss-man. Remember?" Zack barely kept from shouting. It wasn't that he was afraid. He and Scott Flenn had been in worse situations and had usually remained calm. It was just that they were about to lose the tactical advantage. If Sergei allowed them to get much closer, the second truck would have time to swing around and bring their guns to bear.

The Russian must have sensed that too, for just at that moment they heard him shout: "Огонь! —

Fire!"

Kwame sent the missile blazing toward its target, which erupted into a huge fireball as the truck split down the middle, both halves forming a momentary pyramid before totally disintegrating into orange flame. The second truck veered wildly to the left, giving Kwame and

Zack time to reload a second missile. Zack was impressed with his African counterpart's composure. A lesser-trained agent would have excitedly fired a second round too soon after the first, missing the target altogether. However, Kwame took a deep breath and waited for just the right moment.

Whoosh... the missile found its mark and the second truck was no more. Whether fear of survivors or just to be a part of the action, Sergei and Tonanza fired several rounds into the sand surrounding what was left of their assailants' vehicles. A moment later, Tonanza disappeared and Sergei cautioned: "Hold your fire!" Zack hadn't intended to fire toward wounded men, enemy or no, but Kwame had swapped the rocket launcher for the AK-74 in case someone returned fire. A few moments later they heard a series of single shots and then saw Tonanza's giant form walking toward them, silhouetted by the flames. He waited until he stood before the three of them, now gathered beside the Toyota, to give a report.

"Definitely militia," Tonanza reported. "They won't bother us anymore."

Sergei nodded but asked, "You are certain of this?"

Tonanza answered with some sort of guttural noise before opening the driver's door and fetching a canteen. He turned to watch the small fires slowly burn out. Sergei took a deep breath before launching into Kwame and Zack. "You two have any other surprises in store for us?!"

"Bwana?"

"So far we have been assaulted by primeval marauders and Somali militia. What the hell were you thinking when you chose this route?"

Kwame shrugged. "The desert is not for the timid, Bwana. Much can happen out here. That is why runners are paid as well as we are."

Sergei wasn't having it. His adrenaline was high and his military bearing was showing. This was a man unaccustomed to working with civilians. "What else may happen before we reach Addis Ababa? Should we expect an assault from the air next? What is stopping me from leaving you both here in the sand and completing the journey on our own?!"

"You need us, Bwana. The four of us, we are a team, no?"

Sergei's eyes narrowed as he began to raise his weapon. "Not both of you I don't."

Kwame had never seen a white man move so fast. Before they could discern whether Sergei's was an empty threat, Zack dropped his AK on the ground and in one motion zipped behind Sergei, drawing an ugly 9-inch dagger and pressing its blade against the Russian's throat. Tonanza whipped around and pointed his weapon at Zack first but then at Kwame, unwilling to risk hitting his boss. "Let's all just calm down, shall we?" Zack said. "I have no wish to die tonight, and neither do you. None of this could have been foreseen. Understand? It is unfortunate, but we've still got our skin intact so I suggest you drop your weapon, Sergei, and tell your friend over there to do the same. Then we can all drive a few clicks South and wait for daybreak in a couple of hours."

Sergei did as he was told as did Tonanza, although reluctantly. "Forgive me gentlemen," the Russian said, rubbing his throat and then dusting off his shoulders as if brushing away what had just occurred. " I let my emotions get the better of me."

"Cooler heads will always prevail," Zack said, returning the knife to its sheath.

Sergei rubbed his throat a second time and coughed. "Indeed."

"Bwana, my apologies for Tilly's rashness. He is an American; you know how they are."

The Russian just shook his head. "Unfortunately, I do. I've had many dealings with them in the past."

I just bet you have, thought Zack but simply offered a grin instead. Soon he'd find out just what sort of dealings. The interrogation room at Camp Lemonnier was going to be a welcome site.

"Tilly, let's get ready to roll out of here. Bwana, I suggest we distance ourselves another ten kilometers, if that is okay with you."

Sergei nodded. "Tonanza, stow our weapons and get ready to depart." The guard glared at Zack before picking up the canteen he had dropped. When he stood, though, his eyes opened wide in shock. "What? What is it, Tonanza?"

Zack and Kwame saw the big man's mouth fall open just before Tonanza dropped in the sand, an arrow embedded deeply in the base of his neck.

CHAPTER Twenty-Three

Rhodesia; 1975

Students filed into the classroom more slowly today than usual. Although there had been talk of a student protest earlier this morning, so far nothing had materialized. Only a few soldiers roamed the campus—creating a feeling of ease around the campus. Unfortunately, Samuel didn't share that feeling as he stood at the podium to deliver his afternoon lecture. He watched as his students took their seats, some whispering as they exchanged their assignments from over the weekend, checking to see if they'd come up with the same calculations. Emmanuel was not among them.

Samuel didn't know whether to feel relieved or disappointed. He had a speech full of righteous indignation already worked out in his head, full of threats to go to the dean or maybe even the police. He shrugged. It didn't appear that he'd be giving Emmanuel a dressing down after all. He was 10 minutes into the lesson plan when the door opened and a slight figure slipped inside and made his way toward the back.

Emmanuel.

To his credit, Samuel never broke stride but continued with the lecture. Every now and again he would glance at Emmanuel, slumped over his desk in the back of the room, but the young man never looked up, keeping his focus instead on his notes. He was either brave or stupid to show up for class; Samuel couldn't make up his mind which.

At the end of the lecture, some students hurried out the door toward a late-afternoon class, while others, finished with their courses for the day, lingered to speak with one another or to ask their professor a question about some technical detail from the lecture. All the while, Samuel continued to glance at Emmanuel. He was standing now, looking out the window—apparently waiting to speak with him. *Fine,* Samuel told himself, *if he wants to try and explain himself, let him. There's nothing he can possibly say that would justify his actions or his involvement with that group of... of...* he searched for the right word... *of wapumbavu.* And fools is exactly what they were, all of them.

As the last of the students left the classroom, Emmanuel gathered his things and timidly approached his teacher. Standing before him, with his head bowed, he spoke softly.

"I am sorry."

He reached into his pocket and pulled out a wad of bills and placed it on Samuel's desk.

Samuel looked at the money and then at his student. "What is this? Do you think returning my money makes everything right? What about those other people? The women and the old men; are you giving them their money back as well?"

Emmanuel still did not look up. "I would if I could."

The man looked pitiful, yet Samuel was in no mood

to be conciliatory. His eyes narrowed. "How could you?! That monster is nothing more than an opportunist who has seized upon the aspirations and dreams of others and is using them to fatten his own coffers. He's a murderous bully! I looked into his eyes, there is no soul there, no spirit, only greed. He would have killed those people if they had resisted."

Finally, Emmanuel looked up to meet his professor's icy stare. It wasn't what Samuel expected. There was contrition, yes, but something else… something he couldn't put his finger on. Emmanuel was not cowering before him—waiting to be forgiven. Nor was he here to explain. He had something else on his mind.

"That is why I took your money. Because he *would* have killed you. Mukami was in a mood that day. He was hoping someone would fight back; he *wanted* to kill someone that day. Of all the Mpiganaji that I have met, he is the worst." Emmanuel's jaw visibly tightened.

"And yet you have chosen him to be your… your…" Samuel threw his hands up in the air. "I don't know… your leader, your savior?"

Emmanuel scoffed. "Hardly anyone's savior. The man is takataka… garbage."

Samuel was confused. "Yet you follow him?"

Emmanuel walked to the door, shut it, and then pulled up a chair beside the teacher's desk. "Perhaps, Professor, you should sit down."

Samuel refused, still glaring at the student-turned-terrorist.

"I do not blame you for being angry. I had no way of explaining any of this to you on Friday. I thought of coming to your house, but you would have only called the police."

"I still may."

Emmanuel nodded. "Please understand, we would not be having this conversation if I did not feel that I owe you an explanation. What I am about to tell you I have not told anyone else." He took a breath. "I am a spy."

Samuel laughed at the absurdity of it. "Please, Emmanuel, do not try to offer me some ridiculous excuse for your actions. I deserve better than that."

The young man shrugged. "You may choose to believe me, or you may not, but I am telling you the truth."

"How stupid do you think that I am? You are not the sort to help the British."

"You are correct, Professor. I would never help the British. I am working for the French."

Samuel's thoughts began to spin; *perhaps sitting down was a good idea after all.* He took his seat behind the ancient wooden desk across from Emmanuel. "The French?"

"They approached me over a year ago, asked me to help them gather information. They are eager to know anything and everything about what direction the students will take as the British government implodes upon itself."

Samuel took a deep breath. *The kid sounded like he was telling the truth. Still…*

"The last time I checked, the Mpiganaji are not a student organization."

Emmanuel went on. "I have only recently been as-signed to infiltrate Mukami's band of criminals. At first, the French just wanted to know what was happening on campus. They know that I support a free and independent Rhodesia. I was already a member of several student freedom campaigns; they simply wanted me to report on what was being said at those meetings."

"So, you sold out your compatriots." It wasn't a question but an accusation.

Emmanuel's nostrils flared and his gaze hardened. "Professor, I wronged you, for that I am deeply sorry. I understand your anger, but do not insult me. I am not a traitor. I only told the French generalities about the mood of the people, things such as that. I betrayed no secrets."

"Yet you weren't entirely up front either?"

"I come from a poor family, professor. I could not afford to pay for an education were it not for the money the French pay me. Do not misunderstand; my feelings for a free Rhodesia are genuine. There are many, many good people working together to build a new nation devoid of British rule. However, the Mpiganaji are not among them. They are the scum of the earth. When I was offered a chance to infiltrate their ranks and to make a small fortune doing it, I am not ashamed to tell you that I jumped at the opportunity to betray them to the French.

I have experienced no shame at what I am doing," he glanced at the money still lying on the desk, "until now."

Samuel did not want to believe, but there was what his uncle would have called an air of truth in Emmanuel's tone. "How did you ingratiate yourself into this den of thieves?"

"It was easier than you think. Mukami only wants

money. It costs two hundred American dollars to join his ranks. You are then each allotted one-half of one percent of everything Mukami steals. You are right, Mukami has no soul, but he also has no brain. He does not check the background of anyone who wishes to join him. The man is a fool. It was simple enough to convince him that I wanted to become one of them."

"And the money you pay him gets you a uniform and a weapon?"

"No. We purchase our own clothing. The weapons come from the Chinese. They are free; part of their plan to destabilize and then colonialize Africa. The Chinese are in this for the long haul, but one day, perhaps decades from now, they will be even worse than the British. That is why I help the French. France hopes to beat China at its own game."

Samuel shook his head. The speech he had prepared slipped silently away. "I may be a fool," he all but whispered, "but I think I might just believe you." As if searching for affirmation, he glanced at the money resting on his desk. "You told me the other day that they don't know your real name?"

"That's right. They call me Mpenda. It was my uncle's name."

At the mention of Emmanuel's uncle, Samuel thought of his own. *What might Uncle Osuroo say to this young man treading in dangerous waters?* "Emmanuel, you are playing a very dicey game. Surely there is another avenue for you to find money for university?"

"Yes, but I am not just doing this for the money. The Mpiganaji are a disgrace to the free-Rhodesian movement. They cannot be allowed to pass off their racist ideology and their brutal ways as part of our quest for autonomy. I will gladly do everything that I can to stop them. The British are too busy trying to save their own hides to pay them much attention, and the local police are as afraid of them as they are of the police. The French have a plan to turn the tables on these groups, one at a time."

Emmanuel scratched his head. "I am not a fool; I realize the French have their own designs in whatever happens. The Chinese plans will obliterate much of the trade agreements and textile contracts the French have here. And the French know that the British will be out of power soon. They just want to make certain the Chinese don't take over. For my part, if it is a choice between the two, I will take the French over the Chinese."

Emmanuel stood to leave. "Of course, I ask that you not tell anyone what I have just told you. My life depends on it, and so might yours."

Samuel cocked his head. "A threat, Emmanuel?"

"Not from me, professor. If Mukami discovers that I have spoken with you, he would kill us both." Emmanuel turned toward the door.

"Wait."

Samuel glanced down at the money on his desk. "You also took my watch."

Emmanuel nodded. "I gave the watch and your money to Mukami." He pointed to the top of the desk. "That money is from my own wallet. If I owe you more, I will make it good." With that, the student-patriot-spy walked out the door.

CHAPTER Twenty-Four

What a difference a day made. There was something in the air this morning as Samuel strolled across campus for his first class of the day. Judging from the number of military vehicles he'd seen in the parking lot, Samuel knew something was amiss. He could also sense it in the students' demeanor as they hurried past, their eyes darting back and forth. The soldiers he passed seemed on edge, as well.

None of them were leaning against the buildings, smoking, or joking with one another, as they did most mornings. Samuel figured there must be another protest about to start, but he saw no crowds, heard no angry mantra, and saw no placards denouncing the government. *Perhaps something else was afoot.* He turned the corner and was confronted with the gruesome sight of four soldiers removing a body from a tree.

"No one is allowed in this courtyard!" snapped a corporal. "You must leave immediately!" Samuel didn't mean to ignore the order, but he was too shocked at what he saw to move. "Are you deaf?" the corporal shouted. "I said leave!"

"Who… what…?"

This time the corporal raised his weapon. "No one is allowed here; do not make me use force!" Samuel shook himself alert and immediately turned and headed down an alternate path toward his classroom.

My God, he thought, *what has happened?*

"Professor?" a voice from behind him called. "Professor!" It was one of his graduate students. "Did you see?" Samuel didn't speak, only nodded that he had. "I can't believe it! Do you know who did that?" Samuel shook his head, either unable or unwilling to give voice to the macabre nature of what had taken place on campus… on *his* campus.

"It was the Mpiganaji. A custodian said he saw them early this morning. The Mpiganaji had beaten one of the students so badly… he was barely alive when they put the noose over his neck."

Samuel tensed. "The Mpiganaji? Are you certain?"

"The custodian seemed to be familiar enough with the gangsters. He said that they were the same group that attacked the marketplace last Friday. He and his wife were there when it happened."

A horrific thought shot like a bullet through Samuel's brain. "Do you know who it was that they hanged?"

The student shrugged. "No. The custodian didn't know either, only that it was a student, someone he'd seen on campus."

Samuel didn't bother to excuse himself as he turned and ran back toward the soldiers. He was met by a different man in uniform this time. "Please, I must see his face," Samuel begged. "I may know him."

"Corporal?" called the soldier. "This man says he knows the corpse."

Samuel cringed at the word corpse but also saw the

agitation in the corporal's eyes as he turned. "I thought I told you to leave!"

"Yes, yes, but I just heard…" He shook his head. "It doesn't matter. Please, I may be able to identify him for you." *God, he hoped he was wrong.*

The corporal clearly didn't like his orders being defied, however, he stepped aside with a scowl and pointed to the body lying on the ground. Samuel prayed that he was wrong, but as he looked upon the face of the youth, even as badly beaten as he was, he saw the truth. It was Emmanuel. "Holy God," he said, crossing himself.

"You know him, then?"

Samuel nodded. "Yes. He was one of my students."

The corporal shrugged. "Give one of my men his name and then be off. We have work to do."

"But… I think I also may know who did this."

The soldier's eyes narrowed. "So, you have solved a mystery for us, teacher? Is that what you think? We know *who* did this. They're pigs, all of them." He glared menacingly at Samuel. "As are all of your students who stir up trouble and oppose us. Now, this time leave and do not come back, or we will take you with us for questioning."

Samuel knew what that meant.

He turned and left quickly, his gut feeling as if it were twisted into a myriad of separate knots. *The cow-milker must have somehow found out that Emmanuel was a student here and that he had lied to the Mpiganaji. No doubt, Emmanuel's body was left as some sort of sick poetic justice.*

As he walked toward the classroom, Samuel's sorrow turned into anger, and anger into rage. A small owl hooted from a tree nearby. The words of his father came to him: *Always be brave, and always stand against wrong.* His back began to straighten and his gait became more confident. It was time to follow his father's advice.

CHAPTER Twenty-Five

September 1975

The night was cold, unlike the bodies that lay at Samuel's feet. It had taken months--time he had originally planned to be at home in Kenya with his uncle, but he had managed to convince Mukami, the cow-milker, to trust his story about wanting to get revenge on the soldiers who'd arrested so many students on campus.

Samuel had honored his promise to his uncle: He had killed no one. The French commandoes had done that for him. Once he had established a contact at the embassy, the rest had fallen into place rather fast. Mukami had been a simpleton, eager for praise. Once Samuel had won the bully's confidence, convincing the dumb ox that Samuel was in awe of his greatness, Mugami told him everything, even the name of the Chinese contact who was supplying them with weapons. Once the information was verified, the French sent in a squad to annihilate the entire band of Mpiganaji.

Samuel assumed that they would soon do the same with the Chinese arms dealer. Samuel had known where Mukami's thugs would be camped tonight and had led the soldiers straight to the terrorists. He had remained until the carnage was over; he felt he owed as much to Emmanuel. Just before he died, Mukami's eyes had fallen on him. "Yuda!" He spat the word with every ounce of hatred he could muster before closing his eyes and succumbing to the darkness.

Judas? No, he was no Christ killer. Mukami deserved what he got, as did all of these murderers at his feet. They were no different than the Mau Maus who'd killed his family so long ago; no different than that drunken security guard who's murdered Auntie Gemma.

"We are indebted to you for your help in this matter," came a voice from behind him. Although he had only met the Frenchman three weeks ago, he recognized the voice as belonging to Col. Gabriel Bundi, leader of the elite killing force.

Samuel slowly shook his head, remembering his night hiding amongst the boulders. "No, Colonel Bundi, it is you who have helped me."

Puzzled, the colonel reached into his shirt pocket and extracted an envelope folded in half. "Here, this is for you."

Samuel stared at the envelope. "What is this?"

"Ten thousand in American dollars."

"I asked for no payment."

The colonel nodded. "Yes, that's exactly what I was told by the embassy. But we are grateful for your help. These men were the scum of the earth; they deserved what they got. But, even better, you led us to the source of their weapons. My government will be able to use that information as leverage against the Chinese." He pushed the envelope into Samuel's hands. "Take it."

"No, it is blood money. It would just prove that I am exactly what Mukami called me."

The Frenchman pushed the envelope into the waistband of Samuel's trousers. "Give it to others then, if that makes you happy." Colonel Budi walked away before suddenly stopping and turning to face Samuel. "You have a knack for this. You were able to win their trust. I could use a man like you up north. We've been trying to infiltrate a ring of diamond traders." He grimaced. "It's horrible what they are doing to women and children, making slaves out of them." He paused to think for a moment. "If you are willing to help us, I believe we could pay five times what's in that envelope."

Samuel stared at him. It wasn't the money that tempted him, it was the opportunity to stop the cruelty of others. Like most, he had heard the horrific tales about those who traded in blood diamonds. Still, he shook his head. "No. I am a simple professor, that is all. I must go back to my classroom."

"That's a pity. It would be a chance for us to finally stick it to those bastards and right a lot of wrongs."

The words stung. It was as if he was watching his father again as he ran from the boulders to distract the rebels. The colonel was about to let the matter drop when he saw the reaction on the young professor's face and thought there might still be a chance to recruit him. "You sure you won't change your mind?"

Samuel already had.

CHAPTER Twenty-Six

Arrows flew dangerously close as the three men scrambled into the Jeep. "How is that even possible?" Zack demanded to know as they sped away into the night.

"I told you so," was all Kwame could muster.

"We have to go back for the weapons," shouted Sergei.

"Your guns are in their hands now," Zack said, quickly pulling out his .45. There was no need for a charade now; not as far as he was concerned.

"Tilly, what the hell are you doing?"

Zack aimed straight at the Russian's chest. "Making certain he doesn't try to force us to go back to face those Comanches, that's what."

"What in God's name is a Comanche?"

Sergei stared at Zack but didn't so much as blink. "They are American indigenous citizens whose land was stolen from them years ago by bureaucrats in Washington. Correct, Mr. Matteson?"

Zack's eyes narrowed. Kwame almost slammed his foot against the brake. "You're right," Kwame said to Zack, "keep that gun on him."

Sergei laughed. "I must admit that Tilly is an atrocious name. How on earth did you come up with it?"

Zack frowned. "*I* didn't."

"Yes, well… I'm afraid that I don't as yet know your partner's identity, but," he said to Kwame, "if you will forgive me, you don't seem to be cut of the same cloth as your CIA compatriot. I'm guessing you work with one of the West African intelligence offices. Kenya perhaps?"

Zack tilted his head to one side. "You want to hand over your weapons, or should I shoot your man-parts and then take them?"

"I'd rather you did not. I was almost shot there by an angry Chechen when I was a colonel. Nearly ruined both my chances for a family and a promotion."

"But, back there at the brothel…" Kwame stuttered.

"He was buying time," Zack interrupted. You sent a wire with our photographs to Moscow."

Sergei smiled. "Something like that. Tonanza managed to take your pictures when you were otherwise engaged looking at the beautiful women."

Zack motioned with the pistol. "Whatever. Just hand me your weapon."

"I'm afraid you have me at a disadvantage, Mr. Matteson. My only weapons are those from the back of the Toyota—which is also why we need to turn around."

"Stop the Jeep, Kwame. I need to search him."

"You're kidding, right?" Kwame glanced at Zack and saw that he was not. "Okay, okay, just be quick about it."

He checked the rearview mirror for whatever good that would do him in the dark and then stopped the

Jeep. Zack, meanwhile, kept his pistol aimed at Sergei while the three men exited the vehicle. Kwame searched the back of the Jeep until he found what he was looking for: a piece of cording he had noticed earlier. Zack patted the Russian down but couldn't find anything other than an ink pen, which he tossed aside for good measure. Russian spies were known to hide vials of the deadly Novichok poison inside such things. For his part, Kwame kept checking the landscape behind them for any sign of Sandsifters.

"You see," said Sergei, "no weapons. Might I suggest we leave before your Comanches catch up?"

Kwame tied Sergei's hands with a knot he'd used to detain others in the past. It was not one easily slipped out of, which was good since if anyone could get out of a knot, he had no doubt it would be the Russian. "I thought you wanted to go back," Zack said.

"Not *through* them, Mr. Matteson, *around* them. We could make a wide circle, get back to the Toyota, and drive away without them catching up to us."

"What does an FSB agent want with a bunch of newly minted machine guns?" Zack demanded. "You can get your hands on more."

"I never said that I was FSB."

"You didn't have to," Zack said, pointing him back to the Jeep's rear seat. "Besides, the guns aren't important anymore."

"They never were important, except that they will lead me to someone I very much wish to find."

Zack wheeled him around. "I don't suppose you'd care to share just who that is?"

"It wouldn't be my first choice, no."

"Zack?" Kwame said, impatiently.

"How about we just leave you here to be those Sand-whatchamacallits next meal?"

"Zack?"

"You won't do that, Mr. Matteson. It is not your style. Besides, how would you explain your actions back at Camp Lemonnier, or later, to your partner, Mr. Flenn."

"How do you…"

Kwame's patience had worn razor thin. "Zack! Let's go!"

Zack glared at Kwame and then back at Sergei. "Fine. Get in the vehicle. And don't try anything. The jig is up."

"*Ah* yes, I also was told of your use of antiquated euphemisms. Just what is a jig, anyway?"

"Just get in the damn Jeep!"

Kwame jumped behind the wheel as Zack slid into the backseat next to Sergei. He pushed the barrel of his Glock into the Russian's side. "Don't think I won't use this."

"You won't. You care too much about finding out who I am and what my mission is."

Zack pushed it even harder against the Russian's ribs, causing the man to wince. "Guess again. I have no doubt that you are FSB, and like the KGB before, you guys are trained as well as we are not to betray your mission." Kwame stepped on the gas, making certain not to go too fast lest they end up in a sandpit.

Sergei smiled. "I already know *your* mission, Mr.

Matteson. You were sent to Camp Lemonnier to relieve another agent while your partner, Mr. Flenn, lives the life of luxury in Iceland drinking single-malt Scotch."

Zack shook his head incredulously. "How can you possibly... you weren't in that brothel long enough to find all that out."

"We are very thorough, Mr. Matteson, and we do not waste time on small talk. I know a lot more about you, if you'd care to hear it."

"No thanks."

"What I do not know is how you came to be in this Jeep posing as a runner. I assume you disposed of the men that had been sent to escort the Frenchman... just as I disposed of him."

Kwame slammed his palm on the steering wheel. "I knew it! There *was* a Frenchman."

"A horrible man who'd committed great atrocities in the past. He was only in this for the money. He hadn't a clue what was really at stake."

"And you do?" Zack wasn't up for the game. "Kwame, stop here. I don't need this. He's Russian intelligence; it won't do us any good to take him back to the camp. These guys never talk. Leave him here. If those Sandy people don't get him, the desert will."

Kwame did as he was instructed. Sergei laughed. "You are bluffing." In response, Zack shoved him out the door where he fell face down.

"I never bluff." He glanced at Kwame. "Shall we?"

Sergei rolled over, spitting out a mouthful of sand. "You will at least leave me a canteen?"

Zack shook his head. "It would only prolong your

agony. Believe me, I'm doing you a favor." He climbed into the front passenger seat and nodded to Kwame, who put the Jeep in gear.

The Russian made it to his feet, less sure of himself than before. "Wait. I will tell you everything. Just don't leave me here!"

Zack grabbed Kwame's arm. "Hang on a minute." He got out of the Jeep and stood just inches away from the Russian. "Start talking."

"What, here? Now? Those savages will be here any minute."

"Then you'd best start talking fast. The first sign of an arrow and I'm in the Jeep. And Kwame and I are out of here."

The Russian didn't hesitate. "The arms dealer in Addis Ababa. He is more than meets the eye. He has access to a weapon deadlier than you can imagine. He must be stopped and the weapon found."

Zack cocked his head. "Interesting. Go on."

Sergei stood tall. "I will tell you the rest, but only if we all leave now!"

Zack gazed into the night, but only for a second. He knew they shouldn't risk staying any longer. "Fine. Get in. But if you are telling me some cock-and-bull story, I'll personally hand deliver you over to the Sand-drifters."

"Sifters."

Zack glared at Kwame.

"I'm just saying… it's *Sandsifters* not drifters. Why can't you get it right?"

Zack rolled his eyes. "Whatever," he said, sounding like an adolescent as Kwame shifted into gear.

"I mean you can at least learn how to pronounce their…"

"Shut up, Kwame." He turned to face Sergei. "But not you. *You* need to start talking."

CHAPTER Twenty-Seven

Angola; 1979

Dust and debris blew about wildly as eight armed men stood guard over three dozen women and children digging through mud pits near a stream that was both a sewer and source of drinking water for the captives. A fat, squat blob of a man pulled a bandana across his face. No such protection from the frequent windstorms were allowed the prisoners.

"Keep digging!" the blob shouted. "Dig or there will be no food for any of you tonight!" He signaled to a guard on the other side of the stream. "Jafari, I'm going back to camp; you are in charge. If these vermin do not find at least three diamonds by nightfall, shoot one of them." He waved his hand dismissively. "I do not care which one."

Jafari nodded, adjusting his bandana. He knew why Omar was heading back to camp, the fat bastard was going to raid the quarter's refrigerator before the rest of them came in for their evening meal.

The camp had been set up months ago, far away from prying eyes. The Angolan government was collapsing from within. The increasing chaos had allowed for dozens of diamond camps such as this one to spring up in the hinterlands. *Slave camps* was more like it. Mercenaries were hired by the score to raid small villages, kill the men, and capture women and children to work in pits such as this one to pan for diamonds. Opportunistic foreign backers were amassing fortunes, ignoring—and worse—exploiting, the slave labor for their own coffers. Some governments were heavily involved, China and North Korea especially. Neither nation balked at the inhumane treatment of prisoners in their own land, so why raise objections to what happened to these black Africans.

After his boss had left to feed his fat face, Jafari pointed his rifle at a young woman bending low in the water to sift through the silt in a fruitless effort. Everyone but Omar seemed to know that this bed had dried up and that it was time to move on. "You!" he shouted to the woman. "Come with me!"

The woman knew what that meant. She still bore the cigarette burns from having tried to refuse one of the other men. The guards snickered as Jafari pushed the woman toward a clumsily built guardhouse where the mercenaries were allowed occasional breaks from the heat of the sun. Jafari turned at the entrance and winked at his compatriots who cheered him on. Once inside, however, he put his finger to his lips and reached inside his pocket. *At least,* she told herself, *this one will not get me pregnant.* But instead of a prophylactic, he brought out three tiny diamonds and placed them in her hand.

"It will be dark in an hour," Jafari said. "I want you to 'find' these in half that time. Show them to the nearest guard standing next to me. That way I can make certain that he does not try and pocket them for himself."

The woman stared at the diamonds in her hand, unable to believe what he was doing. "One more thing," Jafari whispered. "Tonight, at exactly midnight, make sure all the women and children inside your shack are on the east wall, farthest away from the building where the guards sleep. He stared into her soft, brown eyes to make sure that she had understood him. "It is very important," he added, before whispering the word she'd ceased daring to dream: *Freedom*.

****

At supper that night, Jafari noticed that his regular portion of bread was substantially less than the day before—thanks to Omar. Several of the guards grumbled, but none dared accuse their ruthless boss of being the reason for their skimpy meal.

Since it was Jafari's turn to help guard the prisoners, he was excused from cleanup detail and stepped outside for a smoke. An older man, Mbuzi, whose name meant *goat*, looked the part with a scraggly gray beard and long, uncombed hair. The man, like most of the mercenaries, regularly chewed khat—a stimulant similar to that of cocaine—and it could become a problem tonight. Usually, the guards took turns sleeping, but if Mbuzi would be chewing the leaves it would likely keep him awake. The trick would be getting Mbuzi to agree to hold off on chewing and allow Jafari to take first watch.

As they both stood outside the compound under a gibbous moon, Jafari passed Mbuzi a cigarette. "I wish you were offering me a slice of mutton instead."

Jafari smirked. "If it were, Omar would have already eaten it," he said with a disarming smile.

"True." The lean guard accepted the light from Jafari. "Whose turn is it to go for supplies?"

"I think it is Feechi's turn." Feechi was the smallest and, because of it, the meanest of the lot.

Mbuzi shrugged. "Let's pay the vicious runt to set aside some canned goods where Omar cannot find them this time. I'm tired of being hungry. I'd almost eat that swill we feed the slaves."

Jafari shook his head. "I don't think I could ever be *that* hungry." He leaned in toward Mbuzi and whispered. "Listen, hold off on the khat tonight. I have some cocaine hidden in my pocket. I'll share it with you if you let me have first watch. I'm too awake right now to sleep anyway."

Mbuzi was delighted. "How did you get cocaine up here? Never mind, I don't care how you got it, just be sure to honor your word when you wake me up."

Jafari smiled. "No problem. I have enough to share for two. Just don't tell anyone else. Omar doesn't like it when we hide things from him."

"Food isn't the only thing that piglet wants to hoard," agreed Mbuzi. "If he weren't paying us so well, I'd have left weeks ago."

The two men finished their cigarettes and then made their way to the shack where the prisoners were kept. Once inside, the slaves weren't allowed out until dawn. The shack stank of urine and sweat, causing the guards to take up their station under a large Baobab tree several meters away.

The two men talked for a few minutes before Mbuzi drifted off to sleep. The rule was that one could sleep for four hours before waking to assume the watch.

As the lights dimmed inside the mercenaries' bunkhouse, Jafari checked his wristwatch. It was time. Jafari slowly rose to his feet, quietly reaching for Mbuzi's rifle before tiptoeing into the surrounding brush. All the commandoes, he hoped, knew that he was on their side. He'd learned over the past year that, if anything, the French were punctual.

At exactly midnight, the bunkhouse exploded into a gigantic fireball as not one but two Hellfire missiles found their marks from the drone overhead. Mbuzi jumped to his feet and searched for his rifle, realizing too late that he had been betrayed. A quick burst from somewhere nearby caught the skinny mercenary in the chest. He was dead before his body hit the ground.

While Jafari wanted to rush to the prisoners' quarters and kick open their door, he knew that any movement on his part would be certain to draw fire. Instead, he waited for the soldiers to open the doors and cut through the chains to release the frightened occupants. Terrified, the prisoners rushed outside to find a dozen heavily armed Europeans urging them to come with them. In actuality, there was no reason to hurry since all of the captors were dead; still, the French wanted to clear the area as quickly as possible and get everyone to the landing zone where the helicopters would be waiting.

"Samuel!" called a familiar voice. "Samuel, where are you?"

Jafari saw Colonel Gabriel Bundi standing next to the very woman he had given the diamonds to this afternoon. She was staring at the great fire, a look of deep satisfaction upon her face.

"I'm in the brush, Gabriel. Tell your men not to shoot."

"Why would we shoot the best thing that has happened to our team in years?"

The man calling himself Jafari slowly stood, leaving the rifles on the ground and raising both hands in the air just in case. "You worry too much, Samuel," Col. Bundi said when he finally caught sight of him.

Samuel exchanged a quick glance with the woman from earlier. "These people have been through hell, Colonel. Be sure they are treated gently."

Bundi raised an eyebrow. "In all the missions you have helped us with, have I ever done anything less?"

Samuel's face softened as he turned to the young woman. "I am sorry it took us so long, but I had to find out who was backing these monsters. I couldn't call the colonel and his men until I knew for certain." She was somewhere between an emotional barrage of shock and deep satisfaction at seeing the fate of her captors, but Samuel knew she understood what he was telling her. Eventually, one of the soldiers came and gently escorted the woman into the woods toward the awaiting helicopters.

"Thank you for the intel, Samuel. As we speak, a team is taking out the bastards funding this camp. I just wish we could expose the others. The ones behind desks in Tel Aviv, Hong Kong, and Amsterdam." Col. Bundi glanced around the camp, taking it all in. "You know, no matter how many of these damned operations I've been on, I will never get used to it. How can human beings treat one another like this?"

Samuel looked away. "Do not ask yourself questions without answers, Gabriel."

The colonel shot him a questioning look. "How's that?"

"It is something my uncle used to tell me as a child. Some answers will never come. We must be willing simply to do our job and fight evil, never understanding what it is that drives such people. Besides, if we understood them then we would be just like them, would we not?"

Colonel Bundi shook his head. Whether in perplexity or disgust, Samuel did not know, nor did it matter. It was time now simply to leave this godforsaken place. As they walked into the bush, he thought he heard the hoot of a solitary owl somewhere in the distance.

CHAPTER Twenty-Eight

"I'm telling you that you need to turn around and go back for the Toyota."

Zack was getting tired of this. "You really want to face those men? I had you pegged as smarter than that, Sergei. Besides, those weapons will be gone by now anyway."

Kwame coughed. "*Um*, not likely. The Sandsifters don't have any need for them." Kwame thought he could feel Zack's icy stare on the back of his neck.

"Whose side are you on, anyway?"

"I'm just saying…"

Zack turned to Sergei. "Okay, tell me what's so important about those damn guns."

"I told you: The buyer is someone who has information about a hidden weapon of mass destruction that neither of us would ever want discovered."

Zack wasn't having it. "I find it hard to believe that Putin has sent you on an errand of goodwill."

Sergei looked away.

Zack cocked his head. "Unless… Kwame, stop the Jeep."

Exasperated, Kwame slammed the steering wheel. "What? Again?" Reluctantly, he slowed to a stop.

"You say that you aren't FSB." (It wasn't a question, but a statement.) "Who are you?"

Sergei offered a wan smile. "A friend."

"The hell you say. If you're not with intelligence then how'd you find out my identity so fast."

"As I said: I am a friend… with good connections."

Zack shook his head. "Before I instruct Kwame to risk all of our necks, I need to know more."

Sergei sighed. "I'm part of an organization within Russia that has existed under the radar since World War II. Stalin established our organization originally as saboteurs should the Nazis take Stalingrad. Over time, Stalin went away but our organization never did. During the war, some of our agents got wind of a Nazi plot involving chemical warfare. Hitler had yet to sign onto it; in fact we do not believe he even knew about it. It was developed by a Nazi chemist stationed in Africa."

"Chemical weapons were banned after the first World War."

"Yes, and although the previous generation of chemical weapons were deadly, they were unreliable and limited in scope as to how many they could kill. This one was rumored to be a thousand times more predictable… and lethal. Remember, this was before the atomic bomb. Possession of such a weapon early in the war could have easily turned the tide of the war to Germany overnight."

"And you're telling me that this mythical weapon is still in Africa?"

"We have been secretly searching for this agent since the end of the war. Our people have followed thousands of leads but always came up empty until a few months ago when we found someone who claims to have credible information."

"Who?"

"That, Mr. Matteson, I will not tell you. It is the only reason you will not turned me over to the Sandsifters. You might say it is my insurance policy."

Zack chewed his bottom lip. "If this person is willing to sell you the information, why the guns?"

"You Americans think in two-dimensions," sighed Sergei. "This man has no idea just how dangerous his information is. He only knows that it is a chemical weapon developed in the jungle during the war. He offered it as an afterthought. What he wants is weapons... *my* weapons. I'll never make a deal with him without them. That is why we must go back."

Zack turned to Kwame. "What do you think?"

"I think he's lying," Kwame said. "Ready to move?"

Zack took a deep breath. "Yes."

Kwame reached for the gearshift.

"Take us around the Sandsifters and back to the Toyota."

"You're kidding. You believe this guy?"

"No. But he doesn't strike me as someone who'd risk his neck for a few hundred thousand dollars' worth of machine guns. There's more to this story, and I think it's worth finding out." He glared at Sergei. "If the truck is not there, we are taking you back to Camp Lemonnier where we will find out the truth... eventually."

Sergei scoffed. "Your country's interrogation techniques do not scare me. Besides, I have told you everything I can. Believe me, Mr. Matteson, should this weapon ever be used, it would be catastrophic. We must not let it fall into the wrong hands."

Zack rubbed his chin with the side of his Glock. "And I thought I was the king of clichés."

CHAPTER Twenty-Nine

Archer's Post, 2005

Samuel glanced into the mirror, shocked at how much gray now peppered his beard. Twenty-five years ago, when he'd first started infiltrating gangs of murderers, slave traders, and the like, he'd been clean-shaven. But a beard had become one of many ways he'd altered his appearance over the years. Fine-quality glasses, wigs, cosmetic scars, eye patches—all had been easily affordable thanks to the fortunes paid him by some of the world's wealthiest countries. But that was a thing of the past. *He was*, he told himself, *retiring*.

The smell of bacon, cooked with raisins and chutney filled the house as Osuroo Bankole greeted his nephew from the hallway. "Samuel, my boy, I still cannot believe that you are here." As much as Samuel had aged, Uncle Osuroo was showing the ravages of time that much more. Nearly 80 now, Osuroo walked with a cane and his eyesight was poor, but he had recognized the face of his nephew straight away, even though it had been three years since Samuel's last visit to Archer's Post.

"I am sorry that I surprised you last night, Baba. I know I should have called you weeks ago, but I wasn't entirely certain that I would be able to come, and I have disappointed you so many times in the past."

"Nonsense, child. *You* could never disappoint me."

Samuel grinned as he picked up the razor to shave the beard he'd worn the past six months, gathering intel on the *Lord's Resistance Army* in Southern Sudan. He'd had to learn Bantu before infiltrating the terrorist group. The United Nations operatives had barely stopped a massacre with the intelligence that he had managed to pass to them through his contact in Munich.

"You spoil me, Baba."

"Spoil you? How can I? I hardly ever see you." The words stung, though Samuel knew that his uncle hadn't meant them to hurt.

"Well, I will give you that chance now. I'd like to stay… help you with the farm."

His uncle laughed good-naturedly. "That's what you said three years ago. I believe you were here a month before going out on one of your special missions." Osuroo knew what his nephew did for a living, and had long ago come to terms with it. There was much evil in Africa. *If Samuel could help to stamp out part of it,* he often told himself, *then God be with him.*

As the hair fell into the sink, Samuel began to recognize the face in front of him. The mirror betrayed the years, but it also reflected his determination and strength—both of which he planned to put to work for his uncle now. It wasn't his frequent near misses with death that had brought him home; rather, it was that he had grown weary of the misery. Plus, he'd tired of the people he'd had to work alongside. At times it was difficult to distinguish the difference between the world's intelligence agencies, although the Russians had been the worst, and were the least of the world powers seemingly interested in making the planet a better place.

The Italians hadn't been much better lately, though it was their lack of precision and follow-through that had bothered him the most. It had been hit-or-miss with the Dutch and the Swiss. The Germans had been the most precise; the French, the best at fulfilling their promises. But it had been the Poles who had seemed to genuinely want to effect positive changes in Africa. Samuel still didn't know what interests the Agencja Wywiadu had in the region, but he had found a sensitivity among their agents that had been lacking among the others, except for maybe the original Frenchman who'd first recruited him.

It had been years since he'd heard from Gabriel. The colonel would have long since retired by now, if he was even still alive.

The CIA was the only major intelligence agency he hadn't worked with. Not surprising, given the apathy America displayed toward Africa. Asian and European countries had long expressed an interest in the continent as a whole, but outside of Egypt or Libya, most Americans never heard of what went on here.

Osuroo patted him on the shoulder as he turned and headed toward the kitchen. "Come have breakfast with your old uncle when you are done. I've made you your favorite, kikomando."

"I thought that was bacon I smelled?"

His baba smiled. "Yes, that as well. But I also made a large pot of kikomando. We will feast now that the prodigal has come home.

Samuel couldn't hold back the wide grin. He hadn't

had the avocado and bean stew since he was a teenager.

"Thank you, Baba. After breakfast, maybe you can show me what you would have me do on the farm first?"

His uncle waved his hand in the air. "No. After breakfast I wish to sit and talk with you. We have lots of catching up to do. The farm is in good hands. I will introduce you to my new foreman this afternoon. Finish shaving and then come eat. I want to hear everything about your life these past years." Osuroo turned the corner into the hallway and was gone, but Samuel could still hear his sing-songing: "The prodigal has returned and we must celebrate!"

Later, stuffed with the warm stew he'd remembered from his childhood, Samuel filled his uncle in on some of the nefarious organizations he had helped deal a serious blow to over the years: The Lord's Army, Al-Qaeda, Al-Shabab, Mujao, Boko Haram, plus heinous human traffickers and villainous groups dealing in blood diamonds. He purposefully left out the gory details, reassuring his uncle that never once had he been forced to kill another human being.

"Yet, people have died from your information," Osuroo said with a heavy sigh. "Very bad people." His eyes dropped but rose again. "You did what had to be done, Samuel; I know that. You have done much good over the years… brought an end to much suffering. Your auntie would be proud. I know that I certainly am."

The words were balm to Samuel's soul. "They have paid me well, Baba. At first, I felt guilty for taking the money. But I remembered you once quoted scripture to me that 'the laborer is worth his reward.'"

"They *should* have paid you well. You placed your life at risk every time, Samuel. May I ask: what have you done with this money?"

"I have invested most of it over the years. It has amassed into a great amount. I have no wife, no children. I would like to offer it to you so that you can make your property everything you ever dreamed it could be."

Osuroo shook his head. "But it already is. Nearly a year ago, I hired a foreman who has worked to build up the land, not only here but on my other farms, as well. I now have nearly twice as many cattle as ever."

Samuel took his uncle's hand in his. "That is wonderful, Baba,…but I wish to give you *something*."

"You already have. You have given me a son in whom I take great pride."

"No, I mean something tangible. Something you have always wanted."

Osuroo squeezed Samuel's hand tightly. "You have done that, too, my boy. Do you not remember presenting me the deed to the hill I have always loved? That was an amazing gift. I still do not see how the Twanga family could bear to part with it. Even now, I have Jenga take me there on the weekends. I had him build me a bench on which I sit and dream as I look across the valley below."

"Who is Jenga?"

"Jenga Msaliti. He is the foreman I told you about. He even favors you a bit, when you were younger that is. An amazing man."

Samuel laughed. "If he looks like me, then he must be quite handsome. Come, take me to him so that I may see just how 'amazing' this man is with my own eyes."

Osuroo reached for his cane before making it to his feet. "You will like him. He already likes you."

"How can he? We have never met."

"*Ah*, but he has met *you*… through me. He cajoles me into talking about you all the time. Do not worry, I told him that you work for the French government. He does not know what you really do."

Samuel nodded. "The French, the Russians, the Italians, the Swiss, the Germans, the…"

His uncle raised his hand for him to stop. "Perhaps it would be easier for you to tell me the countries that you *do not* work for."

Samuel laughed again. "Perhaps it would, indeed."

They walked outside and climbed into Samuel's Isuzu truck and headed toward the north end of the large ranch. Beside a creek, three men were offloading hay to supplement the cattle's feed. A tall man with long arms and even longer legs tossed out the bales of hay for the other two hired hands as if they weighed nothing at all. His uncle pointed at the man in the truck. "Jenga."

"He looks like a pencil; how is he able to throw those bales around so easily?"

His uncle smiled approvingly as he watched the man work. "He is wiry, that one. No muscle tone that you can visibly see, but he hides his strength."

Samuel's eyebrows fell. "Let us hope that is all that he is hiding," he said, recalling how the drunken guard had once betrayed them all.

"I admit, I was leery at first. He is not from here; no one knew him. But he soon proved himself to be a hard worker—and just look around. The land has not looked this good in years."

Samuel gazed across the horizon. His uncle was right. The ranch had never looked better, not even when he and his uncle had spent long days working together.

Turning toward the unfamiliar vehicle heading their way, Jenga and two workmen hopped down and stared. Uncle Osuroo stuck his head out the open window and called to them. At once, their shoulders visibly relaxed. They both rushed to the Isuzu, Jenga helping the older man get his balance as he climbed out of the truck.

"I have brought you a surprise, Jenga. My boy, my Samuel, is paying us a visit!"

Samuel grinned. "More than just a visit, Baba." He crossed in front of the Isuzu and held out his hand to Jenga and then the other two hired hands. "I must say, you have done wonders here."

"It is not just us," said one of the men. "There are three more men at the bunkhouse."

Samuel looked at his uncle. "Bunkhouse? Things *have* changed."

Jenga sized the newcomer up from head to toe. "I am so glad to finally meet the great Samuel Kauxho-huena. Your uncle has told me so much about you."

"I'm afraid you have me at a disadvantage," Samuel answered. "I know so little about you."

Osuroo brightened. "Perhaps you will join us tonight for dinner, Jenga?" he said. "The two of you can become better acquainted."

Before Samuel could object, Jenga had already accepted. "I'd be honored, Osuroo."

Not "Bwana Osuroo?" Samuel was surprised at the liberty.

"I have to admit that I feel better knowing that there are six of you doing what my uncle and I used to do all by ourselves."

Jenga frowned.

"I mean no disrespect. It's just that I sometimes felt that I had not served my uncle well in my years here."

Osuroo placed his hand on Samuel's shoulder. "Listen to him, would you? Even as a boy he had strength that would amaze the toughest of the Samburu warriors." Osuroo squeezed Samuel's bicep. "Hard as stone. You are made of granite, I think."

"How does one grow such muscles working for dainty Frenchmen?" Jenga asked in a not-so-teasing manner.

"The ones I worked for were not so dainty," was all the explanation Samuel would offer.

"Then, perhaps you would care to help us unload the rest of the hay?" Jenga replied. It had sounded more like a challenge than a request.

"I would, but you only have four more bales."

The men laughed good naturedly. "We have four more loads to pick up before noon when it gets too hot."

Samuel turned to his uncle. "Would you mind, Baba, if I helped your workers? I am itching to do something on your land again. I need to put these muscles to work."

"It is *your* land, Samuel. Remember? I am only tending it for you."

"Still, may I spend the morning in the fields? It would be a welcome change for me."

Osuroo smiled. "I shall see you at lunch then? I will fry some chicken." Osuroo gestured toward his foreman. "And tonight, I will prepare something special for you both. Come hungry, Jenga."

Jenga smiled. "Don't I always?"

****

An unexpected jolt of the pickup truck hitting a gopher hole caused Samuel to lose his balance and tumble over the siderails of the truck. Jenga signaled for the driver to stop and hopped out. "Are you hurt, Sammy?" Samuel got to his feet and dusted himself off with his sunhat. Overhead, a gray hornbill seemed to be laughing at the sight.

"Only my pride," he said, forcing a laugh even though it did smart a bit. He was getting too old to be falling out of trucks, even if the ground was soft and marshy from spring rains.

"Why don't you ride up front with Tousara for a while? Alexander and I can finish this."

Samuel pushed aside the pain as he jumped back into the truck bed. "What, and have my uncle's foreman think that I am soft?"

Jenga poked him with a stick. "Hey, you are the one who has been prancing around with dainty Frenchmen, remember?"

"As I told you weeks ago, the ones I worked with weren't dainty."

"Maybe so, but they couldn't have been very smart."

"What makes you say that?" Samuel asked his new friend.

Jenga grinned from ear to ear. "Because they never taught you to hold onto the edge of a truck when you sit on the siderails." All three men laughed—Tousara would have too, if he hadn't had the radio up so loud in the cab. "We're almost done here; we will turn back soon. You'll be home in time for supper."

"What, you aren't coming?"

"I think your uncle wants you all to himself tonight. After all, you and I have been together quite a bit lately." It was true. Although Samuel had been suspicious of Jenga at first—*how could he not have been after what had happened to his Auntie Gemma so long ago*—the two had become friends.

"Yes, I suppose I should spend more time with him. It's just that it has felt good to work the land once again." Samuel rubbed his shoulder. "Well, at least it did until now."

The workmen finished their afternoon chores and then headed for the bunkhouse while Samuel made his way inside the house. He could smell the aromatic maafe cooking in the kitchen. Peanut stew had been a staple at his auntie's table when he had been a boy. "Baba?" he called. "Is dinner almost ready. I am starving!"

He walked into the kitchen to find the pot boiling rapidly and his uncle sound asleep in his favorite kitchen chair. Samuel turned down the heat and stirred the pot several times with a wooden spoon to loosen the ingredients sticking to the bottom.

"Leave that alone; you will change the flavor," said his uncle, opening one eye.

"How can setting the house on fire make this taste any better, Baba?"

"I was watching it," Osuroo said defensively.

Samuel chuckled. "You were watching the back of your eyelids."

"What? I was not sleeping."

Samuel laughed. "You were doing an excellent job of pretending, then."

Osuroo stood to check the stew. "I was only resting," he said, unwilling to let the matter go.

Samuel grinned. "You were snoring."

"*Harrumph.* You should hear yourself at night; even the chickens outside are complaining."

"Seriously, Baba, I would hate for something to happen while I am out in the fields. Perhaps it is time we find a woman to come in and help manage things for you."

"A what?"

"A woman. You know, those soft people with the round figures. The ones you could never keep your eyes off of once upon a time… remember?"

"You are mad. I may have occasionally glanced, but I only had eyes for your auntie."

Samuel nodded. "But she has been gone nearly 30 years." He had always wondered: "Why did you never marry again?"

Osuroo evaded the question. "Why haven't you?"

Samuel shrugged. "Never had the time. Not a lot of women in the terrorist groups, at least not in the ones that I've wormed my way into, and certainly not the type of women I'd be interested in."

"*Wormed*? " Osuroo scowled. "If you ask me, that is what they are… nothing but a bunch of worms; not men. Traitors, all of them!"

Samuel shrugged. "Some of them think that they are patriots."

"Then they are delusional worms, as well. Their actions betray all of humanity." He glanced into his nephew's warm eyes. "Tell me again, what is it they call you one they discover they have been the ones betrayed?"

"I go by many different names. But there is one in particular. After I've gone and they realize that they have been betrayed, some have referred to me as the *Yuda Bundi*."

"The Judas Owl?"

"Yes," Samuel answered. "The Judas part is obvious, I suppose, at least from their perspective. However, I'm not sure who first started calling me an owl." He extended both arms and began to flap them like a bird in jest. "Perhaps it is because I swoop down under the cloak of darkness and devour my prey, no?"

Osuroo scoffed. "More likely it is your big eyes…" he grinned as he glanced behind his nephew… "and your fat tail."

"Hey!"

The old man poked Samuel with his cane. "Now go wash up for supper. I have to finish baking the chapati so that we have some flat bread with the stew. And no more talk about a woman in my kitchen."

Samuel did as he was told, but as he helped his uncle clean the dishes later that night, he was even more convinced of the need for a housekeeper and cook.

Finding someone would be relatively easy; talking his uncle into it would be the difficult part. Maybe he could elicit Jenga's help. His uncle trusted Jenga, relied on him—even took his advice on matters pertaining to the farm. *Maybe, between the two of them, they could talk this stubborn, wonderful old man into it.*

CHAPTER Thirty

"Tell me again why we are heading to this part of the stream?"

Samuel was talking with Jenga while stepping gingerly through some marshy bottoms toward a bend underneath a grove of kapok trees. Just ahead, a 10-meter waterfall kept the lifeblood of Uncle Osuroo's land flowing.

"As I recall, this is where the snakes used to spend their summers when I was a kid," he said nervously.

"This is autumn. Besides, I was here yesterday," replied Jenga. "There were no snakes."

Still, Samuel wasn't thrilled to be heading toward a portion of the spring that even the cattle avoided. "I wanted to see if you thought we could build a generator underneath the falls. The two watched the water cascading from above, with Samuel keeping a careful lookout for any sign of the venomous puff adders that used to inhabit this area by the score when he was a child. That was why his uncle had never considered using the waterfall for electricity.

Jenga stared up to the top of the falls. "If my calculations are correct, we could generate a turbine efficiency rate of 37 percent."

Samuel stared at him. "That's pretty damned precise."

Jenga shrugged. "I like being precise, Sammy. I used to help my brothers build water generators. Just one of many things we did with our father. Anytime you raise an object off of the ground it gains potential energy. I have measured the mass flow rate, and if we multiply the flow rate times the density of water at 1000 kilograms-a-meter-cubed we would a rate of 2,00 kilograms a second. Then, I simply multiplied the mass flow rate by the height of the falls to find how much power we will generate. Once I plugged in all the numbers, I came up with the answer. The savings to your uncle would be significant."

Samuel's chin dropped. "Jenga, I had no idea…"

"What? That I am intelligent as well as strong?"

"That's not what I meant. You never cease to amaze me. Engineering used to be my specialty…. why would someone with your aptitude for such things be working as a field hand?"

Jenga looked as if he'd just received an elbow to the gut. "There is no need for insults."

Samuel held up his hands. "I meant no insult. I'm just surprised, that is all."

"What I do is important work—good work. And I am not a *field hand*, as you put it. I am foreman of one of the richest pieces of land in all of Archer's Post."

"I apologize, Jenga. You are correct; I meant no harm… what?" Jenga's gaze had suddenly fallen to the ground behind Samuel. "Ow!"

A snake had struck Samuel just above the boot on his left leg. He whipped around, only to have the giant adder strike again, this time its sharp fangs only met the thick leather of Samuel's right boot.

Thwack!

A knife pinned the adder between eyes and earth, killing it instantly. "Good God, you are an expert with knives, as well?" exclaimed Samuel. "Hurry, help me tie a tourniquet and then get me back to the house. My uncle keeps antivenom in the kitchen."

"There is no time," Jenga said, a bit too calmly for such a situation. "That was a young one; she gave you all her venom." He reached into his pocket. "Here, hold still, I always keep antivenom with me."

He grabbed Samuel's left arm, extending it tightly against his side. Samuel watched as Jenga ripped off the top of a tiny glass vial and extracted the syringe packaged within. Without so much as a second's thought, Jenga inserted the needle into an artery and let the antivenom race the poison through Samuel's heart and spread throughout his body.

"You may feel nauseous, Sammy, but that is normal. Come, let us get you to the truck while you can still stand. I'm afraid you are going to be quite sick for a few days."

Samuel placed an arm around Jenga's shoulder and allowed him to prop him up as they headed for the vehicle. Just as Jenga had predicted, the dizziness came on quickly; whether it was the antivenom or the poison he did not know. Even though the truck was only meters away, Samuel stopped twice to vomit.

"Do not worry, my friend. I only carry the best

antivenom. That adder did her best to kill you, but she failed, I assure you."

As weak as he felt, Samuel still managed to whisper a thank you as Jenga helped him into the truck. Within minutes they were back at the house. Osuroo glanced out the kitchen window where he saw Jenga practically carrying Samuel into the house. He held open the screen door. "Oh, my God! What happened?"

"Snake."

Osuroo headed for the cabinet where he kept the medicine. "I have antivenom for several snakes. What kind was it; quickly, tell me!"

"Puff adder. But do not worry. I had the correct antivenom with me. Sammy will be fine in a day or two. He just needs to rest." Osuroo did his best to help Jenga carry his nephew into the bedroom before removing his nephew's boots and belt."

"Where was it?"

"In the leg. Left one."

Osuroo shook his head. "No; the snake. Where were you when he got bitten?"

"Down by the waterfall."

Osuroo's face turned pale. "The waterfall! Jenga, you know better than to go down there! The snakes have always claimed that area as their own."

"We were scoping it out for a possible generator to help with the electricity."

Osuroo shook his head and mumbled: "Two young fools…"

Jenga's eyes fell to the floor. "It is my fault, Osuroo. I

should not have taken your nephew to the falls. I will go and pack my bags and prepare to leave."

Samuel, who'd been so quiet that both men had assumed he was unconscious, managed to open his eyes and grab hold of Jenga's arms. "You will do no such thing," he whispered. "Baba, Jenga went there yesterday to check to see if there were any snakes. He had no idea." He tried reaching for his uncle with his other hand but he was too weak. "Jenga saved my life."

The old man's brown eyes softened as he looked at his foreman and then back at Samuel. "Yes, yes; you are right. No more talk of anyone leaving. Rest, Samuel. I will make you some tea to help you regain your strength. Jenga, will you stay with him?"

"Yes, of course."

"I will call the tribal medicine man. He's not much at fixing an old man's aches and pains, but he can mend a broken bone and treat snakebites."

"Will he come?"

Osuroo forced a small grin. "He also happens to have a taste for Scotch, and he knows I will send him home with a bottle. He will come."

****

Three red-and-black turacos flew into the sunset until they became nothing more than black dots, the fiery tips of their wings indistinguishable from the brilliant red-orange of the sun. It had been two weeks since Samuel had been bitten. Fully recovered, he was working harder than ever on the farm. He felt he owed it to Jenga to lighten his friend's workload. *After all, Jenga had saved his life.*

For his part, Jenga had made no further mention of building a generator. Just as well. Samuel would've had to have nixed the project to protect the workers, and he didn't want to have to be put in a position to have to turn Jenga down. Not after what Jenga had done for him.

Samuel climbed down from the tractor to inspect a stump that would need to be pulled before next spring. The birds seemed to call to him as they flew overhead. He watched until his eyes could no longer take the rays of the setting sun before returning to plow. If he could get in a half-hour more he'd be finished turning the earth for the next maize crop. The sweet aroma of the soil seemed to refresh his very soul. It was good to be home.

"Sammy!" Only Jenga called him that. He turned to see his friend coming over the small hill. "Sammy, what are you doing? It is getting late."

"I am almost finished."

"So, stop. One of the men can finish this tomorrow."

"Afraid not. Uncle Osuroo has given everyone the day off. Did you forget about the Lake Festival?"

"I hadn't planned on going."

Samuel shook his head. "Not going? You *must* go. I have not been in decades, but it was always the highlight of the year amongst the Samburu. There will be camel races, dances, games—and the most important football match of the year. It is between fathers and their sons. Baba and I used to play long ago. The fathers usually won," he paused at the memory and then smiled, "but not always."

Jenga had made it down the hill now and was pointing to the last acre of ground to be plowed. "Well, then, why don't you let me finish this and you can rest up for the big day."

"I may be ten years your senior, but I can handle a party just as well as you can."

Jenga shrugged. "Maybe I will go just to prove you wrong. Do you think they would allow the two of us to play football with them? You could play with the old men and I with the young."

Samuel laughed good naturedly. "They are boys, Jenga. Twenty years your junior. And," he added, "while we do look a bit alike, only a blind man would think that I was old enough to be your father."

"Keep believing that, old man." Jenga grinned. "You'd best hurry and finish your plowing. You will need your rest if you are going to keep up with me tomorrow!" Jenga walked away laughing, as Samuel climbed back onto the tractor.

"Just watch who you are calling old!" he said, turning the key to drown out his friend before he could reply.

CHAPTER Thirty-One

Laughter filled the air as children in full ceremonial dress performed a centuries-old dance for the crowd. Everyone applauded as two 6-year-old girls stole the show with a spontaneous western-style breakdance that they'd copied from an American movie. Uncle Osuroo clapped the loudest, but it was less about the children and more about his joy that he and Samuel were here together. It had been too long since he'd been able to share the Lake Festival with someone he loved.

No one knew just how long the festival had been taking place, although there were tribal accounts of an annual event nearby, where the Uaso Secondary School was now. It had purportedly been a day of frivolity, not unlike the Lake Festival. Lake Sungura had been built by a small band of Germans before the war. The men were later taken prisoner by the British in a country-wide sweep to round up of Nazi infiltrators attempting to win the hearts of the indigenous. Fed by the rains, along with a channel from the Ewaso Nigiro River, the lake had been the site of an annual gathering ever since the end of World War II. No one knew what had happened to its creators, nor had anyone ever asked.

Although the war had not been felt as deeply in Kenya as it had in North Africa, nearly 100,000 Kenyans had been recruited into serving the British against the

Italian and German troops. Under British law, troops were kept segregated and no black man could rise above the rank of warrant officer. Sacrificing black lives over white ones became the norm whenever the opportunity arose and it was not long before the growing seeds of discontent spread throughout the country. Many said that the roots of the Mau Mau uprising lay in such abuse by white troops during the war.

But today was not a day for painful remembrance but of merrymaking. Beer flowed freely, as did Chang'aa—a potent home-brew, distilled from millet, maize and sorghum. By the time the camel races began, half of the gambling crowd were betting with reckless abandon—too inebriated to care which camel had the most powerful legs or the best reputation of being fast on its feet. One of the few who'd not imbibed during the day had been Osuroo's foreman.

"Come on, Jenga," Samuel encouraged as he helped his uncle into a folding chair near the finish line. "One beer won't hurt you."

"Leave the man alone," Osuroo grunted as he took another sip of Chang'aa. "One of us has to be able to drive home when this is over. And considering how much you and I have already had to drink, it certainly won't be either one of us."

"I'm as alert as a cheetah," Samuel groused.

"A cheetah whose been drinking beer and Chang'aa all afternoon," Jenga said.

Samuel plopped down on the ground next to where his uncle sat in one of the metal folding chairs placed earlier for the elderly in the crowd. "And why not? It has been a long time since I've been surrounded by my people." He reached up and squeezed his uncle's arm. "My loving baba and my wonderful new friend."

He held up his beer in an attempted salute only to slosh half of it out of the paper cup. "To the man who saved my life!"

"Which is what I will be doing again later tonight when I drive the two of you home," Jenga joked as six more camels were led to the starting gate.

"Samuel," instructed Osuroo, "go put 10,000 shillings on that tall one right there, Number Eleven; I feel lucky."

"What you feel is drunk," scolded Jenga good naturedly. "Why throw away $100 dollars on that worthless, flea-ridden carpet. Check out Number Four. That one is a winner for sure!"

"What do you know about camels?" Osuroo groused.

"My father used to breed them."

Samuel was quiet, knowing absolutely nothing about the beasts. "That's good enough for me," Osuroo said. "Change that to Number Four." Samuel struggled to his feet.

"Number Four it is," he said. "I need to get another beer anyway." He glanced at Jenga. "How much are you wagering?"

Jenga laughed. "Not a single shilling. I have to save my money for the trip."

Samuel raised an eyebrow. "What trip is that?"

Jenga looked down at the smiling Osuroo, half asleep in the chair. "You have not told him?"

"Told me what?"

"I am planning a trip to England in a couple of months; that is, if I can save enough money."

"England, why England?"

"I have always wanted to go. My father spent some time there during the war. He said the countryside was beautiful, and that if I ever got the opportunity I should visit."

Samuel shrugged. "Your father sounds like an interesting man. Is there anything he did not do?"

Jenga shook his head. "Not much."

"Where in England are you heading?"

"My father always spoke of York and Durham. I'm planning on starting there."

At the mention of Durham, something in the back of Samuel's throat felt like it turned to sand. *His father had spoken to him of the graveyard at Durham Cathedral… and of what was buried there.*

"Do not worry; I will be gone only while the land is dormant. I will be back in time for spring planting."

"It is not that," Samuel managed to say. "It's just that…" he glanced down at his uncle, "…we will miss you, that is all."

Jenga smiled. "I have an idea, Sammy. Why don't you go with me?"

"What?"

"It would be good for you," Osuroo chimed in. "You deserve a break, son. I will be fine."

Samuel's head was foggy from too much beer, but he couldn't help wonder if providence was whispering in his ear. *After all… Durham! What were the chances he'd be asked to go there?* Durham was where his father had hidden what he used to refer to as "Hell's Elixir."

"Let me give it some thought," he said, as a cold shiver worked its way up his spine.

Jenga shrugged. "I hope you will say yes. We could have a wonderful time together exploring England's countryside." He smiled. "Maybe I should be the one to refill that beer for you?"

"What? Oh, yes, thank you." Samuel was no longer in a festive mood. Try as he might, he was unable to focus on the races or the other festivities that afternoon. Thoughts of an ancient graveyard and the secret that it had kept hidden for decades allowed little room for anything else.

CHAPTER Thirty-Two

Grand Bara Desert

They hadn't seen the ravine until it was almost too late. The Jeep complained loudly as Kwame stomped on the brakes. Zack and Sergei nearly tumbled out onto the sand.

"Kakogo cherta!" shouted Sergei.

"What the hell, indeed!" Zack echoed.

Sergei stared at Zack. "So, you speak Russian? I suppose that is a good thing for a spy."

Zack climbed out of the Jeep. "Just like you speak English, right?"

"I told you already; I am not FSB."

"Yeah, yeah. Look, even if we believed that cock-and-bull story of yours, we're on a different mission you and me—don't you forget it."

Sergei lifted his shackled hands. "How can I?" Kwame checked his GPS. We are only half a kilometer from where we left the other vehicle.

"Let's just hope our sand buddies aren't hanging around," Zack quipped.

"Untie me and I will run ahead to check."

"And leave you with an entire arsenal at your disposal? I don't think so." Zack walked around the small ravine until he found solid ground to the right.

"Kwame, drive over here; just take it slow." Kwame did, and soon the three cautiously approached the spot where they'd been attacked. They carefully drove past the two burned-out trucks before chancing an approach to the Toyota. "Sergei, this is where you get your wish. Hop out and make sure one of those sand bunnies isn't hiding inside."

From the look on his face, that was clearly not what the Russian had in mind. "Not unless you untie me, first."

Zack pointed his .45 at the Russian's kneecap. "Then, perhaps pain is something you enjoy."

"You see too many spy movies, Mr. Matteson. You are not going to shoot me."

Kwame pulled a long knife. "Neither am I, but unlike my friend, I have no qualms about inflicting a bit of pain when necessary."

"Chert," Sergei swore as he managed to climb out of the backseat. "Just keep me covered," he said with an audible sigh. "My mission is too important for it to end here."

Kwame put the knife away and picked up the AK as he and Zack took positions on either side of the Jeep. Sergei made his way toward the Toyota slowly, looking like a shorn lamb waiting to be slaughtered. When nothing happened, he peered into the vehicle through the windows and then turned and hurried back. "They didn't post a guard," was all he said.

"See. I told you, Tilly."

"Quit calling me that," Zack groused. "Grab that launcher and the last missile and I'll get the gas can."

"Be sure to bring the water. They will have taken whatever water was in the Toyota." Sure enough, the petrol can in the back of the Toyota was untouched, but all the canteens were gone. "Okay, Tilly, now what? Are we just going to leave the Jeep here?"

Zack thought for a moment before coming to a decision. "Hand me you knife." Sergei's eyes grew twice in size as Zack approached him. "Give me your hands," Zack demanded before cutting the Russian loose. "I don't like the idea of leaving both vehicles here in case one breaks down. But I can't watch you and drive at the same time, so you're going to follow us in the Jeep."

He made sure he caught Sergei's eye. "But if you try and drive away or have any thoughts of escaping, we will shoot you down and call it a successful mission."

"What is it you Americans say? You're the boss."

"Just make sure that you remember that. When we slow down, you slow down. When we stop, you stop. We'll ditch the Jeep when we get out of this giant litter box and back to civilization. That's when I want to hear more about this supposed mission you are on."

"You still do not believe me, no?"

Zack grunted in disgust. "I haven't made up my mind."

Sergei, for his part, remained silent.

"Tilly, the Sandsifters will figure out we've doubled back by now."

Zack tossed Sergei the keys to the Jeep. "Then let's go before we wear out our welcome. And get all the weapons from the Jeep first." He rolled his eyes. "And for Pete's sake, would you *please* stop calling me that!"

****

Zack slept most of the way as night turned to dusk and dust to dawn. Kwame kept an eye in the rearview mirror to make certain Sergei stayed close. At last, he poked Zack with his elbow to wake him. "Come on, Tilly, time to go to work."

"What?" Zack said, his brain not fully embracing the transition. In his dream he'd been in his back yard playing with his daughter.

"Earth to Matteson. Come in, Matteson."

Zack stretched and wiped his eyes with the back of both hands. "Where are we?"

"Desert. Remember?" Zack turned to look out the back. "He's still there," Kwame said. "I'm thinking we should stop before he realizes how close we are to civilization and tries to get around us.

"Good idea. How much farther do we have to go?"

"We should be seeing an actual road within the next five kilometers."

"Okay. Let's stop. I need to use the sandbox anyway."

"Your colorful metaphors never cease to amaze me."

Zack rolled his eyes. "Well, excuse me, your grace, while I trip the light fantastic to the loo."

Kwame shook his head, but the truth was that nature was calling him as well. No doubt, Sergei would also welcome a private moment in the sand. He slowed and then came to a stop, as did Sergei. The three men climbed out of their vehicles in like mind and mission. Afterward, as Sergei approached the Toyota, Zack positioned himself near the rear of the vehicle in case the Russian decided to go for one of the guns.

"We're travelling in one vehicle from this point on, Sergei. Hold your hands in front of you."

"While it may sound strange to you, Mr. Matteson, I pose you and your partner no threat. Had I wanted to harm you I would have already done so."

Zack held his hand out to Kwame for the piece of cord to tie Sergei's hands. "Pardon me if I'm not convinced. You did, after all, need us to get you across the desert."

"I needed runners to make me look like a legitimate arms dealer." Somehow, the words *legitimate* and *arms dealer* didn't mix well in Zack's brain. "But, when I discovered that you are CIA, I considered how you might be of some assistance to my mission."

"Tell you what, Sergei, or whatever your real name is, while Kwame is topping off the gas tank, why don't you finish that little story you were telling me." Zack wrapped the cords around both of Sergei's wrists individually before tying them together in a manner worthy of the handlers of the Great Houdini.

"I have told you more than enough to get me killed," he sighed… "but I suppose there is, as your people say, no escaping it now. You will not assist me otherwise, no?"

"Assist *you*? I'm not the one with my hands tied, buddy boy."

The Russian stared at his bonds before reluctantly adding to what he'd already told them. "The chemical I spoke of, it was crudely made in a German outpost by a self-serving officer who was a chemist before the war. Kreps was his name. He was with the SS; the equivalent of a Russian major. We believe the natives told him about a compound that occurs in nature, a deadly poison, that he managed to synthesize in such a way as to make it deadly enough that a few drops released in the air could kill hundreds in the blink of an eye."

"Just how did you Russians get wind of this?"

Sergei hesitated; he was obviously uncomfortable telling Zack any more. "A certain British leftenant came across the officer's notes when the English took the outpost. He was unable to read German, but his wife could. She secretly worked for us."

"A spy?"

"Technically, no. We were all on the same side back then."

Zack scoffed, but allowed him to continue. "She told her husband they were nothing of importance, but her handler in Leningrad was a decent man, well placed within our army's intelligence service." Even though Sergei was much too young to have served, he sighed heavily as if the memory of the war weighed on him personally.

"Things were going badly in my country; thousands of our people were dying every day. Stupid decisions were made which cost many innocent lives. The intelligence officer knew the high command would stop at nothing to find this poison. He thought it wise to conceal the information until after the war. Fortunately, this man survived. He was even decorated by Stalin and given a position within national intelligence. Not long after, he formed his own highly secretive organization of a few former military officers and civilian scientists. They have served under many covers across the decades: diplomatic attaches to Africa, tourists, even Orthodox missionaries. We have tried to find evidence of what became of the poison. Alas, we have found very little; nothing of the actual formula, only the stories of the families of people Kreps experimented upon. There was, however, enough for us to continue our search; and now, we believe we are closer than ever."

"Tell you what," Zack said. "I'll get you back to Camp Lemonnier, and then to Washington and you can tell this to my superiors at Langley."

Sergei's eyes widened as he said with a trace of mockery, "The same superiors you have detested for years?" He waited for the words to sink in. "I told you, I am not FSB, and I am not. Our organization is small, but we have run circles around the KGB, the GRU and the FSB for decades. We are very knowledgeable… and capable." *Was that a threat?* The corner of the Russian's mouth turned upward. "While at the brothel, I was able to get plenty of information about you, Mr. Matteson."

"Yeah, that's what you said."

"Your wife's name is Donna," he recited. "Your marriage is not on the firmest footing. You have $73,301 in your savings account, you married in Edinburgh with your partner, Scott Flenn, acting as your best man. At the time, you were chasing down an Iraqi traitor who'd almost poisoned the two of you—shall I continue?"

Zack glared at him. "Not necessary."

"Are you certain? I know other things, as well. For

instance, you do not share your partner's affinity for following procedure. You also like to make your own decisions, independent of the bureaucrats and pencil-pushers at Langley. Correct?"

Zack inhaled deeply before answering. "You continue to have me at a disadvantage. How about telling me your real name and about your military training?"

Sergei nodded. "Very well, Mr. Matteson. Indeed, you are correct. I was an officer in the Russian army. I suppose something about me must still bear witness to my command training, no? It does not matter. It will do you no good to try and find out more about me when you finally contact Langley. There have been hundreds of officers who would fit my description."

Zack offered one of his trademark grins. "Frankly, Sergei, I'm not as interested in you or your so-called mission as you seem to think I am."

Sergei's eyes narrowed. "You should be! I am not lying to you about this. We are closer now to finding information about the poison than we have ever been. So close, that I am willing to take you, an agent for the CIA, into my confidence! I have not made this decision lightly. As much as it pains me to say this… I *need* you, Mr. Matteson. And as cliché as it may sound: The *world* needs you."

CHAPTER Thirty-Two

May 30, 1941

Kenyan recruits weren't often given a day off, and when they were, there were tight restrictions on just where they could and could not go while in England. From what Corporal Osmann and his brother, Kifo, had heard, the attitudes of the whites in Durham weren't nearly as bad as those in London. Of course, neither compared to the disdain many of the American troops had toward the blacks. Still, Osmann made certain to distance himself from the local people out for a Sunday afternoon stroll as he made his way to the giant cathedral at the top of the hill.

Durham Cathedral was one of the approved sites African soldiers were allowed to visit. Fewer than 200 Kenyans had been brought to the north of England to serve the officers and new recruits of the Durham Light Infantrymen. Already, the D.L.I. had raised a dozen battalions, sending soldiers to fight in France, Burma, North Africa and Italy. Surprisingly, Durham had not yet been bombed by the Luftwaffe, although rumors were that the town was living on borrowed time. Residents had spent weeks preparing for one of the many night raids that had plagued the rest of the country.

Osmann walked across the beautiful Framwellgate Bridge over the River Wear. Most people ignored him, although a portly, professorial looking man with wispy hair offered him a friendly smile. Just over the treetops, he could see the great Norman tower of Durham Cathedral and to its left, the façade of an ancient castle. Framwellgate Bridge itself was a masterpiece, dating back to mediaeval times.

Osmann was amazed at the amount of traffic the ancient masonry was able to accommodate, much of it military traffic, with trucks disguised to look like commercial delivery vans. So far, the Germans had not discerned the importance of Durham to England's war efforts, and great lengths were being taken to keep it that way.

The huge cathedral was unlike anything that he had ever seen. Indeed, the city of Durham itself was magnificent. Osmann was unsure of what other European cities were like, but Durham was a stately place with its ancient buildings and picturesque views. *If the rest of Europe was anything like this, why on earth were the Germans bent on destroying it?* But if Sturmbannführer Hans Kreps had been an example of what the Nazis were capable of, he understood the Allies determination to stop Hitler at all costs.

Osmann thought of the box that was hidden away in his small trunk back at the barracks for African servants. He had brought the poison with him with the intention of turning it over to the highest-ranking British officer he could find, but working on kitchen detail these past months had not provided him with an opportunity to meet any officers other than the brash second-leftenant who often complained about the way his eggs had been prepared.

Kifo, of course, knew about the poison, but the war had changed him. Osmann wasn't certain that he trusted his brother anymore. In the beginning, Kifo had spent days trying to convince Osmann that they should sell the nerve agent to the highest bidder. Osmann had told him that he had destroyed the evil elixir, and had been silent about just what had happened to the rest of the Sturmbannführer hellish concoction—how he had brought it with him to England.

Standing before the great cathedral, the wind blowing damp and cold from the West, Osmann removed his cap as he marveled at the site before him. Durham Cathedral dated to 995, when monks from Lindisfarne brought the remains of Saint Cuthbert to the top of this hill. But Osmann had no knowledge of any of that as he walked underneath the huge stone archway and past a gruesome bronze figure affixed to the huge oaken doors where sinners had once sought sanctuary. Inside, he found the most beautiful man-made vision he could ever hope to see. Words like Romanesque, Gothic, medieval-symmetry, were meaningless to him, but other words, such as holy and magnificent, sprang immediately to mind.

The ribbed vaults of the great stone columns rose from the floor to the massive stone ceiling above, while artfully crafted pews were neatly aligned in perfect rows on either side of a wide aisle. Directly ahead was a gigantic carved spire encompassing a marble baptismal font. At the other end of the long aisle was the high altar, behind which was a chapel dedicated to an English saint named Bede. Just beyond the shrine were nine more altars, lined up against the rear wall of the great church. He overheard one of the priests explaining to a group of finely dressed women that each altar had been built to accommodate the crowds who had visited the cathedral over the centuries to worship at the shrine of Saint Cuthbert.

A bit of a religious man himself, Osmann thought he owed it to himself and his late parents, both devout Christians, to visit to the shrine. He passed a cleaning woman with a mop and bucket and climbed the steps underneath a blue banner boasting a gold cross. Inside he found a simple altar on one end, surrounded by four tall candles and a statue of a man holding his own head. The strong odor of detergent caused Osmann to wrinkle his nose as he wondered what the headless statue was about. A placard underneath simply read: *King Oswald*. And a rectangular slab of marble with a Latin inscription was surrounded by rails to prevent tourists from trampling on it.

This apparently was Saint Cuthbert's tomb. Above, was a gigantic imposed image of the risen Christ in a virtual rainbow of colors. It seemed magically suspended above the slab of green marble. A shiver ran down Osmann's spine as he stood in front of the prayer desk at the foot of the tomb. Although no one else was in the room, he felt what seemed like two hands pressing against his shoulders forcing him to kneel. Prayer wasn't what he had come here for, but pray he did, as if the fate of the world depended on it... and, perhaps it did.

Lord... Osmann prayed. *...I'm a simple man from a faraway place, but having seen the grandeur of this holy place I* *believe that some part of your spirit must dwell here. Show me what to do with this horrible thing you have entrusted me with.*

There was, however, no voice from on high or white dove alighting upon his shoulder. Instead, the cleaning lady stuck her head into the chapel and rudely said, "'Ere now. There's a service beginning in 'ere soon. Be off with you. Gentlemen and ladies will be a worshippin' in 'ere."

The charm of the ancient church faded as he made his way back outside. *He probably could have insisted on staying for the worship service. After all, he was in a British uniform. But why should he after the way he'd just been treated.* Instead he strolled through the cemetery until he stopped at a gravestone which was barely readable, except for a date, 1691, and only one name which was readable. He could hardly believe it.

The stone clearly read *Osmann*! *Was this the sign he'd asked for?* His stomach dropped. It fell even further when he swore he heard a single word carried by the breeze:

Tonight.

CHAPTER Thirty-Three

2005

"Tonight?" Zack repeated. "That's when we're supposed to meet your contact?" Sergei simply nodded as they drove past shell-pocked gray-and-brown buildings on the outskirts of Addis Ababa with the skyline of Ethiopia's most modern city on the horizon. Heavily clothed women with baskets on their heads and men carrying older Russian and Chinese-made automatic rifles stopped to stare at the Toyota as it passed the battle-scarred buildings.

"What's the story here?" Zack asked Kwame. "These people look like they've never seen a Toyota before."

"It is you which interests them. Perhaps you should close your window. A white face attracts attention in these boroughs."

Zack did as he was instructed. "What's with all these messed-up buildings?" The shell of half of what might have once been an apartment building jutted angrily toward the sky.

Kwame shrugged. "Who knows. There have been many battles fought in these neighborhoods. The guerillas' names and purpose change as often as the shifting sand."

Zack turned to the Russian. "Looks like the people down here mean business. So do I, Sergei. If you try and double cross us at any point, I will not hesitate to kill you; do not underestimate me. Understood?"

"I suppose suspicion comes naturally to people in your profession, no? We will be in the city soon; you will see that I mean you no harm."

"About that?" Kwame added. "Your contact is the one who sent the runners that we dispatched, how do you plan to pass us off?"

"I will tell them the truth."

Zack's eyes narrowed.

"By that, I mean that I will inform them that the men died in the desert. I will tell them of the Sandsifters. No doubt they will have heard of them, yes?"

Kwame frowned. "No doubt."

"What about us?" Zack snapped.

"You will pose as my bodyguards."

Zack didn't come close to trusting the Russian but he was intrigued enough to allow the man to take him to whomever it was that was expecting him. He wanted to know more about Sergei's contact. Gun-running was one of the nastier trades in the Sahara, and any knowledge he could bring back would prove useful.

"Just so long as you understand that the two of us will never be out of site. Any attempts to betray us will end very badly for you."

"Mr. Matteson, I understand your reticence to believe what I have told you, but I have no intention of betraying you. I cannot stress how important it is that this man believes that you are who I tell them. He is hoping to buy weapons, yes, but he is also expecting to sell information to me on what he calls the ultimate weapon." Sergei took a breath. "For an exorbitant price, of course."

"Of course." Zack glanced at Kwame to see if he was buying any of this, but he couldn't get a read from him. "So, what is your plan?"

"I need a meal, a shower and to rest. You provide that, and I provide you with more answers, yes?"

Zack rolled his eyes. "We nearly get killed in the desert and he all he can think about is the Hilton."

Kwame shrugged. "A shower does sound good. How about it, Tilly?"

Zack slunk into his seat. "You're not going to quit calling me that, are you? Fine. Whatever. Just make sure you help me keep an eye on him. You may buy this bit about an ultimate weapon, but I don't."

"Which is why you want me to find a hotel and not a friendly embassy, right? Who're you kidding? Admit it, he's got you hooked."

"No such thing. You're right, take us to the U.S. Embassy. That's what the rules dictate."

Sergei tensed but Kwame raised an eyebrow. "You are certain?"

Zack scowled. "No. Find the damn Hilton or Sheraton or someplace decent."

Kwame laughed. "I knew it. I was told that Zack Matteson enjoys living on the edge."

"Oh yeah, what else were you told?"

It was Sergei who answered. "That you don't like following the rules, perhaps?"

"Precisely," laughed Kwame. "Tilly here is his own man." His eyes narrowed. "But, Sergei, he is correct when he says do not double cross us. If I sense that you are even considering it, he won't have to do it; I will kill you without blinking an eye."

Sergei shook his head. "My work has led me down many roads, gentlemen, but I am not a spy, whether you believe me or not. I am not accustomed to all the deception you people have to weave. Tonight, you will see that I am telling you the truth."

"Pray that we do," was Zack's only reply.

****

Zack and Kwame had taken turns watching Sergei in the hotel room, but all the Russian had done after taking a shower and having a meal brought up by room service was to take a nap. Zack and Kwame had both managed to rest, as well, taking turns sleeping and standing guard. Zack had rented the room with a special credit card, issued by the home office, which allowed them to know his whereabouts—*just in case*.

Zack watched Kwame as he lay motionless in the other bed, Zack's Glock resting within reach on the coffee table next to him. Even if the Russian were telling the truth, which Zack doubted, he'd make certain that the man in the white suit would accompany him back to Camp Lemonnier when this was finished. He and Kwame had discussed matters while Sergei had been in the shower. If the Russian tried something fishy at the rendezvous tonight, they'd be ready. *Sometimes it truly was best to shoot first and ask questions later.*

But one thing kept nagging him. What if there really was a doomsday chemical? Tens of thousands had succumbed to poison gas in the first world war. The Geneva Gas Protocol of 1925 banned the use of chemical weapons and had been signed by most of the world's countries, although it had not stopped many of those same nations from continuing to develop them. Zack had firsthand knowledge of one U.S. underground laboratory that continued to develop biological and chemical weapons even while a great deal was being made of destroying older chemical weapons at places like Fort McClellan in Anniston, Alabama.

Of course, the argument was always that these underground experiments were only to understand how to create defenses against them, but Zack knew too well that unused weapons resisted staying that way forever. *Had not Iraq used them against Iran with hardly more than a slap on the wrist from the world's superpowers? What would prevent other nations from future use? Even now, Chinese and Russian laboratories were thought to be developing highly sophisticated poisons that could target particular ethnic groups.*

That thought sickened him. Maybe that was why he'd agreed to see this through. It wasn't mere curiosity; it was more of an "Oh, my God, what if..." that drove him.

Zack ran his hand across the length of his pistol, but it brought little comfort. Conventional weapons were passé. Battles of the future were already being fought through complicated technology and cyberattacks. Biological warfare might even now be on the horizon again now that rogue Middle Eastern nations were successfully arming terrorists with enough information. *God forbid the industrial nations from deciding to use, or even accidentally unleashing such a weapon.*

Sergei opened one eye and stared at the Glock. "I sincerely hope you are not considering using that, Mr. Matteson."

"Not as long as you behave yourself."

Kwame stretched as he awoke. "Is it time?" he asked.

Sergei checked his watch. "Soon." He sat up and arched his back, twisting his neck until they all heard a pop. "*Ah*, yes, that is better." He glanced at Kwame. "Something I received in Tajikistan; the surgeons never quite corrected it."

Zack stared at him. "So… now what?"

"Now, I use the wash closet, and then I will inform you of what you need to know," he said, heading toward the bathroom.

"Just leave the door open; I don't want you going all MacGyver on me."

Kwame wrinkled his face. "Mac who?"

"He's a guy who can make weapons out of anything. Like a toilet handle and a tube of toothpaste," said Zack.

Kwame appeared genuinely impressed. "Indeed? I would like to meet such a man."

"It is only a television program," came Sergei's voice from the bathroom.

It was Zack's turn to be impressed. "How do you…"

"What," Sergei said appearing in the doorway. "Do you think I am only a soldier? I, too, have leisure time.

Many of your American television programs are shown in Russia these days."

Zack waved with his Glock for him to sit. "Cut to the chase, Sergei. How are you proposing that this go down tonight?"

Sergei sat on the edge of the bed and leaned forward. "The man I am scheduled to meet is one of three brothers. The eldest was killed in some sort of accident when he was a teenager. We have lost track of the youngest brother but this man's name is Gesi."

"Last name?"

"You will forgive me if I keep some things to myself, Mr. Matteson. I would not wish you to end this operation and turn over the information to your superiors. My organization has worked for decades trying to unravel this mystery. I will not have it jeopardized by a cowboy."

"Cowboy?" Zack mulled the term over in his mind. It was a word used by the CIA to refer to agents who didn't play well with others. Had it not been for his unique partnership with Scott Flenn, it might well have been used about him.

"Gesi," Sergei continued, "has been a small-time weapons dealer for many years. He deals in Chinese and Syrian guns mostly. When we discovered that he had information about the chemical, we offered him brand-new Russian AK-74s at a cheap price. He jumped at the opportunity."

"Just how did you learn that he had information?"

Sergei offered a practiced smile. "Again, Mr. Matteson, some things are not necessary to be shared at this precise moment." He waved his hand in the air as if fanning away smoke. "As I was saying, he jumped at the opportunity. When our people were able to convince him to sell us the information, he asked us for twenty million American dollars."

Kwame gave a low whistle.

"We offered five…"

Zack nodded. "And settled on ten; yeah, yeah, get on with it."

Sergei shrugged. "You are an impatient man, Mr. Matteson. If there is one thing I have learned, impatience leads to mistakes."

"And if there's one thing I've learned," Zack's eyes narrowed, "it's that people who double-cross me end up in body bags."

"There is no need for continued threats, Mr. Mattson. I fully appreciate your position. After tonight, perhaps you will appreciate mine."

Kwame interrupted. "Will you two quit the posturing and get on with it?"

"Yes, quite right, gentlemen. Gesi has agreed to receive the weapons as an advanced payment toward releasing us the information."

"You're giving them the weapons for free?"

"Zack, let him talk, will you?"

"Not free, Mr. Matteson. He is going to tell me what he knows. He has agreed to furnish me with the whereabouts of the weapon, once he receives his final payment."

"Ten million," Zack said smugly.

"Eleven. But it does not matter. Once the information is secure, Gesi will no longer be useful to us."

Zack knew what that meant. He also knew what it would mean for him and for Kwame once Sergei had determined that they were also of no use to the Russian. That was why he would end things sooner than Sergei expected. Of course, Sergei would be watching him closely. Things were about to get interesting, of that Zack had no doubt.

"You will go with me tonight posing as my guards. Once we have the information and have handed over the rifles, we will come back here."

Zack raised an eyebrow. "That simple?"

Sergei nodded. "Dah; that simple."

Kwame glanced at Zack before speaking. "It has been my experience, that espionage is never simple. Your two bodyguards will each be carrying one of those AKs with a full magazine."

Zack nodded. "Primed and ready to rock'n'roll."

Sergei turned his eyes to Kwame. "I do not suppose that you would allow me the loan of one of your pistols?"

It was Zack who answered. "Fat chance."

CHAPTER Thirty-Four

England; 1942

A fog that years later would be dubbed "Saint Cuthbert's Mist" descended upon the sleeping town of Durham as Osmann crept silently through the cathedral's graveyard. With the help of a flashlight, what the English called a *torch*, he found the tombstone after only a moment's search. Other than the sound of a lone dog barking in the distance, all was still.

Osmann didn't have much time. If he were found missing from the barracks, the consequences could be brutal. *The Brits were hard enough on their own soldiers, so no telling what they would do to him.* The Kenyan recruits brought here for training had never once challenged their superiors. Most of them were so relieved to have been rescued from the hands of the cruel Nazis, that they hardly seemed to care about the harsh stares they received from the English or that their rations were nowhere near as good as their British counterparts.

Osmann had slipped away after the evening meal. He hadn't even told Kifo his plans for the night. He didn't dare. His younger brother had changed lately. Osmann was never certain whether it had been the cruelties of war or something else going on in the recesses of Kifo 's deepest self. His brother had become increasingly moody; silent one day, talkative the next. Together, they had seen more suffering than a man of great years should have seen, but Kifo was only 18. Osmann had not understood his brother's dark, depressive moments, which Kifo seemed to slip into almost weekly; nor did Osmann understand Kifo 's frequent, unpredictable turnarounds to outright exuberance at times. It was as if Kifo were two different people trapped within the one body. At times his brother's soul seemed as if it weighed heavily against him, but then things would spin around and for days it was as if he thought himself indestructible. Osmann no longer trusted his brother the way that he once had. It was as if someone had stolen the essence of Kifo and replaced it with someone unrecognizable.

Osmann reached into his small knapsack for the trowel and a steel box he'd brought along. He'd convinced himself that it was best to bury this box here on holy ground where no one would ever suspect such a vile object would exist. Aside from casting the damned thing into the depths of the sea, this would have to suffice as the next best thing. Osmann now realized that no government could ever be trusted with its contents or allowed to decipher its demonic formula. *No, he would bury it here and then go back to the base and trust that the cathedral's patron, Saint Cuthbert, would stand a watchful guard.*

He quietly dug a small hole in front of the tombstone of the mysterious "Osmann" from centuries ago. *Perhaps it had been divine guidance that had led him here after all.* He dug about 2 feet deep and then pushed the box into the soft earth, covering it quickly, though taking enough time to place the grass carefully back into place so that the hole would go unnoticed. He'd left the key to the small, gray, metal lockbox back in the barracks, uncertain of just what to do with it. The key would not be needed by someone willing to smash the box open—*God help them, if they did*—but still Osmann had felt better keeping the key separate from the box.

Kifo had tried to persuade him to sell the poison; he had even suggested selling it to the Nazis at one point. But Osmann had refused. *No one must be allowed access to such a thing, ever.* He hadn't told Kifo where he'd hidden the box of vials after he'd shot Sturmbannführer Kreps that day in the village, nor even when the Brits liberated the outpost. Kifo might have suspected that his brother had brought the poison to England, but if so, he hadn't said anything about it.

Satisfied that no one would notice the slight indentation in the dirt come the morrow, Osmann stood and gave a last glance in all directions to make sure no one had seen him in the fog. A strange feeling came over him as he looked back at the grave. It was a feeling of peace—something he hadn't known in a long time. He stared at the outer wall of the cathedral and wondered if what he was feeling had been a gift from the saint interred within.

Although he had not done so in years, Osmann crossed himself before quickly walking away. In the distance he thought he heard the engines of a fighter squadron; it was only later that he learned that a Luftwaffe mission to bomb the train depot and the great cathedral that very night had been thwarted by the thick mist, and the German bombs had landed instead in a cow pasture outside the city. For some reason, Hitler never again tried to bomb Durham.

What he had not noticed was the man who had followed him here and who, even now, was crouching behind a gravestone on the opposite end of the cemetery. "Osmann is a fool," Kifo allowed himself to whisper. His brother could deny himself if he chose, but Kifo vowed to return some day and claim that fortune—the fortune that was rightfully his.

CHAPTER Thirty-Five

The city of Addis Ababa seemed to roll on forever, or was it just the horrendous traffic of late afternoon they'd found themselves trying to navigate through? Whichever, Zack was impressed by the sheer size of the city. "You know, when Americans hear about Ethiopia, all we hear is about poverty and starvation. Just look at this place. Modern… contemporary… not at all what I pictured."

"Believe me, there is enough poverty and starvation to go around," Kwame said as he surveyed the bustling sidewalks on both sides of the six-lane thoroughfare. "Even here there are those who cannot find enough to feed their family. Disease and malnutrition plague much of this land."

"Still," Zack said, straining to see the tops of the skyscrapers, "I'm impressed."

Kwame made a sound of disapproval not unlike Zack's wife, Donna, when she was perturbed by something he'd just said. "Americans. You know so little about this continent."

"No offense, Kwame, but we *have* been busy over the last century with two world wars, two more in Asia and a bitterly cold one with Sergei's friends."

Kwame was unimpressed. "Yet, I wager that if I

were to ask you to describe Minsk, Cairo, Paris or London you would have no trouble at all."

Zack shifted his weight as if he'd suddenly become uncomfortable. "That's different. Those are important cities."

"And Addis Ababa is not?" Kwame shook his head. "Do you know that more than two million people live here, or that it houses one of the largest manufacturing centers in all of Africa? Do you know the city's reputation as home to some of the greatest athletes in the world?"

"And textiles," added Sergei from the backseat. "Do not forget textiles."

"Great. I'm stuck here with two representatives of the Ethiopian Chamber of Commerce."

Kwame managed to just avoid hitting a young boy chasing a chicken out of the way of oncoming traffic. "I'm only saying that you Americans aren't interested in the world unless a nation somehow affects your commerce. I have listened to many of your news broadcasts; rarely is Africa ever mentioned. As opposed to the BBC, which features something about Africa every day."

"Sure. Britain is a lot closer."

"China is farther away, yet it seems to hold your interest."

Sergei leaned forward. "Perhaps you had better quit while you are behind, Mr. Matteson. I believe you are losing this one, no?"

Unwilling to concede, Zack pointed out the window to a U.S. flag hanging in a storefront window. "Yeah, well, how do you explain that?"

Kwame glanced at the shop. "They obviously sell

American goods there. Blue jeans, Jack Daniel's, Pop-Tarts. That's the reason for the flag."

"Pop-Tarts?"

"Considered a treat by many."

Zack's own penchant for sugar was beginning to beckon. "I don't suppose we will pass a candy store somewhere along the way?"

"Jelly beans?" asked Sergei.

Zack turned in surprise. "How…?"

The Russian simply grinned.

"This guy is starting to give me the creeps."

Kwame cocked his head to one side. "Creep? Oh, like creeping around? Because he is a spy, no?"

"Forget it."

Ahead lay a labyrinth of skyscrapers and other tall buildings, churches and statues—not at all what Zack expected. "I don't get it. The city seems a lot like any other metropolis; what gives with all the militias you told us about, like the welcoming committee we ran into last night?"

Kwame shrugged. "Does not Los Angeles have its street gangs? New York? Chicago? You have your troubles; Africa has hers. Only here the struggle is often about such things as water rights and food shortages."

"Desperation brings about its own kind of villain, does it not, Mr. Matteson?" Sergei said with a note of condescension in his voice.

"Which your government has taken advantage of time and time again," snapped Zack.

Sergei crossed his arms in front of him. "Oh… and America has not?"

Zack turned to look out the window. "I admit, America's got her faults; never said she didn't. But at least we don't…"

"Stop!" Sergei called out.

Kwame peered at Sergei in the rearview mirror.

"We missed our turn."

"You've been here before?"

The Russian nodded. "I memorized the map of the city."

Zack shook his head. "How is that even possible."

"Each person in my organization is chosen for possessing unique gifts, Mr. Matteson. One of mine happens to be that I have an eidetic memory."

Kwame looked at Zack for guidance. "You best turn around," Zack said with just a hint of a sigh.

"We are meeting my contact in an Anglican Church. They leave the doors open at night for the homeless."

"Which is the way I feel right now," Zack muttered. "Kwame, once we get there, don't let him out of your sight. If you feel so much as one hair rise on the back of your neck, shoot first and ask questions later."

"You know many idioms, Mr. Matteson."

Kwame shook his head. "You don't know the half of it."

"And many idiots," Zack added. "So, don't become one of them. It will be the last thing you ever do."

Sergei sighed. "I hope that after tonight you will both understand that I mean you no harm."

"Just don't count on us feeling the same way, buddy boy."

Kwame turned down three other streets until Sergei

was satisfied. "Slow down," he said, "it should be just ahead, on the right."

A small, Gothic framework of wood and brick was sandwiched tightly between two concrete structures, all painted white. The bright red door on the church seemed warm and inviting, compared to the cold, gray doors of nearby structures. A few bedraggled people wearing not much more than rags leaned against the church. Two were speaking with each other and one to herself. Three more were sitting and one was sprawled on the sidewalk, apparently unconscious.

"Nice place," muttered Zack.

Sergei simply shrugged. "It is where he said to meet him. No doubt he will be watching us from somewhere inside. I must ask you both, as distasteful as I am certain that it will be for you, to pretend that you work for me. They will expect you to be tough, but servile."

Zack shook his head. "Distasteful doesn't begin to describe it."

"Tilly…" cautioned Kwame. "Remember, it is for the greater good."

"It sure as hell better be." Zack climbed out of the car and waited for Kwame to join him before opening the door for Sergei. For his part, the Russian instantly resumed his former demeanor—a man accustomed to being in command. He straightened himself to his full height, only about 5-foot-6. But thrusting his barrel chest forward, he appeared a man not to be challenged. Zack leaned forward and whispered: "You double-cross us and the first bullet belongs to you."

Sergei ignored the remark as he strode past homeless men and women toward the red door.

"*Um,* not to be a spoilsport, but if we're going in there, who's to say that they won't just take the Toyota and leave us here?"

"It is theirs when they want it," Sergei responded. "It is a down payment, remember?"

"Anybody given any thought as to how we get back to the hotel?" Kwame muttered under his breath.

"What?"

"Nothing." Kwame opened the door and peered inside. "Just a handful of people in the church; I don't think they are our guys."

As they entered the nave, two woman busily placing blankets on pews gaped at them in horror before quickly disappearing out a side entrance. Another woman calmly approached them. She neither appeared to be one of the homeless or a member of the church's hospitality team. "You are late," she said, matter-of-factly. "He is waiting in the pastor's office," she said to Sergei before turning and pointing toward an open door behind the lectern. "Down the hall and on the right." She glared at Zack and Kwame. "Leave your weapons here. I will watch them."

"Like hell," was all Zack said as the trio made their way toward the door.

The hallway was darkened except for a light at the opposite end emanating from the pastor's office. Zack wondered about the cleric, and whether he had willingly given permission for his office to be used in such a fashion. Doubtful. Hopefully the man had simply been away, and not fallen prey to whoever these people were.

A mousy dark-skinned man had stepped out of the hallway when he'd heard them coming. There was a .38 tucked into his waistband. He turned and said something to the room's occupants before a larger man, carrying a Chinese assault rifle stepped over the threshold.

"Dondosha silaha yako," he said, raising his weapon toward the Russian.

"What'd he say?"

"He wants us to drop our weapons," answered Kwame.

"I'll drop him first."

It was Sergei who answered in Swahili. "Wanaume wangu wameapa kunilinda..." he began.

Kwame translated as Sergei spoke: "My men are sworn to protect me. They will not harm you unless you try to harm me. If you wish to do business, then it is you who must put your weapon aside. I have come on good faith; I suggest you do the same or this transaction ends here and now." Zack's finger moved toward the trigger housing.

A voice from inside the office gave the big man and the mouse new directions; they both lowered their weapons and stepped aside. Sergei entered the office first along with Zack; Kwame stood just outside to keep an eye on the two guards.

A lean, balding man with temples of silver sat opposite a small metal desk with both of his arms crossed over his chest. No weapon was in sight, but even if the man had wanted to there was no way he could extract a pistol from a desk drawer or inside his shirt before Zack could cut him down—nor did that reality seem to cause the man much trepidation.

"Sergei." The man slowly stood and offered his right hand across the desk. "You made it," he said in nearly perfect Russian.

Sergei took his hand and pumped it several times. "I was beginning to think otherwise."

The African arched one eyebrow. "Trouble?"

Sergei nodded. "Last night in the desert, some barbarians shot at us with bows and arrows. It was incredible."

The African simply nodded. "Yes, the Sandsifters. They are not friendly to trespassers. I would assume the runners I sent would have steered clear of them. Where are they by the way?"

Zack tensed as Sergei's mouth turned into a frown. "I'm afraid that they both perished in the raid, along with one of my bodyguards. We barely escaped with our lives."

The man shook his head. "Most unfortunate. They were valuable to me."

"I am certain that we will be able to lessen the pain of your loss... if the information you have for me is verifiable."

If the arms dealer was insulted, he did not show it. "I originally had hopes that my brother, Msaliti, would be here when this day came. Our father would have wanted it that way, but, alas, my brother and I had a falling out some time ago. Ironically, it was over the very information that I am about to pass on to you. He wasn't interested in the money, only in using the weapon to amass power for himself."

Sergei grinned. "Money *is* power, is it not, my friend?"

The African shrugged. "I suppose for some it is; but not for you and your friends, *eh*, Sergei?" The Russian cocked his head slightly to one side and laughed. "If money equaled power I do not believe you would be so willing to give so much of it away."

"An interesting point, Gesi." *Zack now had not one but two names to go on—Msaliti and Gesi.* "And while I would love to discuss philosophy with you some other time, my mission is to bring you the guns in exchange for information. No doubt your men have already verified that I have lived up to my part of the bargain."

Gesi stared greedily at him— looking like what Zack thought Fagin might have had Charles Dickens been an Ethiopian. "You have the money also?"

"Not with me, no. That was our deal, remember? I bring you a good faith gesture of a truckload full of new AK-74s and you tell me where I may find the poison gas. The money will follow."

Gesi leaned against the small desk, placing his hands on either side. Zack constantly watched those hands. Weapon or not, he'd kill Gesi in a heartbeat should the man make the wrong move. "Then, Sergei, you will understand that I will only give you part of the information you seek. When you bring me the money, you may have the rest of the details."

Sergei's pale complexion became even more so. "You do not have the weapon with you?"

"I'm not a fool. Such a substance is too dangerous even for me." Gesi brightened. "But not for you and your friends, *eh*? You would be capable of handling such a substance or you would not be here. After my men have relieved you of your cargo, I will be delighted to tell you some of what I know. The rest will have to wait until you have the money."

He tapped his forehead. "Where are my manners? I have had a meal prepared for us." He clapped his hands and the woman from before stepped inside.

"Everything is ready," she said.

"*Ah*, good. Sergei, let us step across the hall to one of the classrooms. I have food and wine. We can sit and speak more of this terrible weapon and the grief it has caused my family. My men will unload your vehicle while we eat."

"What about the priest of this parish?" It wasn't Zack's place as a bodyguard to speak, but he did anyway.

Sergei raised his hand dismissively. "Tilly, I'm certain that our host has taken all necessary precautions. Let us not decline his hospitality. Have Yazid join us, will you?"

Zack wasn't about to leave the two men alone to talk, so he stuck his head into the hallway and gestured for Kwame. The three men followed Gesi into a small classroom where two chairs had been set up around a folding table. Olives, tomatoes, sandwiches and some sort of sautéed chunks of meat were arranged in earthenware. A bottle of red wine and a bottle of Amarula, an African cream liqueur, were set in the center of the table. "Gentlemen, please, help yourselves."

Zack was tempted to do just that, especially when he saw several chocolate straws arranged neatly in a separate bowl. He knew, however, that as a bodyguard his job was solely to keep watch. "They are not hungry," Sergei said dismissively. "Let us sit and eat, Gesi, and you may tell me this story of yours."

The Russian and Ethiopian did just that while Kwame and Zack took servile positions at opposite ends of the room. The meat smelled delicious, and Zack was hungry, but it was the chocolate he kept eyeing until the story began to unfold.

"Sergei, may I ask: what is your relationship with your father?" Gesi asked as he stuffed an olive into his mouth.

"My father?" Sergei obviously hadn't anticipated that particular question. "He died when I was very young. Why do you ask?"

"So, you never got to know the man? Pity." Gesi poured them both a second glass of wine. "I was very close to my father over the years; more so than my younger brothers. They were more interested in making a name for themselves. But my baba..." he closed his eyes for a moment, "...he and I were always together. He used to tell me that family is everything. Which was strange because of the family life dealt him. He lost his parents at a young age and had only his traitorous brother."

Zack wasn't sure where this was leading but he admired the way the Russian was playing the game. "Your uncle was a traitor?" asked Sergei, reaching for an olive.

Gesi scowled. "To my father he was. After the war he disowned my father. Never once did he attempt to contact us." Gesi looked away. "It hurt my baba very much. It was why he came to Ethiopia."

Zack glanced at Kwame, who was pretending not to be paying attention to the arms dealer but was likely making mental notes of his every word. For his part, Sergei sipped his wine and waited to see where this was heading.

"For years, there was no contact between them. Then one day my father discovers that his brother is living up north in the land of our ancestors. He tried to mend the divide between them but my uncle would have nothing to do with him. My brother and I have hated the man ever since. All the more when my baba told us what had divided them."

God, how long was this going to take? Zack had heard somewhere that story-telling was a favorite pastime on this continent; he just hoped this one wasn't going to go on forever.

"My father and uncle had been conscripted by a Nazi officer who was a chemist of some kind. Baba would not go into many details about the horrors he had seen. The Nazis experimented on the villagers with his nerve agents until he developed one so lethal that even the tiniest droplet could kill hundreds." *So far, Gesi's story was checking out with everything Sergei had told them.*

As the tale progressed, Zack's curiosity was piqued; even his interest in the chocolate disappeared. For his part, Sergei had quit sipping from his wineglass and was leaning slightly forward.

"My father rose up against this man. He told us how he killed the Nazi Sturmbannfuhrer and fought off half of the contingent of Germans stationed in that village before taking all that remained of the chemical with him. His cowardly brother, Osmann, was of no help during any of this, of course. Yet, my father took pity on him. They took the chemical to the British, who, instead of listening to them, convinced them to join the Kenyan regiment and go to England for training." Gesi made a face.

"Bah! Training indeed. All of the black Africans were nothing more than mtumwa... slaves to the English. Shining their shoes, cooking their meals, pressing their clothes. My father was a hero. He said he took the chemical to England, hoping to give it to the British government," here Gesi gesticulated with his hands while raising his voice, "but they were not worthy!" Gesi lowered his voice and then reached for his wineglass before releasing a long and embellished sigh. "And that was when my uncle took advantage. He stole the locked box that my father kept, along with the key. He ran away one night but..." and here Gesi smiled... "but my baba was clever. He followed him in the shadows and watched my uncle bury the box."

Sergei was starting to show signs of impatience. "But you have retrieved it, no?"

Gesi looked at the Russian as if he had gone completely mad. "Do you take me for a fool? There is no telling what my uncle did to that box. He likely wired it to explode if the correct key was not inserted."

Sergei's eyes narrowed. "And you do not have this key?"

Gesi sighed in earnest this time. "Alas, I do not. But I am positive that your well-funded organization would be able to properly handle such a contingency, would you not?"

The Russian was silent for the longest time before speaking. When he did, it was in the most threatening of tones. "Am I to understand that I have come all this way, handed over expensive weapons—very expensive weapons—and you neither have the poison nor the means to acquire it?"

Gesi held up the palms of both hands. "I have plenty, Sergei. I am the only man who knows exactly where it is and how to find it." The single bead of perspiration on Gesi's forehead told Zack that he was lying… *but what exactly was he lying about?*

Sergei picked up his paper napkin and slowly dabbed at the corner of his mouth. "I apologize for my burst of anger. It is just that my people have sought this box of your father's for many years. We will, of course, be happy to honor our part of the bargain once we have verified all that you have said."

"Verified?"

"Da. Once we have the box in our possession then we will pay you what we agreed upon."

"I will tell you what you want to know but only after I have received the payment."

Sergei stood. "Then I am afraid we are at an impasse. Your men have the weapons; I can do nothing about that. But I will not pay for a story of what might be a… a…," he stammered, searching for the right phrase.

"A wild goose chase," Zack offered. Sergei glared at

him. Zack pressed his lips tightly together. *Sergei had been telling him the truth after all… at least some of it.*

The man thought for a moment and then said, "I will bring you the map my father made tomorrow in exchange for half of what you have promised to pay."

"A man such as you could disappear with a large fortune such as that."

Again, Gesi seemed indifferent to the insult. "A man such as me would not settle for such a paltry sum when he could easily double that amount with the Americans."

Sergei allowed his eyes to fall to the floor. Zack thought he saw a flash of red around the tips of the Russian's ears. Finally, after taking a deep breath, Sergei said, "I will look at this map of yours. If I am impressed, my people will wire you one million… only one," he said again. "The remaining will be paid to you if we then find the box and it contains what you say."

Gesi nodded repeatedly. "It will; it will."

Zack stared at the two men. *While Sergei was playing the game of the clever negotiator, inside he must be dancing on a cloud— to be so close to fulfilling his search. With his ability to memorize things instantly, he would no doubt take a look at the map and never need send the gun runner a dime. And, if what the Russian had said earlier was true—and it appeared now that it was—then Sergei was closer now than his organization had ever been to finding this elusive super weapon.* Something that Zack knew must never be allowed to happen.

CHAPTER Thirty-Six

Darkness enveloped the eerily deserted Ethiopian street as well as Zack's thoughts. At one level, he was relieved to know that Sergei had been telling them the truth, but at another, the ghastly knowledge that such a compound existed and could potentially be found by just about anyone was sickening. *Had it only been good fortune that no one had stumbled upon this box and its devilish concoction all these many years?* Zack chewed on his bottom lip as they walked down the back alley and into the street.

As Gesi escorted the trio out to find their truck he visibly tensed. "What is it?" Kwame queried, raising his weapon.

Gesi stared down the street, first left then right then left again. "Quickly, back inside."

"What?" Zack asked just a split second before a bullet ricocheted behind his head. Gesi and Kwame dropped to the ground, leaving Zack standing with Sergei. Zack's automatic rifle was at the ready but he had no idea where to aim. A deafening silence fell over them for the briefest of moments, and then a burst of fire from around the corner—one of Gesi's men providing cover for them to get inside.

Zack heard shouts, from Gesi's men or whoever was now returning fire. But above the noise he heard the arms dealer shout. "Inside, now!" This time they all obeyed.

Kwame said something to Gesi in Swahili, but Gesi didn't answer. Instead, he motioned for them to follow him deeper inside the church. "Come," he finally said in Russian, "they are after the weapons."

"Who?" Sergei and Zack both retorted in unison.

"The Forty Brothers."

Kwame froze.

"Who the hell are the Forty Brothers," he said to Kwame.

"Very bad people." He said something again to Kwame as they made their way past frightened, homeless people ducking behind pews.

"What the hell's going on?!"

Kwame pushed Zack from behind. "The Forty Brothers are a gang of religious zealots who have no qualm killing anyone and everyone, so I suggest we do as he says and keep moving."

"How do *you* know who they are?" Zack shouted at Gesi.

"They have been clients of mine on occasion."

Zack kept a close eye on Sergei in case this was some sort of ruse. "So this is how they thank you?"

"Clearly, I've been betrayed."

At that moment they heard glass breaking behind them, Zack turned to see a heavily armed man crawling through one of the church's classroom windows. "Yours?" he shouted to Gesi.

"No!" Gesi shouted back.

Zack opened fire. The man was dead before he hit the ground.

"Tilly, give me a gun!" Sergei demanded.

Crap. No way in hell was Zack giving the Russian a gun, but that would spell the end of their charade. "Don't worry, sir, we have you covered," Zack said, hoping it was enough to convince Gesi. The men ran around a corner and into a kitchen where the woman from earlier lay sprawled across the floor in a pool of blood. "They're already inside!" He'd no more blurted that out when a man sprang from the pantry and opened fire, catching Gesi full on in the chest. Kwame fired twice and the man fell back into the shelves. Dozens of canned goods clattered across the floor as Sergei bent down to check Gesi for a pulse.

"Which way now?" Zack asked as Kwame rushed to the threshold and chanced a glance down the hall. No one was in sight. Sergei knelt beside Gesi to check for a pulse—there wasn't one. Zack pointed to the dead man from the pantry. "He had to have gotten in here somehow. There must be another door!"

They exited the kitchen to the left and followed the hallway to another classroom... empty. "There's a door in here," Zack shouted from the next room. "Let's go." The door led to an alley where Gesi's men were engaged in a firefight with the Forty Brothers. "Damn!"

"We can't go back through the church," warned Kwame. "No telling how many of them are already heading this way."

Zack peered out the door again. All the action was to the right of the alley. The left was clear for now. "Sometimes, gentlemen," offered Sergei, "one has to march through the flames of hell…"

Zack recognized the Russian parable. "…to find the release of heaven." He glanced at Kwame. "He's right; it's our only choice."

Kwame forced a grin. "Then what are we waiting for?"

Sergei started for the door. "Nope. Kwame first, then me, then you," said Zack.

Sergei returned Kwame's grin. "Your friend wishes to use me for protection against the bullets. Frankly I am not surprised."

A commotion at the end of the hallway told them the time was now. "Let's go!" shouted Zack.

Zack took a breath and then nodded to Kwame. "In for a penny, in for a pound," he said as the trio bolted into the alley.

Shots ricocheted off block walls sending tiny puffs of disintegrating cement into the night. The three men rounded the corner out of the alley and continued running away from the carnage behind them. Sergei was surprisingly fit for a man his age, although by the time they'd found their way across several blocks and into a small park they were all breathing hard. They stopped in front of a large statue of a horse and rider, Zack checking for any sign that they were being followed. It was Sergei who spoke first. "Vot eto pizdets!"

Zack nodded. "Yeah, putting it mildly. Although I think I can come up with some other choice words."

"He was our only contact," Sergei muttered. "Gesi

Kauxhohuena." Zack saw Kwame react to the name. "He promised us a map. Now, where do we turn?"

"We've got to get rid of these weapons," said Kwame, searching for somewhere to dump his automatic rifle. "We can't be seen with them." Although there was no one in sight and the sound of the gunfire was now distant, Zack was reluctant to part with his protection. "We still have our pistols, Zack, they will suffice."

"They could still catch up with us," said Zack.

"More than likely the police will if you don't do as Kwame suggests," Sergei offered. "Perhaps you should leave those rifles here with this statue."

"No way; a kid might find them."

Kwame pointed across the street to a rusted dumpster. "There. That's the perfect place."

Dubious, but outvoted, Zack followed them across the street where Kwame relieved him of his AK-74 and threw it in the dumpster with his own. "Now what?" asked Sergei.

"We have to keep moving until we can find a taxi to take us back to the hotel," said Kwame.

"Who died and made you boss?" griped Zack.

"You got a better plan, big man?"

Zack glanced in all directions before admitting that he did not.

"Fine, let's go." Kwame didn't wait for the other two but quickly made his way past closed shops and deserted buildings toward where they could hear sounds of traffic. When they slowed, Zack noticed a blood stain on the Russian's white suit.

"Are you okay?" he asked.

"It is nothing, just a scratch."

"Let me see it," Zack said. The Russian opened his coat to reveal a nasty gash along Sergei's ribcage. "That doesn't look like a scratch to me."

The Russian peered down at the wound. "I've had worse. The bullet didn't penetrate. It just left a trail, that is all."

Kwame stared at the torn flesh. "You need a doctor." He glanced up at Zack. "He needs a doctor," he repeated.

Zack's eyes widened as he shook his head slightly as if to say, "How the hell do you propose we do that?"

"I'm fine gentlemen, really."

Kwame thought a moment. "I've got an idea. First, we need to find a taxi. You think you can make it?"

"Have I slowed you down yet?"

Zack couldn't conceal a grin. "Tough bastard," was all he said.

The trio made their way purposefully toward the sound of beeping horns, taking a shortcut through another alleyway before erupting onto a busy thoroughfare as if expulsed from a catapult. They paused to catch their breath before Kwame spotted a taxi. Kwame signaled and the driver simply shrugged before motioning for them to cross the four lanes of traffic toward his car. The effort was nearly as treacherous as the scene at the church had been, since cars showed no signs of stopping and barely swerved to miss them as they crossed.

"Reminds me of New York," groused Zack as they made their way to the cab. Kwame spoke in Swahili hurriedly, causing the cabbie to stare at Sergei for a long time before answering.

"He's going to take us to a doctor who doesn't ask questions, but he wants a hundred dollars, American."

"So," Zack said, "give it to him."

"You're the man with the money; you give it to him."

Zack reached into his wallet and found five twenties. "Fine, but for this fare I expect it to be next door to a candy shop."

"You know, Mr. Matteson," Sergei said with a grimace as he climbed into the taxi, "perhaps you should have stuck with cigarettes. They are much easier to find than jellybeans."

"Shut up and move over."

CHAPTER Thirty-Seven

Cascades of light penetrated through his eyelids with the force of a jackhammer, pounding every nerve in Samuel's brain and forcing him to seek refuge under his pillow. "So, are you planning to sleep the day away?" Uncle Osuroo's voice sounded close and yet far away at the same time.

"What time is it?" came the hoarse reply from underneath the pillow.

"Nearly noon. I can tell that you haven't done much drinking while you have been away. You have the tolerance of a schoolboy."

It was true, Samuel had rarely consumed alcohol, and had never used drugs, unwilling to allow himself to lose control during an assignment. One slip of the tongue could have cost him his life. Right now, with the enormity of his hangover, he wasn't all that sure that life was worth holding onto.

"I brought you a sandwich and something to take the edge off. "Come sit with me on the porch once you are able."

"I should be helping Jenga," Samuel feebly protested.

"It is the Lord's day, no one is working, remember?"

"Ugh."

"You were raised a Christian, how is it that you have no memory of what day it is?" his uncle teased.

"Shh!"

The sound of Osuroo's laughter as he left the bedroom triggered the jackhammer again. It was nearly a half-hour before Samuel was dressed and able to face the day. Uncle Osuroo was sitting quietly in a rocking chair on the verandah. A cool breeze caught Samuel by surprise since yesterday had been hot and dry. Osuroo pulled his sweater a bit tighter across his chest. "So, I see that Lazarus has finally arisen."

"I wasn't quite as dead as I thought."

"Could have fooled me. Come sit down with your uncle. I wish to discuss a matter with you."

Samuel obeyed, pulling a second rocking chair close to his uncle. "Are you all right?"

"I'm 82 years old; no, I'm not all right. But that isn't what is concerning me."

Samuel raised an eyebrow. "What is it then?"

Osuroo gazed past the old barn and across the land he'd devoted his life toward a grove of almond trees. "I am going to ask you to do something; well, two things. One may not sit well with you."

"What are they?"

Osuroo took a deep breath. The first is that I want you to accompany Jenga to England in two months. I know that you want to stay here and take care of me, but I will be fine for a few weeks. He can't really afford this trip, but he says he has always wanted to go. I want you to help pay for some of the expenses. Don't let him think it is charity though, he's a proud man."

"Well…"

Osuroo held up his hand. "I'm not finished. I think the trip would be good for you, as well. God knows what you've seen over the last twenty-five years. I know from what you leave out in your stories that you are sparing me from the details. I also know that it has taken a toll on you; I can see it in your eyes." Osuroo stopped rocking.

"You are not young anymore, Samuel. You have never taken a bride, had children, gone abroad to see the wonders of the outside world. No, you have spent your life uncovering Africa's underbelly, trying to destroy the evil that ravages our people and prevents our development."

Samuel looked away. "If only I could have been more successful."

Osuroo nodded, staring out at the almond grove. "A hole can always be dug deeper, but you have done more than most. Evil is like a single hyena. By itself it is afraid and will do little harm, but when it finds others to form into a pack, then the danger is multiplied. You have helped isolate many hyenas, kept them from growing into larger packs. It is time now for others to take over."

Samuel sighed.

Intuitively, Osuroo reached over and squeezed his nephew's knee. "A man does what he can, Samuel."

"Okay, Baba. I will go, since it seems to please you. What is the other matter, the one that will displease me?"

"I wish for you to give Jenga the farm in Maua when I die. As you know, I have had you sell the land in Meru and Isiolo. Maua is all I have left outside this estate. Jenga does not speak of his family much, but I sense he has nothing to go home to, and I know that he has little money. The land in Maua is good land, fertile. The cattle there are all sold, but he could buy more with the money I am leaving to him in my will."

Samuel sat quietly, mulling over what his uncle was saying.

"He has been a great help to me. You did not see the farm before Jenga arrived. He has poured his soul into this place and has brought the land, the barn, even the house back from years of neglect." Samuel felt guilty for not having been here to help his uncle, but knew that Osuroo did not blame him for that. "Jenga is young. He can make a good living and raise a strong family at Maua. Do not worry, I'm leaving the rest of my money to you."

"Baba, I have money. More than you can possibly guess. What I do... what I *used* to do... was quite lucrative. While I never intended to profit from doing what was right, the governments that I worked for have taken good care of me."

"Then you do not mind that I wish you to give Jenga the farm at Maua?"

"I do not care whose name you put on the deed, Baba. I know that you gave me the titles, but as far as I am concerned, the land is yours until the day you go to heaven. If you wish Jenga to have Maua, that is fine. I will be content right here with my memories of you."

Osuroo nodded. "And your Auntie Gemma."

"And Auntie Gemma."

As the breeze blew again, colder this time, Osuroo

struggled to fasten his sweater. Samuel reached over and helped him with the buttons. "You are a good son, Samuel."

Samuel smiled. "Only because I had two good fathers to show me the way."

CHAPTER Thirty-Eight

The cold blue of a bare fluorescent light overhead dimmed and brightened as if by sadistic whim, compelling Zack to step out of the makeshift operating room. The cabbie had taken them to a nondescript three-story building at the end of a street of two dozen other looka-like tenements. Kwame seemed unbothered by the flickering light, so he stood guard over the Russian as the doctor sterilized and sewed Sergei's wounded side. Sergei was tough. Zack would give him that. As the white jacket and shirt had come off, Zack had noticed two other similar scars garnered from who knew what skirmish or vendetta.

The doctor's outer office consisted of nothing more than a small refrigerator, a desk and chair along with a dozen other folding chairs in a double-line against the far wall. No filing cabinet, no reading materials, no carpet on the bare cement floor—little to make this look like a place of healing. The cabbie had said the doctor took cash only, two times the normal rate after dark.

The physician had not asked any questions, simply studied Sergei's wound, named his price and set to work. Three hundred dollars was an extraordinary fee in an impoverished land such as Ethiopia, but Zack had been expecting more. Back in the States, such a doctor would have charged a few thousand for his silence.

Zack had told the cabbie to come back in an hour and he'd give him another hundred for a lift back to the hotel. This had been a horrific night on top of an equally horrific three days. Tomorrow, he would call it in and request transport back to Camp Lemonnier. Enough was enough. Zack leaned against the wall and yawned twice. He craved sleep. He stared at the refrigerator. He also craved sugar.

He opened it to find several vials of medicine and a single can of Pepsi, which he willingly claimed for the caffeine and calories. Scott Flenn often chided him about his sweet tooth but Zack never seemed to put on a pound. Sergei had been right, he'd quit smoking some years back and had substituted popping jellybeans in his mouth every time he'd wanted a cigarette. Over time the craving had become one for sugar instead of nicotine.

Zack checked his watch; the cabdriver should be here in a few minutes. *Hopefully, the doc would be done and they could get the hell out of Dodge by the time he arrived.* He stuck his head back into the examination room just as the doctor was putting some finishing touches on the wound. The doctor handed a small bottle to Kwame and offered what Zack assumed were instructions, but it was in a language unfamiliar to Zack, though not Swahili. Kwame nodded as Sergei dressed himself in the blood-stained white shirt, placing a carefully folded jacket across his arm.

"It appears, gentlemen, that not only do I need a new wardrobe, but I am in this man's debt. He said that matters were a bit worse than I had perceived them to be, but with his stiches and antibiotics I should be, as the English say, 'right as rain' in a few days."

"Peachy," groused Zack.

"You speak Amharic?" Kwame said, his left eyebrow arching slightly.

"Not as well as you, but enough to get by, I suppose." Sergei looked to Zack. "Is our driver here yet?"

"A few more minutes."

"*Ah*, good; then shall we all wait for him where the light is not so, *ah*, temperamental?" The trio exited into the outer office while the doctor cleaned up from the procedure. Sergei pointed to the medicine. "Kwame, would you mind if I kept that on my person?"

Kwame shrugged and handed the bottle of pills to Sergei. Outside a horn honked once. Zack carefully peered through the blinds. "Thank God for small miracles," he said. "That's our ride."

"Are you certain?"

Zack checked again. "Yep, same guy."

"Excellent. Then would you two mind placing your pistols on that desk for me, please?" From underneath his jacket, Sergei extracted a .38 revolver. "Our friend, Gesi, had no more need of this so I relieved him of it while I checked his pulse." He motioned with the pistol toward the desk. "Now, please. I wish you no harm, but I will use this if necessary."

Zack and Kwame exchanged angry glances before doing as they were told. "You didn't check him?" Zack griped.

"I didn't see *you* patting him down either," Kwame shot back. Outside, the horn honked again.

"Please, gentlemen. My driver is in a hurry." He glared at Kwame. "Oh, and I believe you made mention of a knife earlier. Please place that on the table as well." Kwame frowned but did as he was told.

Sergei dropped his jacket and scooped up the weapons, tucking them into his waistband. He looked at Zack after opening the door. "When you make your report to Langley," Mr. Matteson, "please assure them that once we find the poison it will be disposed of properly. The world already has too many dangerous playthings. Oh, and one more thing: If anyone follows me out this door, I will shoot with no reserve."

With that, Sergei slipped outside, closing the door behind him.

****

Zack slammed his fist against the candy machine in the lobby of the hotel. "Come on damn it, I put the money in the slot!"

"You have to pull the knob first," Kwame instructed, offering a reassuring glance to the startled night clerk. "Let's get to the room and then we can order room service, unless you want that candy bar to be supper."

Zack ignored him and started for the hotel clerk, checking his anger. "Sir. My friend and I need to exchange our room for tonight." He slipped his last two 20-dollar bills under the porter's bell on the counter. He'd need to find a bank in the morning and replace what he'd spent.

"Is there something unsatisfactory about your present room, sir?" asked the man, eyeing the money.

"We'd like a different view; that's all. Perhaps something across the hall?"

The clerk checked the computer before reaching for the money. "You are in luck. I have a room across the hall and just three doors down from your present room. Will that suffice, sir?"

Zack forced a smile. "Perfect. Put any extra expenses on my card." He started to turn, "Oh, and if our friend returns please tell him that we have checked out."

The man offered what he assumed was a knowing glance and a nod. "Certainly sir. I will be most discreet."

Kwame let out a laugh as soon as they were in the elevator. "You know that guy thinks we're some sort of threesome and have had a lover's quarrel, don't you?"

"I don't give a damn what he thinks."

Kwame sighed. "Come on, Zack. It's not your fault."

Zack stared at the numbers changing above the elevator door. "What's not my fault?"

"Sergei's grabbing that gun and pocketing it while we weren't lookin. At least he did not use it."

"Yeah? Why don't you try explaining that to my boss at Langley?"

The elevator door opened. They passed their old room on the way down the hall to the new. "At least, if he comes during the night we won't be there." Zack swiped the pass key and turned on the light.

"He will not come."

Zack turned on the television to see if any local news station was covering what had happened on the streets just a few hours ago. "What makes you so frickin' sure?"

"He is not interested in us. Sergei is a peculiar kind

of man. I have seen his type before. He's a man on a mission. We were an inconvenience, nothing more. Once he saw an opportunity to rid himself of us, he took it."

"Yeah, well he's no better off than before without Gesi's map." Zack snapped off the television after finding nothing about the street battle. "Who the hell was that group anyway?"

"The Forty Brothers? Insurgents… mostly criminals. They're one of many such organizations in Ethiopia and South Sudan. Addis Ababa appears calm, but only on the surface. The Horn of Africa has been much like your own Wild West, I think. Periods of peace, intermingled with periods of outlaws and bandits."

"I didn't think you watched American television?" Zack opened the blinds and stood in front of a large window. Kwame excused himself to the toilet while Zack stared into the night.

"Have you given any thought to this poison of Sergei's?" called Kwame as he dried his hands on one of several white towels perfectly arranged underneath the bathroom sink.

"That's for better minds than mine. I'm done."

Kwame leaned against the doorframe with a puzzled look on his face. "Really? You are abandoning this? I would think you would have been convinced by the events of tonight." His eyes narrowed. "Leave Africa for the Africans, *eh*?"

"Stop that."

"Why? Isn't that what you are doing? Leaving a potential weapon of mass destruction for Africa to figure out?" Kwame didn't try to hide his disdain. "Not America's problem, right, Zack?"

"No," he snapped and then closed the curtains angrily. "It's not."

"What if the Russians find it; what then?"

"Like I said, he doesn't have the map."

Kwame shook his head. "Not yet. What is to prevent him from discovering where Gesi lives and ransacking it until he finds the map?"

Kwame was right. Sergei would do just that. The Russian was, as Kwame had said, a man on a mission. "So, what do you want me to do about it? Find the house first?" *That would be exactly what Flenn would have said.*

"There is no need." Kwame grinned. "We have something better."

"Better?" Zack stared at him. "What the hell are you talking about?"

"More than you can possibly know."

"Kwame, quit talking in riddles. If you know something, spit it out."

Kwame pointed to the phone between the beds. "First, order us something from room service. I am hungry. Afterward, I will tell you everything. I am certain that you will be most fascinated."

CHAPTER Thirty-Nine

When the hamburgers and fried potatoes were delivered to the room, Zack realized he was hungrier than he'd thought. He eyed the chocolate cake but decided to save it for last. "Okay," he said, impatiently, "food's here… what's this secret of yours?"

Kwame shook his head. "Allow me to at least get something on my stomach first. You had a chocolate bar, remember?"

Zack tore into his burger ravenously. "Whatever."

They ate for a moment and then Kwame began: "Tonight, after he was killed, Sergei let Gesi's last name slip. Do you remember it?"

"Kah-who's-hyena something or other."

Kwame glared at him. "Your lack of understanding of African culture never ceases to astound me. Did Washington not consider that before sending you?" He rolled his eyes. "No, of course not. Why did I ask?"

Zack speared a potato with his fork. "Okay, okay, so I can't pronounce some of your odd names. So what?"

"Who is the current president of Poland?"

Zack stuffed the potato in his mouth and still managed to say, "Aleksander Kwaśniewski. Why?"

"And the prime minister of France?"

"What, his whole name? Okay, it's Dominique Marie François René Galouzeau de Villepin. Again, why?"

Kwame shook his head in disclination. "And you did that with your mouth full of potatoes. Ugh. The name was Kauxhohuena, Zack, Kaux—hoh—uena. It is not difficult."

"Okay, okay. I was close."

Kwame took a bite of hamburger to keep himself from saying what he wanted to say. "Gesi Kauxhohuena is known to us, as is his entire family. Gesi is a gun-runner…"

"We already knew that," interrupted Zack.

Kwame glared at him. "Are you going to allow me to finish?"

Zack sighed. "Fine, fine. Go ahead, break a leg."

"I may in a moment, but it will not be my own." Kwame started over: "Gesi is a gun-runner." He held up his hand to prevent Zack from interjecting again. "So were his brothers. One was killed, the other we lost track of a couple of years ago. He may also be dead; we do not know. Their father's name was Kifo—Kifo Kauxhohuena. He was a man of many talents before becoming a notorious smuggler. He died some years ago. Shot, I believe, by another smuggler."

"And?"

"And… Kifo had an older brother; they served together as conscripts during the war but afterward became estranged from one another. The older brother settled in Kenya and became a low-level official with the British while Kifo came here to live—he and his sons after him. The elder brother was killed in the Mau Mau Rebellion along with most of his family. Only a son survived. The son went on to be adopted by his mother's sister and her husband."

"I know you guys like long stories, but could you cut to the chase?" Zack turned his attention to the last of his burger.

"The reason that I know this story is that the son is well known to us. He has worked to help right many wrongs throughout the continent. He has worked for African and other intelligence agencies to help stop hundreds of atrocities." Kwame's jaw muscles visibly tightened. "Atrocities that your country has not been the least bit interested in, I might add."

"You don't miss a chance, do you?"

Kwame ignored the remark. "As the brother's child, he may also know something of this poison. Perhaps he can fill in the pieces for us. Gesi did say that his uncle was the one who hid the poison. We should find Gesi's cousin and discover what he knows."

"Don't you think he would have said something before now?"

"Perhaps; perhaps not." He shrugged. "What else do we have? Besides, I have a feeling about this. I've had it ever since I heard Sergei speak that scum's name."

Zack was halfway through his Himbasha cake and eyeing the untouched piece on Kwame's plate. "How do we know that this man is not somehow tied in with his cousins?"

Kwame shook his head. "No. Not him. He is a righteous man. He would have no tolerance for his evil uncle's family."

"Okay. Next question. Do you know how to find him?"

Kwame's eyes fell. "Sadly, I do not. I have worked with him many times, but he is very secretive. He has had to be to survive. Only a select few know how to locate him; but I know one of them. I will attempt to reach him tonight on the telephone."

Zack thought a moment before taking a deep breath. "Might as well give it a shot. It's not like we have anything else to go on." He finished his cake but not before adding, "Although, as far as I'm concerned, I'd rather get my hands on that white-suited-Ruskie and make him turn over the map."

"He may not even find it."

Kwame's suggestion about locating Gesi's cousin was their best chance at finding the poison. *And, perhaps Sergei as well,* Zack thought. *After all, if they were both on the track for the poison it would be the most likely way their paths would ever cross again.* "This cousin got a name?" he finally asked.

Kwame nodded. "He goes by many. But he is known to his enemies as the Judas Owl."

CHAPTER Forty

A lone hyena ran from underneath the almond grove as Samuel drove up the hill to find the stranger. He had come to the grove when he'd seen a man standing at the top of the hill staring down with binoculars. Clearly the man had also seen him. Samuel had watched as the figure turned and nailed something to one of the trees and then left. Grabbing his uncle's rifle from the back of the truck, he headed for the crest but the man was long gone by the time he got there. He found the tree and what had been nailed there: a yellow piece of paper flapping in the gentle breeze.

Even though Samuel knew the stranger was gone, he searched the landscape. He saw dust coming from the faraway road and assumed that whoever it was must have had a vehicle just out of sight.

The wind tried its best to separate paper from tree but it was Samuel's large hand that accomplished the job. His heart pounded within his chest the moment he read the words:

I have need of the Owl's services. Meet me in the school playground at dusk.

Damn! They had found him. Only a select few around the world knew his true identity. Samuel wondered which one had come calling. *It did not matter;*

he was no longer going to play that horrible game. How dare they come here to his home!

Samuel gazed across the rich farm land he'd cherished all his life. Righting wrongs had once been a crusade for him—a crusade he now had gladly set aside. He crumpled the piece of paper and threw it on the ground. "No," he said to the wind. "I will not go. I am done with that life… no more."

Even as he said it, however, he knew that "that life" was not done with him. Despite every instinct telling him not to go to the school, he knew he had to, or else they would make their presence known in more direct ways. The last thing he wanted was for his uncle to be disturbed by such people. He cursed aloud, before stomping back to the truck. *Yes, he would be at the playground at dusk, but only to tell whomever it was to go to hell.* His days as the Judas Owl were behind him.

****

It had been years since Samuel had walked behind the small village school to the playground. Two little boys were going up and down on the same lone seesaw that he had once played upon as a child. It was rustier now, of course, as was the old swing that he'd loved. He smiled. The ancient hedgerow was still there. He could still remember the nights he'd stolen away to meet his girlfriend behind them.

A skinny man who was all limbs appeared from out of nowhere. "I am glad you came," he said. "I wasn't certain that you would."

"Merde! It's *you*! I should have known. I thought it might be the French."

Kwame smiled. "I doubt the French remember. They have too much on their mind these days. They've given up trying to stop the Chinese from taking over."

"Too bad."

Samuel watched the boys playing so late in the day. Neither one was taking interest in the two men talking beside the giant hedge. "You have come a long way for nothing. Whatever it is you want, I can tell you right now that you are wasting your breath. I am finished with my former life. The Judas Owl is no more."

"You and I worked well together against the Lord's Resistance Army a few years ago; you know that you can trust me, Samuel."

Samuel continued watching the children. "Trust has nothing to do with it. I am not interested."

"What, you do not want to hear what I have to say to you?"

"I believe that is what I just said."

The taller man cleared his throat. "Not even if I tell you that it could affect the Samburu?"

"Just go away, Kwame. I have no interest."

"Fine. I will do as you say. But remember when you are walking in the ashes of your uncle's home that you had a chance to stop this before it began."

Samuel grabbed the lanky man by one of his long arms. It was like grasping onto a scarecrow. "My uncle? What are you talking about?"

"A group of stupid North Koreans are convinced

that the Samburu land is covering a great field of oil," he lied.

"There is no oil here," Samuel scoffed.

"I said they were stupid."

"The Samburu will never sell this land."

Kwame locked eyes with Samuel. "They are stupid, but they are also vicious. They plan to hire thugs out of Nairobi, an entire gang to burn the people out. The people who are left after a year of killing, raping and house fires will face the Samburu, who will gladly sell their property, and at a fraction of what it is worth."

"So, stop them."

"I have no jurisdiction here; you know that."

"I know just the opposite. You have great influence throughout Africa. You can at least go to the authorities."

The man rolled his eyes. "Since when have the authorities cared what has happened to the Samburu?"

Samuel's eyes flashed fire. "Surely there is some-one!"

Kwame nodded. "Yes there is, and I am looking at him."

Samuel shook his head. "No! Find someone else. I will tell my uncle and the people. We will be ready for trouble."

The story was a complete fabrication, of course, but it had been the only one Kwame could think of to set up a meeting between Zack and Samuel. If there was any chance that Samuel was in league with his cousin Gesi—even a remote possibility—Kwame couldn't risk mentioning the poison yet.

"You won't see it coming, Samuel. And even if you

do, can you guarantee that your elderly uncle would survive? If the gang doesn't kill him, seeing the destruction of his land will."

Kwame was right. Uncle Osuroo could not bear seeing his land destroyed.

"How do you know all of this?"

"The CIA."

"Since when have they cared about Africa? I don't recall them coming to Rwanda's aid."

"No one came to Rwanda's aid... until it was too late."

That wasn't enough for Samuel. "You and I have worked together in the past, Kwame. You know as well as I do that America doesn't give a damn about us. Their drug companies experiment on our people, their oil barons pay us pennies on the dollar, their..."

"You can go on all you want, Samuel. But the rest of the world's no different. Maybe the French were once. Perhaps the Brits..."

Samuel shot him a warning glance. "Don't even start to defend the British. You know perfectly well what their colonial past did to this continent."

"And you should know better than most that those days brought as much good as they did bad to Africa."

"Kwame, I do not wish to stand here and argue sociology and politics with you. What is it you want?"

The lanky intelligence officer smiled. "I merely wish you to meet with a man... an American."

"CIA?"

Kwame nodded. "He has his faults, but he is a good

man, although do not tell him I said that. He and I have spent time hunting diamond traders together."

Samuel's left eyebrow shot up. "Blood diamonds?"

"He helped me free an entire camp of women and children three weeks ago." That much was true. It was what had led them to the desert in hopes of gathering information from runners about other camps.

Samuel could still recall the looks on the faces of the people he'd helped Col. Bundi free so long ago. "It is a despicable trade. Why in God's name must it still go on?" He nearly spat the words.

"Because there aren't enough people like us to stand up against it. This gang of North Koreans in Nairobi, they are just as ruthless as the traders in blood diamonds. Would you have such people wage war against the people of Archer's Post, against your uncle?"

"Of course not."

"All I am asking is that you meet the American. Let him tell you his plan."

"Why can't you do it?"

Kwame had thought through every aspect of the lie. "North Korean intelligence has a dossier on me. They broke into the files in the home office; who knows what else they have now."

Samuel understood. "Perhaps a dossier on me?"

"No. There is no file on the identity of the Judas Owl."

Samuel tilted his head slightly. "And you have told no one else?"

"Correct."

Samuel mulled over what Kwame was asking him.

"Why does your CIA man care? Americans don't give a fig about Africa."

"Maybe not, but they *hate* the North Koreans."

"And that's the reason this American of yours is wanting to help my people?"

Kwame did the last thing Samuel expected. He laughed. "Who the hell knows why Zack Matteson does anything. He's his own man. I do trust him, though. What he has planned will only take a few days."

"And then you will no longer bother me?"

Kwame didn't answer.

CHAPTER Forty-One

Zack stared at the receipt the bellhop had slipped under his door during the night and wondered how he'd talk Langley into approving a bill for three nights at the lavish Sankara Hotel, one of Nairobi's best. Sure, he and Kwame could have stayed at the Radisson Blu for less—*no doubt Flenn would have insisted upon it, Dudley Do-Right that he was at times—but why not live it up a little?*

He threw on some gym shorts along with a tee shirt that he'd purchased in the hotel shop and went downstairs for a workout in the gym. Afterward, he went to the room to change and back downstairs to eat a breakfast of sausages, eggs and chapati—the closest thing on the menu to a sweet roll. He stopped by the gift shop but the woman had never even heard of a jellybean. He wound up buying a large pack of chewing gum instead.

The man known as the Judas Owl wasn't due until 5 p.m., which gave him nine hours to fill. This wasn't Zack's first trip to Nairobi; he and Flenn had tracked a shipment of uranium through here two years ago. The boys in Washington had sent a veritable legion of agents when it came time for the bust, relegating Zack and Flenn to the sidelines and stealing all the credit for their months of undercover work. Flenn had said to let it go, but Zack hadn't been about to, especially after finding out Marshall Webster was the lead agent who'd sideswiped them—the same guy his wife had said had been coming on to her. Just the memory of it made him boil.

Zack considered taking in a movie at a nearby theater, but there wasn't anything worth watching, so he strolled through a park where he found a flier advertising helicopter tours over Nairobi National Park. With nothing better to do, he fished out his phone and dialed the number, jotting down the directions for a flight after lunch. He'd be back in plenty of time to meet with the Owl. With any luck, he and Kwame would discern whether this guy had any fealty to his gangster cousin and also maybe even get a lead on where the poison might be stashed.

From the air, Nairobi looked like any other modern city with towering steel-and-glass architecture reaching up to the clouds, but just outside the city Zack spotted herds of giraffes, elephants, a number of wildebeests, and impalas. The pilot pointed out a herd of buffalo—of all things and much to Zack's surprise—and they even managed to spot a pride of lions, all just a few kilometers outside the city. Zack suddenly found himself wishing he had someone to share the experience with. There hadn't been much time for romancing Donna this past year, what with all the assignments he and Flenn had been given. *Hell, even Flenn would be a welcome companion.* Flenn's time in Iceland should be ending soon. If Zack could wrap this thing up, he reasoned, he might be able to connect with him before Langley got used to the two of them being apart and gave them separate assignments.

The tour came to an end and Zack tipped the pilot

before taking a taxi to his hotel where he ordered a bourbon on the rocks at the bar before heading up to his room. The Judas Owl was due to arrive any minute now. Zack turned on the television and nibbled on a chocolate bar as he watched a football match between Kenya and Manchester United. Soccer was more Flenn's thing; still it was a way to pass the time.

The knock didn't come until 5:45 p.m. Palming his Glock with his right hand, he checked through the door's peephole and saw Kwame's familiar face. He opened the door to find Kwame with a second man, a number of years older. "This him? I expected someone younger."

Samuel glared at the agent. "Funny, you are exactly what *I* expected."

"What's that supposed to mean?"

Kwame pushed between them. "Shall we all go inside? I'd really like to close this door, gentlemen."

Inside, Samuel and Zack sized up the other; both a quick study of men. The two men had a similar build and appeared equally muscular, and both were wondering who'd come out on top in a fight. Neither could help it—occupational hazard. "So, you're the Judas Owl?"

Samuel scowled. "It is not a name I would relish were it not for the type of man that calls me that."

Zack stuck out his hand. "Zack Matteson." Samuel was slow to return the handshake but made certain that his grip was equally firm.

"Okay," Samuel said with a shrug. "So, America has an interest in Africa now?"

"Why not?" Zack replied, rubbing his right hand, and leaving Samuel with a feeling of satisfaction. "After all, you and I seem to have something in common. You might call this North meets South."

Kwame couldn't help saying it: "More like Owl meets Jack Ass."

Irritated and bewildered, Samuel asked: "Just what it is it that you and I can possibly have in common?"

Zack pointed to a couple of chairs in the room. "Why don't we sit down." He poured himself a bourbon from a bottle on the credenza. "I understand that you are an old friend of Kwame's." Zack forced a disarming grin. "I'll try not to let that influence me."

Samuel shrugged. "He and I have worked together; that is all."

Zack nodded. "In Uganda the last time, I believe. Group of religious terrorists? Where are my manners… can I pour you a drink?" Samuel accepted, but only after he'd watched Zack take the first sip. Zack sat on the edge of the bed and slowly nursed the bourbon. Samuel knew the game—he'd played so many over the years—but he was tired of it. He tasted the bourbon and waited for the CIA man to make his pitch.

They'd nearly finished their drinks before Kwame broke the silence.

"Enough, Zack. Just tell Samuel what it is you want from him."

"I suppose an apology is in order, Mr. Kauxho-huena. I'm afraid that Kwame hasn't quite told you the truth." Zack waited to see how the man some called the Judas Owl would respond, but Samuel didn't so much as raise an eyebrow. Such things were par for the course in the world of espionage.

"Lies are a part of your trade, are they not?"

Zack responded with a grin. "At times, yes. But we weren't sure how you would respond to the truth." He got up and poured another bourbon for himself, raising the bottle to offer Samuel a second drink. Samuel refused. "You see, it is a rather delicate matter. It has to do with your cousin Gesi." At the mention of Gesi, Samuel's eyes flashed fire. *Aha, now I've got your attention,* thought Zack.

"I know of the man, but I have never met him," answered Samuel. "I only know what others have told me. He's an arms dealer. Total scum. Has no conscious; keeps terrorists supplied with weapons." Samuel glared first at Zack and then at Kwame. "You, of all people, should know that I don't have any dealings with my father's brother or his family." He turned his gaze toward Zack. "Let me guess, you want me to help you meet him?" Samuel stood. "I'd sooner have vultures pick my bones in the desert."

Zack shrugged. "We don't need you to help us meet him. We've already done that."

Samuel was confused. "What then could you possibly want me for, then? *Ahh…* you've taken him prisoner and want my help in interrogating him. Is that it?"

"Gesi is dead," Zack said flatly.

"From your mouth to God's ear."

Kwame nodded. "No, he speaks the truth. Your cousin is dead."

"Please do not continue calling that vermin my cousin. His father was a criminal and so was he. If he is dead, I will not grieve."

Zack scratched the top of his head. "You don't know your uncle's family?"

"Only through the stories of my childhood and what my aunt told me."

"So, you'd have no problem helping us undo a bit of a problem that your cousin... *um*, Gesi... left for us?"

"Was Gesi in league with the North Koreans?"

Zack looked puzzled. "North Koreans?" Kwame had neglected to fill Zack in on the details he'd used to convince Samuel to meet with them.

"Mr. CIA," Samuel stated, "do you see that door over there?" Zack glanced at the door which led to the hallway. "I am about to walk out of that same door and bid you adieu. You apparently have nothing for me; and I, sir, certainly have nothing for you."

Time to fish or cut bait, Zack thought. "Not even if I told you that Gesi was trying to sell a weapon of mass destruction?"

Samuel hesitated. "What sort of weapon?"

"A terrible one," offered Kwame.

"Aren't they all?" Samuel quipped.

"Yes, but some are worse than others. This one was developed years ago, by the Nazis."

Zack watched as the blood seemed to drain from the man's face. *Bingo!*

"The thing is, Samuel, I don't know whether we can trust you or not. Despite what you say, you and Gesi might have been in this together."

Kwame had heard enough. "This man has infiltrated more than two dozen rogue terrorist groups. He's worked with intelligence organizations from all over the world."

Zack stared at Samuel. "Is that where the 'Judas' comes from? Been playing one spy against another?"

"You are a cynic as well as an ass," exclaimed Kwame. "The name comes from the terrorists. They started calling him that a few years ago. They say he is a traitor who is as stealthy as an owl and who can slip in and out of their presence virtually unseen."

"I never thought of an owl as stealthy."

It was Samuel who spoke. "That is because you have never spent any time around them."

"And you have?"

Samuel did not answer. There was no reason to give this American any details about his past. "What is it you really want from me?"

Kwame spelled it out. "We need your help finding a nerve agent developed by the Nazis in Kenya years ago. We have to find it before the Russians do."

Samuel's jaw muscles tightened. "By *we* you mean that the Americans want to find it."

"No. Just Matteson and me. We know a Russian agent is on its trail. I realize that you distrust the Americans, but if I remember correctly, not half as much as you do the Russians."

"Neither can be trusted."

"Look at me, Samuel," Kwame implored. "You know that I am a man you *can* trust. I am sorry I misled you about the North Koreans, but it was the only way I could get you to respond quickly. Yes, I agree, Zack Matteson is a jackass…"

"Hey…"

"…but he is also someone I trust with my life. I understand you don't believe *him*, but please… believe *me*. There is a deadly and potent poison out there somewhere and we wish only to keep it away from people who might use it."

Samuel took a breath. "And why is it that you think I can help you?"

"Because from what we heard, your father and your uncle apparently helped make it."

"That is a lie!"

Matteson set his glass down. "Look, Samuel is it? I'm a latecomer to this party myself. All I know is that there's a Russian agent who is trying to find a map that your uncle passed down to his sons. A map with directions to this nerve agent. We know what Russia does with nerve agents. We don't need another one in their arsenal. Is there anything that you know or can think of that will help us?"

"Samuel, as you can see, we're pretty desperate. I am sorry that I misled you but I could not risk you not coming to speak with us. If there is anything, anything at all, that you can think of…"

"Like any maps your father may have given you, any special papers?" Zack added.

Kwame nodded. "Anything that might help us find this thing and destroy it."

Samuel thought of the key his father had given him as a child. A key that he had stored under a loose plank in his uncle Osuroo's attic on one of his return trips home years ago. He considered the key and the unseen box that had lain undisturbed for so many decades in a cemetery so far away. Then he turned his thoughts to what the white man had just said. "A map?" *Could there possibly be such a thing? Had his uncle Kifo known all this time where the poison was? What if the Russians were looking for it? What if they found it? Yet, what if the CIA found it?*

He shook his head. Even though he did trust Kwame, he would not trust this American. He realized what he must do. No nation could be entrusted with the key to the gates of hell. If the Russians and the Americans were both looking for it then it would only be a matter of time before one of them found it.

Samuel stood. "I am sorry. But I cannot think of anything that would help you." He nodded toward Kwame. "Perhaps you can give me a telephone number in case I come up with something."

"No," said Zack, "that won't be necessary. I'm sorry we troubled you."

Samuel did not hesitate but headed straight for the door. *He had to get to England, and fast. He and Jenga would just need to advance their upcoming trip. Uncle Osuroo would understand.*

After he'd gone Kwame swung around. "Zack, why in hell's name did you not allow me to tell him how to contact us? He might think of something."

Zack shook his head slowly. "Unless I'm off my game, I'd say that he already has."

CHAPTER Forty-Two

"But, Samuel, I thought we weren't leaving for another two months?" Jenga was taken completely by surprise. "Why the change?"

Samuel had been ready for this. "I was able to get an amazing deal on the airline tickets. It was so good, that I went ahead and paid for yours, as well. I've checked with Uncle Osuroo; he is fine with us leaving earlier than we'd planned. Jafari and Omar can handle things while you are away."

"You paid for *my* ticket?"

Samuel wore his most practiced grin. "Yes." He placed one arm around the younger man's shoulder. "I have been thinking. You deserve this. You have taken such good care of Uncle Osuroo while I was not here." He looked across a field that would soon be tilled and readied for planting season. "I hate to admit it, but the farm has never looked better." He squeezed Jenga's shoulder. "And we owe that to you. I've decided to pay your way to England to express my gratitude."

He squeezed Jenga's shoulder again, tighter this time. "What do you say? Let's go have an adventure, *eh*?"

Samuel could tell Jenga was mulling it over in his mind. He assumed his uncle's foreman was simply having difficulty letting go of his duties and responsibilities, although it really didn't matter what Jenga decided.

Samuel was going with or without him. It simply looked better to be impetuous than to leave Jenga behind on a trip that they'd been planning to take together.

"But, why does it have to be tomorrow?"

"That was the deal with the airline. Come on; it will be fun."

Jenga rubbed his forehead several times before slowly beginning to nod. "Well, what else can I say? Yes!"

Samuel threw his arms around his friend. "Wonderful! I am delighted. We will have…what is it the British say… a jolly good time."

Jenga laughed, though a bit nervously. Samuel understood. It had to be difficult for Jenga to put everything aside and leave someone else in charge. Still, Samuel had been most convincing. He would use the cover of his trip with Jenga so that Uncle Osuroo would not worry about his sudden departure. No doubt, if he'd just left on short notice, the way he'd always done in the past, it would be too great a strain on his baba. *No, this way, his uncle would not worry.*

Sending Jenga to notify the field hands, Samuel went inside to pack. With any luck, they would be halfway to England before Kwame and the American knew he had disappeared.

Alone in his room, Samuel could hardly believe the recent turn of events. His father, convinced that the world's super powers could not be trusted with such a deadly weapon, had hidden the poison in as safe a place as he had been able. But it had plagued Samuel all those years. *Why keep the key, and why tell the story to a child?* Memories of that day, the day the Mau Maus killed his family, came flooding back. He sat on the edge of his bed and thought of his father luring the rebels away from the boulders… and Samuel. It had been nearly 50 years, but the events of that horrible day had been seared into his memory.

"Always be brave, and always stand against wrong." He had tried to make his father's words form the very credo by which he lived his entire adult life, freeing victims of cruelty and working to destroy evil from within. He'd lost count of how many terrorist cells and guerilla militias he had infiltrated over the decades. He seldom thought of the vile men he'd betrayed to the authorities but chose instead to think of the people he had helped rescue from misery. *Would his father be proud of him?* he sat and wondered. "No, not yet," he said aloud. *Not until one last thing was accomplished.*

He stepped out into the long hall and listened for his uncle. It was the time of day when Uncle Osuroo usually fell asleep in a padded rocker in the main living room. Sure enough, Samuel found his uncle with his head back and mouth slightly open, snoring gently as he slept. Samuel climbed the stairs to the attic and found the spot where he'd hidden the key for safe keeping. He removed the loose board and spotted it exactly where he'd left it. Samuel took a deep breath before reaching for the key that he had once worn around his neck, the same way that his father had before him. The key was still on the same chain his father had worn. *No one made keys that looked like this anymore.* He picked it up. It was heavier than he remembered. *Or was it the weight of what he knew that he had to do?*

As he knelt in front of the small opening in the floor, he remembered not only his father but also his Auntie Gemma, and Emmanuel. *God in heaven, all of that was so long ago, a lifetime.* Samuel stared at the key.

He would go to Durham with Jenga. It would be easy enough to lose him at night in a pub or tourist attraction. He would go to the great cathedral his father had told him about and find the tomb marked with the same name as his baba. Once he dug up the poison, he would take it to the sea. He wasn't exactly sure how, but he would find a way. He had no other choice. Hopefully, if heaven allowed such things, his father would be with him to help finish the task he himself had begun.

The reservations were made. He and Jenga would leave in the morning. The more Samuel thought about it, the more hopeful he became that neither the CIA nor this mysterious Russian of whom Kwame and Matteson had spoken, would ever know anything about what awaited him in England.

He was wrong on both counts.

CHAPTER Forty-Three

Jenga stared at the mammoth house of worship known as York Minster. His eyes couldn't take it all in as he gazed 236 feet toward the clouds at the creamy limestone towers. "I feel as out of place here as a sparrow in an eagle's nest," he told Samuel.

"I know what you mean," answered Samuel, himself agog at the majestic structure in front of him. "I have only been out of Africa once, and that was to Paris. I felt the same way when I saw Notre Dame."

Jenga gestured toward the towering spires above them. "Was it anything like *this*?"

"They are both massive, but I believe this is bigger. Shall we go inside and take a look?" Samuel and Jenga had arrived in Manchester three nights ago. They'd taken a couple of tours of the city before taking a train to York. Tomorrow, they would take another train to Durham. At some point, Samuel would have to come up with an excuse to go off on his own. If he did, it would mean that he'd decided to take matters into his own hands.

"I will leave that up to you, Sammy. Where you go, I shall gladly follow."

That could prove to be a problem once they got to Durham. "Well," Samuel said with a smile, "my father used to tell me stories about the British. I say let's go inside and see what it is they have to say about the Almighty."

Jenga nodded. "I'm not religious myself, but I know that your uncle is. He has had me drive him to the village church many Sundays. I'm sure that he would approve our exploring this further; although, I must say the church he attends is nothing compared to this."

"I'm certain that it is to him." Samuel frowned as he gazed at the magnificent towers above. "I have known many who confused wealth and power with greatness. It has always been their downfall." He thought he saw a flash behind Jenga's eyes, as if he had struck a nerve.

Inside the Minster, stone arches framed both sides of the grand nave. Such grandeur he had only encountered once before— at Notre Dame. This, however, seemed even more impressive with its expansive utilization of space and light. The exquisite hand-carved stones and the centuries-old stained glass left Samuel with an impression of holiness and grandeur. The impression it appeared to be making on Jenga, however, was different somehow, although Samuel couldn't quite place his finger on it. Jenga kept wondering aloud about the cost it would take to run such a place and what secret treasures might the minster hold. As if to accentuate the latter, they wandered into the undercroft and witnessed a vast array of British splendor. Jenga was first drawn to the giant silver candlesticks which had once adorned the altars, and next to the bejeweled gold rings worn by former archbishops. For his part, Samuel was fascinated by the ancient illuminated manuscripts and the Horn of Ulf, an elaborately carved elephant tusk gifted to the great church by a Viking lord more than 1,000 years ago.

After the self-guided tour, they found a nearby pub

where they both ate their fill. Samuel was impressed by a local dark ale the barkeep had recommended. Afterward, they found their way into an unusual network of narrow, medieval streets that were lined with shops and cafés. They spent most of the afternoon wandering in and out of woolen stores and souvenir shops, the likes of which neither man had ever seen. Tomorrow, they'd head for Durham, where they'd spend three days before heading to Lindisfarne and the Farne Islands.

They came across an exhibit of the hull of a Viking ship which, according to the nearby placard, had sailed up the Thames and then up the Lea on its way to York— *Jorvik*, the Vikings had called it. It brought to mind Samuel's plan to bury the Nazi poison in the North Sea. On the flight, he had figured out just how to do it. Once he had the poison in his possession, they would travel to a seaside ruin called Lindisfarne. Last night he'd read that he could charter a touring boat from there to the Farne Islands. From what he could tell on the map, it appeared to be the perfect place to sink the treacherous thing.

Other than being booby-trapped by the Nazi major, he couldn't recall his father ever saying much about the actual box itself, whether it was wooden or metal. Samuel hoped for metal. A wooden box might have decayed under the earth over the years, leaving the substance vulnerable to whatever explosive charge the Nazi monster had placed inside. Of course, the man might have been lying about the charge just to keep his apprentices at bay. Still, Samuel would exercise the utmost caution when he dug it up. He'd bring along a padded box for extra stability. He'd purchased it in a giftshop this morning. He told Jenga it was a present for his uncle's prayer book and Bible.

Jenga read the inscription underneath the Viking boat out loud: *"Up the Thames, and then up the Lea, and along the Lea to its source, then in a straight line to Bedford, then up the Ouse to the Watling Street.* What do you suppose that means, Sammy?" he asked.

"It appears to be a quote from a Viking map."

Jenga shrugged. "I do not know much about Vikings except what I have seen in movies. They were pillagers, no?"

"Not just pillagers; there were also artisans and craftsmen among them. England and France remember them as annoying raiders, but there was a whole other side to them."

"I suppose there is to all of us," Jenga said nonchalantly before moving on to the next exhibit. Samuel scratched his head, wondering what, if anything, his friend had meant by that.

****

The two East Africans weren't difficult to follow. Zack had left Kwame back at the Kisumu International Airport a few days ago, with a promise to keep him in the loop after they had discovered Samuel's purchase of two tickets to England. "Told you so," Zack had told Kwame. "We tell him about this weapon of mass destruction— which he denies any knowledge of—and the next day he books a flight to England."

Kwame had agreed with Zack's plan to follow

Samuel while he stayed behind and tried to find out what he could about the other man, Jenga. All Kwame had been able to discover so far was that he was some sort of farmhand for Samuel's uncle.

Zack was already working on his second bag of jellybeans for the day, both of which he'd procured at a candy shop in York. He sat in the back of the minster and watched for the two men to resurface from the undercroft. He wasn't particularly interested in the mammoth building as a place of worship but couldn't keep from marveling at the medieval Gothic architecture and stained glass. His father had been a carpenter, and Zack had inherited an eye for quality workmanship.

Tourists milled about, often with heads tilted backward, straining to see the ceilings. One little boy stood with an attractive Asian woman and a pudgy middle-aged man; the boy leaned back and peered at a heart-shaped rose window through binoculars. Zack was beginning to wonder if he should have followed Samuel downstairs to the exhibit rooms. His map of the great church showed all the exits were on the main floor, but they had been gone an awfully long time. He stuffed the rest of the candy into his pocket and stood up just as he saw the two men ascending the stairwell.

Zack quickly turned his attention to a gold-trimmed memorial dedicated to a wealthy parishioner from the 16th century. *Money may have once been called the root of all evil by the founder of Christianity,* he thought as he stared at the statuette, *but the church he left behind certainly didn't seem to see things that way.* Over the centuries, the wealthy had been entombed within walls of opulence, such as this, while the poor were buried in mass graves—their only memorial, the impression they'd left on others.

The Judas Owl hadn't left much of an impression on Zack. *What was he after?* So far, the Kenyan had been playing the role of a tourist taking in the sights, but Zack wasn't buying it. Kwame had said that Osmann and Kifo had been stationed in Durham for four months during the war, along with other Kenyan recruits. *There had to be a connection... but what?* Zack had no idea what ties bound these two men together—any more than he knew what connected a deadly Nazi nerve gas and the peaceful hills of Northumberland. As he watched the two men heading toward the exit, however, *he sure as hell was going to make it his job to find out.*

CHAPTER Forty-Four

Zack had taken the car behind Samuel and the other man at the depot. So far, neither had spotted him, and he planned to keep it that way. The train from York Station listed multiple stops, meaning that the two men might be heading anywhere. Zack would have to get off at each stop to see if they were disembarking.

The life of a spy was nothing like what was portrayed in the movies. Most of it was spent waiting and watching. *Flenn had more patience for this side of the job than he did. Too bad he wasn't here,* Zack thought, realizing yet again just how dependent he had become on his partner's wisdom and advice. *He and Flenn were like two sides of the same coin—counterbalances on the proverbial scale of life. Why the home office had deemed it necessary to split them up for a few months was beyond knowing.*

He was sitting next to a buxom 30-something blonde who reminded him a bit of Donna, except that Donna was seven months pregnant with their second child. Zack had sworn he'd be home before the baby came, and would have been packing to go back to D.C. now had he not followed Kwame into the desert on what was supposed to be a simple assignment to track a couple of diamond smugglers for a few days.

The rolling hills and ancient hedgerows of the English countryside didn't impress Zack nearly as much as the number of sheep he saw grazing. They seemed to be everywhere—farmland, churchyards, graveled roads, and ancient cemeteries. "What's with all the sheep?" he finally asked the blonde.

She peered out the window. "Eee, thas' a reet gradly lot, *eh*? Many a buint o'r, from the look of 'em."

"*Um…* yeah, that's what I thought." What he lacked in understanding his eyes made up for in appreciation of her shapely figure. Not that he was tempted. He'd said goodbye to his playboy ways years ago when he'd married Donna. He knew in an instant that she had been the only girl for him.

Sadly, the years hadn't been easy for either of them. He was constantly on assignment and she was left home alone with their little girl, Michelle. Now, with another one on the way, he knew he'd have to convince his superiors to give him assignments closer to home. Technically, the CIA was not supposed to collect information on American soil, but that rule had become laughable over the years.

There was even a secret center in Florida that schooled agents in the art of working around the FBI and local law enforcement. *Of course, the feds would go into a tirade each time they discovered Langley's fingerprint on their turf, but most of those thundering dunderheads never had a clue.*

"I n'er met a Yank a'fore." The blonde ran her hand lazily through her long hair, brushing it away from her forehead. "What type of bizness brings ya' 'ere, love?"

"I sell rat traps."

He enjoyed the look on people's faces when he used

that cover. However, it didn't seem to deter her. "Do ya' now? Well, jes' las' n'ght me mum tol' me 'er ca' 'as a fa' ra' stashed in t'coil 'oyle."

"In the what?"

"T'coil 'oyle."

Zack was totally lost; he'd hoped the rat trap line would have been enough to deter her. "Is that a fact?" he responded, not knowing what else to say. "We see that a lot in our line of work." He stood and fumbled in his pocket. "If you'll excuse me, I'm going to make my way to the snack bar." He knew better than to ask if she would like something. It would only have encouraged her flirtations; even worse, he wouldn't know just what the hell she'd asked him to bring her.

An elderly couple was standing in line in front of him. They both ordered a cup of Costa coffee and a scone with raspberry jam. The way they'd said *raspberry* seemed cute to Zack. He looked at them and wondered what he and Donna would be like at their age. Zack searched the candy counter but the selection was limited, and unfortunately no jellybeans. Flenn always teased him about how much sugar he consumed, even though Zack never gained an ounce. He weighed the same he had in college—benefits of a high metabolism.

He ordered a Pepsi and decided to try one of the scones with lemon curd. He ate it at the counter, unwilling to risk another encounter with blondie. Ordinarily, he was quite the innocent flirt with beautiful women, but this one seemed too eager. Flenn had told him that he was the only man he knew who could go from being a curmudgeon to Casanova in the blink of an eye if a pretty girl was around. With his rugged good looks and enigmatic smile, Zack could charm the pants off of anyone… in fact, that was how he had won Donna.

The conductor announced that the first stop would be Durham. Zack stepped from the railcar and peered ahead in search of his mark. As luck would have it, he spotted the two Africans as they made their way through the turnstile, rolling their luggage behind them. Zack had brought nothing with him, buying whatever he needed when opportunity afforded him access and discarding what he couldn't carry on his person. The company credit card he carried had its drawbacks, though. Langley would be able to follow him should one of the many bean-counters be paying close attention. Likely, he'd soon be receiving a call or a visit from another agent asking just what the hell he was doing in England. *Until then, he'd follow these two wherever they went like white on rice.*

Durham Station was small, with only a coffee service, newsstand, and a café/bar, which was closed at the moment. Samuel and his companion stopped for coffees and then purchased a map from the newsstand before climbing into one of the white, multi-passenger taxis with large numbers painted in blue on the side. Zack searched for a second cab and found one while the driver of the other vehicle waited for more passengers before pulling away.

Forever a practitioner of overused idioms, as well as a devotee of old spy movies, Zack delighted in telling the cabbie: "Follow that car."

****

"I feel as if I've stepped back in time," Jenga said, staring out the taxi's windows at the streets of Durham. Two- and three-story brown and white ancient buildings lined each narrow road and alleyway as hundreds of people representing every possible race walked along the sidewalks. Some jaunted by with purpose while others strolled slowly past, stopping in front of shops and bakery windows to admire the treasures on display.

Samuel was equally impressed. He'd only been out of Africa once before, having been summoned to Paris to brief senior government ministers on the rise in terrorist organizations in East Africa. He glanced at Jenga. The man was mesmerized. "I've only known one big city in my life, but Addis Ababa was nothing like this," Jenga said.

"I didn't know you'd been to Ethiopia," Samuel said. It was a place he had long avoided. His uncle's family were rumored to be involved with a crime syndicate there.

Jenga scratched his head, never taking his eyes off the street scenes unfolding in front of him. "Tell me, Sammy, is this anything like Paris?"

Samuel smiled. He peered out the window at a steep hill. "Not really. Paris is more modern, at least the parts I saw. I was only there for a few days. This is what I imagine a Charles Dickens novel would look like, only cleaner."

"Charles who?"

"An English author from a long time ago. In my work, I've had opportunity to read quite a bit."

"You know, it's funny, Sammy. I don't know much about your work; you never seem to want to talk about it."

Samuel offered a practiced shrug. "Not much to talk about, really. What about you? I've known you for three months and I've never heard you say anything about your own past."

Jenga offered a warm smile. "And yet here we are, good friends, almost family."

Samuel had often wondered what it would have been like to have a brother. Sometimes, late at night, he still thought about his little sisters and wondered what life could have been like were it not for that fateful day. Jenga was not the same as family, but he was the next best thing.

"So, where do you want to go first, Jenga? I mean after we check into our hotel. Durham Castle, perhaps? The Heritage Centre? How about the university?"

"Durham Cathedral." Jenga hadn't hesitated.

"The cathedral? I thought you would have had enough of churches back in York. I thought you said you were not a religious man."

Jenga shook his head. "I am not. But I would like to see how the church here compares with York Minster; see what treasures it is hiding."

Samuel didn't know about treasures, but he did know the horrible secret that the cathedral's cemetery had kept hidden for decades. He too needed to see the church grounds and figure out a way to do what he had come here to do. His father had been right, the world could not be trusted with such a secret. True, even worse weapons had been invented since then but he was not about to allow that CIA or the rumored Russian agent to place one more hideous addition to the to the world's arsenal. "Durham Cathedral, you say? Well, why not. It looks quite impressive in the brochure."

After unpacking and grabbing lunch in a pub with a white elephant painted on the window, the duo walked across Framwellgate Bridge over the River Wear. Samuel enjoyed watching students from the University of Durham gathered in small groups on the riverbank, listening to their professors. He peered into the cloudless sky and closed his eyes as the warmth of the British sun caressed his face. For a moment, he was able to just exist and drink in the peacefulness of the moment. He opened his eyes and watched the students below.

"What is it, Sammy?"

Samuel sighed wistfully. "I was remembering my life as a university professor."

Jenga nodded. "Rhodesia. Your uncle told me." Jenga looked at Samuel and then at the scene below. "Why did you leave?"

"More important work presented itself." The thought snapped Samuel back into the moment. *He was here for one reason only; it was foolish to allow himself to become distracted.*

Jenga pointed to a road at the end of the bridge. "According to the map, both the cathedral and the castle are at the top of that hill."

Samuel managed a smile. "Then, let's go."

As they trekked up the steep hill past pubs, gift shops and a university bookstore, Samuel felt something odd. Trepidation perhaps? Nervousness about the task at hand? *Or was it something else?* Thoughts of his father hiding him behind the boulder popped into his head. He had long ago ceased hearing the sound of his father's voice but he had never forgotten his admonition that day: "Always be brave, and always stand against wrong."

It wasn't a lack of courage that filled him now or confusion about whether he was doing the right thing. No, this feeling was more like a presence—like something, *or someone*, was standing next to him encouraging him to follow through with his plan. Was God leading Samuel someday to dispose of this horrible thing? Was that it? Since his father had been unable to return here, was God here with *him* now? Or was it simply the memory of his dad?

Just knowing that his father had walked up this same hill half a century ago filled him with a sense of awe... and dread.

Jenga pointed up ahead. "Look, there it is!" Two massive Norman spires rose majestically in the air. It took them several more steps to the top of the hill before they could see the great cathedral in its totality. Jenga gave a low whistle. "Just look at this place!"

The sandstone walls and rectangular towers of the cathedral bore no resemblance to York Minster with its white Gothic transepts and multiple pointed spires. Architectural words like *Romanesque* and *Gothic* meant nothing to Jenga. But Samuel, who had once taught aspiring engineering students, marveled at the differences in style. Both great churches were ancient, Durham having been built in the 11th century and York

Minster a century later. Unlike the limestone of the minster, the sandstone cathedral in front of them appeared to be half-church, half-fortress, sitting as it was on top a high hill on a peninsula surrounded by the River Wear.

A huge, weathered stone relief on the north façade of the gigantic edifice, which depicted a monk and a milkmaid with her cow, was puzzling to both men. They knew nothing of the legend of how Saint Cuthbert's remains had been brought to this hilltop by Lindisfarne monks led by two dairy maidens.

To the right and below was what Samuel had come for—the cemetery. He feigned only moderate initial interest in the plethora of granite, slate, and marble markers protruding upward from the ground like so many skeleton fingers from a bad horror movie. Instead he and Jenga made their way to the massive oaken planked doors. Jenga stared at the garden of ancient tombs and gravestones for a moment before turning to enter.

A hideous door knocker shaped as a goblin— surrounded by flames and eating a human being— conveyed anything but peaceful sanctuary within. Nevertheless, the two East Africans entered the colossal nave and could not help but be struck by the contrast to York Minster. Durham Cathedral was darker for one thing, and quieter. The echoes of tourists' voices were more subdued, although that could be because there were fewer people here than Samuel and Jenga had seen in York. High above them was a ribbed, vaulted ceiling unlike anything Samuel had ever studied. He had no way of knowing that this ceiling was the first of its type in the world. He would have been even more amazed had he been able to see the massive flying buttresses high in the roof of the triforium (the arcade above the arches of the nave which gave extra support to the vaulting).

Inside, large-ribbed columns rose well over 6 meters, not even halfway to the soaring stone ceiling, a marvel of engineering in itself. The pointed arches in the Norman nave caught Samuel's attention immediately, while Jenga seemed more interested in the rounded pillars with their zigzag, indented patterns. The grandeur of the stone high altar at one end of the nave stood in stark contrast to the spired baptismal font at the other. Two signs were nearby, one directing visitors to the Shrine of Saint Cuthbert, the other to the Treasures of the Cathedral. Samuel wished to investigate the shrine while Jenga was more interested in following directions to the ancient treasure trove. As Samuel watched Jenga disappear down a long, marble staircase, he considered rushing out to the cemetery to search for the stone bearing his father's name. Yet, his interest in the shrine was real, and it would afford him a momentary distraction from the real reason he'd come to England.

The shrine was breathtaking. A spectacular gold-trimmed canopy of deep blues and reds depicting the risen Christ was surrounded by symbols of the four Gospel evangelists. Directly underneath was a polished, green marble slab with a single Latin word: *Cvthbertvs*. Samuel had no idea just who Cuthbert was or why the church considered him a saint, but judging from the magnificence of the shrine he must have been someone especially important. He sat alone for several minutes in one of the chapel chairs gazing at the tomb and the depiction above. A statue of a man holding his own head was a puzzle, but one he decided would simply have to go unanswered. After several minutes soaking in the solemnity and silence of the shrine, he stood. It was time to walk amongst the dead.

Samuel stepped to the door with the grotesque goblin and outside into the graveyard. He was surprised to find Jenga already there, wandering amongst the stones. "Were the treasures disappointing?" he called, startling his friend.

"Nothing down there but crosses and religious items."

Samuel nodded. "For some, that is treasure enough."

"Ha," Jenga scoffed, "hardly enough gold to hold anyone's interest."

"So, you thought you'd search out here?"

Jenga shrugged. "Just waiting for you, Sammy."

Samuel walked amongst the graves, hoping to catch a glimpse of the one his father had told him about long ago. "Look at some of these dates, Jenga. Can you believe how old they are… here's one that says 1511." Pretending to be interested in the dates would allow him some time to search the names carved into each… at least the ones that had withstood the years and the English weather.

"Here's an older one," Jenga called. "It says 1443."

"Oh, here's another one, even older than that." The two men called out dates to one another until, at last,

Samuel found the very stone for which he had been searching. It was directly underneath the sculpted woman and cow high above. He pretended to look past it but glanced a second time and felt his heart skip a beat. Although the second name was impossible to read, he knew this was the place. It read:

Osmann La…tlu.. 1691-17..

The date of death was illegible, and Samuel didn't wish to call attention to the marker. He would sneak back here tonight and retrieve that which his father had left buried here. An ugly reminder of an uglier war in which 73 million people had lost their lives. More than that, really. Rarely did the European-based textbooks ever mention Kenyans or other Africans who'd died during the war. The number was thought to be either irrelevant or too difficult to retrieve, and so, like most things African, the West chose to ignore it.

Thank you, Baba, for leading me here, Samuel silently prayed. *Now, I will complete the task which you began.*

"Come, Jenga, I am thirsty. Let us find one of those pubs we passed along the way." However, Samuel would only have one beer. He needed all his wits about him for tonight and the task at hand.

CHAPTER Forty-Five

The great church loomed shadowless against the gray sky, reminding Zack of the opening scene from some black-and-white horror movie he had seen as a kid. *What was this fascination these two had for big churches? First York, and now here in Durham.*

As he watched the main entrance from a coffee shop across the parking lot, Zack sat eating a slice of lemon pie and drinking a ginger ale. A slight teenager with auburn hair and a tiny Union Jack tattooed on the inside of her wrist brought him a second piece of pie at his request. "Will 'at be all, suh?"

"Yes, thank you," he answered, not taking his eyes off the entrance where Samuel and his friend had entered a half-hour ago. He still hadn't heard from Kwame about the other man's identity. *Maybe he'd hear something later in the day.* "Oh, there wouldn't be a candy shop hereabouts, would there?"

"Oh yes, suh, 'tis a 'reet' gran' one, jes' do'n the street. 'Tis on the left; ya' canna' miss it."

Zack smiled at the accent. He'd spent plenty of time in England, but most of it in London. Northumberland was entirely different aesthetically, and had a much slower pace along with its unique accents. He and Donna had married only 120 miles from here, in Edinburgh, but that was as close as he'd come to ever having visited the North.

He glanced at the darkening sky and wondered how long before the rain came. *Just what in the hell was he doing here? In only a matter of days he had exchanged sand-filled boots for Oxford loafers. He and Kwame must have spooked the Judas Owl into coming here, but why England of all places?*

The answer came in a phone call. Zack set his fork down to answer the phone. "Can you talk?" came Kwame's voice over the receiver.

Zack couldn't help it. "Better than most of the people around here," he said.

"*Ah...* Northern England," Kwame said. "I spent some time there myself a few years ago. Charming people."

"Yeah, if you can ever figure out what the hell they're saying."

"Never mind. I've gotten some intel."

"You find out who this man is with the Owl?"

"Not yet, but I'm working on it. I've got something even better though."

Zack could hear the excitement in Kwame's voice . "Lay it on me."

Kwame did. He reminded Zack of how Samuel's real father had been killed in the Mau Mau Rebellion back in the early '60s, and how, before that, his father had been a Kenyan conscript for the British. "Yeah, yeah; old news," was all Zack said. Kwame didn't explain just how he had gotten this new bit of information, but apparently his resources rivaled Zack's own.

"Here's where it gets interesting," Kwame said into the phone.

"*Ahh*, the plot thickens, does it?" Zack picked up his fork and started on his pie just as Samuel's traveling companion darted outside the main entrance and headed straight for the cemetery. He appeared to be searching for something amongst the gravestones.

"I'll say. Samuel's father's name was Osmann, right?"

"I remember."

"There is an old record of a young man named Osmann having been forced to aid the Nazis in the early days of the war. He was assigned as one of the lab-rats for a Sturmbannführer Hans Kreps. Sound familiar?"

Zack released a low whistle. "Bingo. That corroborates what Gesi was telling Sergei back at that church."

"I'm not done yet. Seems after they freed themselves from the Nazis, Samuel's father and his Uncle Kifo were conscripted into the British army and later assigned to a base in Durham for a few months."

Zack stared at the man in the cemetery searching amongst the tombs. "Oh my God!"

The waitress seemed to appear out of nowhere. "Is 'nethin' amiss, suh?"

Zack assured her that he was fine and sent her away. "Do you know what this means?" he asked Kwame. He didn't wait for an answer but this time he at least made sure to lower his voice. "Samuel's father and uncle must have brought the poison to England. It's here, and Samuel must know where. We spooked him into coming here. He doesn't trust us and wants to make sure we don't find it first."

"I'm guessing the same, but could it just be a coincidence?"

"How many coincidences would it take to convince you, Kwame?"

"I never thought I'd say this, but I agree with you on something. Samuel must have gone to England to find the damned thing. Have you been able to watch them closely?"

Zack stared out the window at the man searching amongst the graves. "Close enough. He's a smart one, though. He's been acting like a tourist the whole time. Spending a lot of time in pubs and churches."

"Churches?"

"Cathedrals. That's where we are now. Durham Cathedral." At that precise moment, Samuel stepped out of the great doors and joined his friend hunting amongst the gravestones. An idea flashed to mind. "You don't suppose…"

A similar idea must have come to Kwame. "What? That Osmann hid the poison in the church?"

"Not necessarily *inside*. Listen, I've got a hunch. Call me the minute you find out who this other man is with the Judas Owl."

No longer interested in the pie, Zack hung up the phone and stared out the window as Samuel and the stranger seemed to be calling out names on the stones. This was it! It had to be. The poison was buried somewhere in that cemetery!

CHAPTER Forty-Six

Samuel had waited until he was certain that Jenga was asleep before creeping out of his hotel bed and quietly slipping out of the room. He took a taxi to Framwellgate Bridge and walked the rest of the way just to make sure no on was following. Music and laughter filled the late-night air as revelers took advantage of various pubs before closing time. There were few people strolling about outside, for which Samuel was grateful.

He made his way up Silver Street and then turned toward the cathedral. The farther he walked up the hill the less the lights from the pubs below illuminated the road in front of him. A heavy fog was rolling in, diffracting the lights of the great church away from the cemetery below. That would make it more difficult for any security cameras to pick him up. The last thing he needed was for some bobby to arrest him for desecrating a grave. He wondered if his father's heart had been beating that night as fast as his was now. It was frightening, yet oddly comforting, to know that he was walking in his dad's footsteps.

The continual chittering of a nightjar set Samuel's nerves even more on edge as he approached the tombstone he'd spotted earlier. That afternoon he had slipped away from Jenga long enough to purchase a small trowel, which he'd slipped into his trouser pocket.

As he knelt on the soft earth, he marveled at the fact that he was really here… about to fulfill his father's hope of ridding the world of this awful thing. Disposing of the box in the North Sea would be simple enough; finding it might be the hard part. With no other way to go about it, Samuel carefully pushed the trowel into the earth and began to dig, thrusting the pointed end of the miniature shovel in every direction as he probed deeper, hoping to make contact before anyone caught sight of him. As luck would have it, fewer than five minutes passed before he felt something hard underneath the soil.

Hoping it wasn't merely a stone, Samuel dug carefully until he'd unearthed a small, rectangular metal box. He paused only a moment to reflect on both the fact that his father had been the last person to hold this box, and its deadly contents, before carefully placing it in the cloth bag he'd brought along with the trowel. Tomorrow, they would go to Lindisfarne where he'd charter a boat and dispose of this ghastly thing once and for all.

Samuel covered the hole as best he could before standing in the quiet of the foggy cemetery. Fortunately he'd been able to escape detection from cathedral security and the local police. Not so fortunately… and unbeknownst to him… three pairs of eyes had been watching his every move.

Zack Matteson stood quietly in the recessed entranceway of the darkened coffee shop. From there he could just make out the silhouette of a man kneeling in the cemetery. More worrisome was the other figure who had darted behind a hedge on the opposite side of the courtyard. From his vantage point Zack could see that the second person crouched behind the shrubs was also watching Samuel's every move. Zack was careful not to betray his position and simply waited to see what either man would do next. He didn't have to wait long.

Minutes later, Samuel hurried passed him and down the hill, and a dim figure behind the bushes stepped onto the pavement and began walking directly toward Zack. He had not had time to acquire a weapon, although he could certainly handle himself in a fight. *Hopefully it wouldn't come to that.*

The figure stopped only meters away from where Zack remained hidden in the shadows. The man reached into his pocket and pulled out a mobile phone, calling for a cab, which arrived less than a minute later. As the headlights fell upon the mystery man in front of him, Zack retreated deeper into the shadows of the café doorway, but not before getting a good look at the man's illuminated face. It was the same fellow who had traveled with Samuel from Africa.

"That's odd," he whispered as the taxi sped away. "Why is his friend spying on him?" Zack turned it over several times in his mind. *Maybe the friend had just followed him, not knowing the reason Samuel had come here under the cover of darkness. Or worse, maybe he did know.* Zack scratched his head. *Either way, Samuel had no clue that his travelling companion had been spying on him.* "Damn, Kwame, when are you going to find out who this guy is?"

Zack thought of calling Kwame, but it was nearly 1 a.m. That meant that it was almost dawn back at Camp Lemonnier. Kwame would be awake soon; he'd give it another hour. *First things first… he needed to get back to the hotel. Now that Samuel had the poison in hand, his next move would be the most telling of what he planned to do with it.*

As Zack made his way down the steep hill toward the sound of folk music from the nearest pub, another obscure figure stirred from the far corner of the courtyard. As he watched Zack disappear into the night, the towers of the cathedral bathed him in a halo of diffused light. The man was grateful that he'd exchanged his customary white suit for black jeans and a black shirt. Sergei was not in a hurry. He knew where all three men would be heading… to the hotel for the remainder of the night.

He would wait and follow them tomorrow… and then kill them all.

CHAPTER Forty-Seven

"Where in God's good name are you guys going?" Zack said into the ether as he tried to keep several cars' distance between his rental car and the little blue sedan driving through twists and turns, past endless meadows of wooly sheep and ancient hedgerows.

Fortunately, he had awakened early and had gone downstairs for a sweet roll when he saw Samuel along with his shadow from last night standing in line at the hotel's rental car kiosk. He'd waited for them to secure a reservation and head back to the elevator, presumably to pack, before renting an even smaller Ford Fiesta for himself. He'd waited in the car until he'd seen them toss their suitcases in the trunk of a blue Vauxhall Corsa and drive away.

Zack had limited experience driving on the wrong side of the road but it proved easy enough until he came to what seemed like an endless series of roundabouts. How he'd managed through them was nothing short of a miracle.

The countryside would have been more impressive had he not been concentrating on remaining undetected––and in the correct lane. All Zack knew was that they were heading Northeast. He'd seen directional signs for some place named Seahouses—*an odd name for a town*—

but so far, he'd seen no signs of civilization; nothing but pastures and roundabouts.

Once, on a joint assignment south of London, Flenn had gone on and on about the moors, the ancient hedgerows in the shire, and the seemingly endless bright-yellow gorse growing along the roadways. But Flenn was like that. It was rare for Zack to notice, or care, about the beauty of nature. On that same trip he'd seen the moors as open ground where someone could get a clear shot at him, the hedgerows as places an assassin could easily hide, and the gorse as a thorny preventative for anyone fleeing on foot. He couldn't help it; that was just how he viewed the world.

Today as he drove, Zack wondered about last night. *Why had Samuel's companion followed at a distance? Did he not know what it was that his friend was really doing here in England? If not, why the cloak and dagger?* Zack wondered if Samuel was on his way to try and dispose of the box he'd exhumed from the cathedral's graveyard last night... *what other reason could he possibly have for coming all this way to dig in a cemetery in the middle of the night? From what Kwame had told him, Samuel was not the kind of man who would try and sell it as a weapon, nor one who could ever actually use the damn thing. No, Samuel must have a plan to dispose of it.* And Zack was going to find out what that plan was. If, as he presumed, Samuel was taking the box to another destination to hide it again, then Zack would mark where and make certain that Sergei never found it. But, if Samuel's traveling companion proved not to be the friend Samuel thought him to be, Zack would be there to prevent the man from making away with the box full of poison.

"Something is rotten in Denmark," he said out loud. *What was that; Shakespeare? Flenn would know. Flenn read Shakespeare and a lot of that other girly stuff.* "He probably even enjoyed it," Zack mumbled, with a shake of his head.

Times like these, Zack missed his partner. Scott Flenn was the jelly to Zack's peanut butter. Flenn would have called it something fancier, maybe something about yin and yang or some such, but the truth was that over the years their skills, their personalities, and their alternate universes had just seemed to mesh. Although he would never admit it to Flenn, he'd be glad when their temporary assignments were over. After the baby came, he and Flenn could once again become the dynamic duo.

Oh my God—Donna! He'd been in England three days and had yet to call her. His wife didn't expect many calls while he was in the field on assignment, but it would have been easy enough to phone her now. He made a mental note to call as soon as they got to wherever it was that Samuel was going.

Only two cars separated the Fiesta from their Corsa. He eased his foot off the accelerator and pulled over to allow two more cars to pass. If he and Kwame had already spooked the Owl into coming to England it was certain that he'd be checking to see if anyone was following him. As they drove down endless country roads, Zack began to wonder if he should call Flenn. He couldn't risk telling him what was going on over the phone, but it would be good just to hear partner's voice.

He reached for his phone just as it began to ring. It wasn't Flenn, though; it was Kwame.

"Matteson, are you sitting down?"

Zack checked the speedometer. "You might say that, yes. I'm in a car following your friends."

"Friend." Kwame corrected. "I just got confirmation on who the other man is. You won't believe it."

"Try me."

The man's name is Msaliti… Msaliti Kauxhohuena."

Zack nearly swerved off the road. "Kauxhohuena? "This guy with Samuel is Gesi's younger brother? The one you thought…"

"The one we thought might be dead, yes. Turns out he is very much alive. He's been working for Samuel's step-uncle all this time."

Zack could feel his face turning red. "So, the whole damn family is in on it!"

"I don't think so. Msaliti has been working under an alias. He calls himself Jenga. He managed to get himself ingratiated with the Owl's uncle and become a foreman on their farm while Samuel was away."

"They don't know who he really is? That doesn't make sense; Msaliti is Samuel's first-cousin for Chrissake."

"They were aware of one another but they've likely never met. Their fathers hated each other."

Zack stared hard at the little blue sedan as it crested a hill in front of him. "It doesn't make sense. Why would Msaliti go to work for Samuel's uncle under an alias?" Kwame was silent, waiting to see if Zack would come to the same conclusion.

"Oh, my God! He's after the poison and Samuel has no idea."

"I would wager that Msaliti's father told his sons the family secret. Gesi went after it his way while Msaliti followed a different tack. He must've assumed Samuel would know exactly where the weapon was hidden. He went to work for the uncle knowing that Samuel would eventually show up at the farm. I believe he spent months worming his way into the old man's trust."

"Son of a bitch!" Zack said. "And, we lit the match."

"What?"

Zack pounded his fist on the steering wheel. "Unbelievable! We scared Samuel into coming here. We even told him about Sergei. He's afraid of what might happen if the United States or Russia get hold of this thing."

"Wouldn't you be?"

Zack didn't answer. Instead he filled Kwame in on what had happened the night before as he passed a sign that read:

Seahouses, 19 km.

"Damn! I think I know what he's planning. He's going to try and dump that thing into the North Sea."

"Msaliti will never allow that to happen. Zack, you've got to stop him!"

"I'm one step ahead of you buddy boy. Time for some direct action." He mashed the accelerator and passed three of the cars in front of him.

He never noticed the black sedan behind him. The same black sedan that had been following Samuel and Zack since they'd left the hotel.

CHAPTER Forty-Eight

The English countryside was a stark contrast to the terrain Samuel had been accustomed to all his life. Africa is a continent of diverse landscapes, but life in the Northern Hemisphere had developed on a completely different trajectory. For one thing, there was green grass everywhere. Many of the trees were identifiable, but just as many were not. He and Jenga had seen little wildlife other than sheep, various kinds of fowl, and, on one occasion, a spotted deer. Wide open hilly glens where sheep grazed were interspersed with thick forests. Often a side road appeared from out of nowhere, seemingly less traveled than the one they were on this morning. Signs pointed to unseen inns and pubs down those roads, and were it not for the task at hand, Samuel would have been tempted to explore more than one of them.

"Sammy, tell me again where it is that we are going?" Jenga asked.

"I told you... to a place called Lindisfarne."

"I looked it up on the map. There doesn't seem to be anything there worth visiting."

Samuel checked the speedometer; the last thing he needed was to be pulled over for a traffic violation, especially when he was this close to the end of his journey. "*Ah*, but there you are wrong, Jenga. This was the home to one of England's greatest saints. A man by the name of Cuthbert led a group of Christians here when England was still largely a pagan land. I read about him back in Durham."

Jenga scratched his head. "I didn't know you were so religious."

"My father was. I think he would have wanted me to come. Besides," Samuel glanced at Jenga, "Lindisfarne was also where the Vikings first invaded England."

"Still," Jenga added with a shrug of indifference, "I'm curious why we should go there when the great Scottish city of Edinburgh is so close."

Samuel offered a practiced laugh, not about to tell Jenga the real reason for his trip to the island. "Humor me, Jenga. We will only stay a day or two. I want us to charter a boat and tackle the North Sea for an afternoon. That will be exciting, no?"

"Excitement? Is that why you wish to go out to sea. Or is there another reason?"

Samuel laughed again, a bit more forced this time. "What other possible reason could I have?"

"Perhaps to dispose of the poison you unearthed last night?"

If it were not for the cars behind him Samuel would have come to a screeching halt.

"What on earth are you talking about?" He glanced at his friend, only this time Jenga was holding a small pistol.

"Jenga! Where did you get that thing?" The grin that Jenga had on his face was something that Samuel was more accustomed to seeing on the jackals he'd help track down over the years: dealers in blood diamonds, human traffickers, and drug smugglers.

"England is no different than back home. Anything can be found here… for a price. I took a bit of a side tour in one of the seamier back alleys in York. Why are you slowing down, Sammy? Keep your foot on the gas, and do everything I tell you."

"Jenga, I do not understand. Why do you point that gun at me?"

"Simple, Sammy. I want the weapon."

"What weapon? I have no such weapon."

"Cut the pretense, Sammy. I know exactly what you have. Your father buried it during the war, and now you have it. I thought when I mentioned to you that I was coming to Durham your interest would be piqued. I was right. I do not know why you suddenly changed our travel date, but all the better for me. I assume you have it in your suitcase?"

Samuel usually could take command of most any situation, but this time he was the one who'd been betrayed. "I am telling you that I do not know what you are talking about. Have you gone mad, Kwame?"

Kwame simply smiled. "You may stop calling me by that name. My name is Msaliti. Now, keep your eyes on the road," Msaliti barked, "and do as I tell you!"

Samuel stared at the road in front of him, hardly registering the trees and hedges that went by. "I do not understand."

Msaliti laughed. "Your father would have. It is funny, no? All these years you have been the traitor, and now, your new best friend has—what is it the Americans say—'pulled one over on you.'" Msaliti laughed. "You were much easier to fool than I had presumed you would be. I suppose it helped that I had earned your gullible uncle's trust while I waited for you to come home." Jenga never took his eyes off Samuel. "How in hell's name did you ever deceive so many, Sammy? You have quite the reputation, you know."

"How do you…"

"How do I what?" He laughed again. "How do I know that you are the Judas Owl? I am smarter than you thought, no? Also a good actor. You and that old fool bought the entire act." He cocked his head slightly to the side. "You are quite famous among some of my associates, Sammy. They would have paid me dearly to know what I know." He raised the gun slightly. "But I believe what is in your possession is far more valuable. My brothers and I have planned many years how to find what our fathers were too afraid to claim for themselves."

Samuel's grip tightened on the steering wheel. He was looking for a way to crash the vehicle into a wall or a tree without setting off whatever booby-trap the Nazi Sturmbannführer had placed within the box. *"Our fathers?" Jenga's real name… Msaliti… Oh my God!* "Msaliti," he repeated, his brain feeling as if it were on fire. "Msaliti! The son of my father's evil brother!" Samuel had mistakenly thought this jackal's grin couldn't grow any larger.

"Evil? Is that not a religious term, cousin? I thought you said you were not religious."

"I may not be religious, but I have seen evil up close. I just never thought…"

"What, that you would be the one betrayed? Looks like the great Judas Owl has lost his wings."

"How did you do it, Jenga? How did you find me?" Jenga' laughter was more than just annoying as the shock at having been bested started to dissipate. What he needed was to keep the man talking, keep him distracted, find a way to turn the advantage.

"My father kept up with your family. He had originally thought you were all killed during the insurrection. That was long before my time. Too bad, really. I would have enjoyed being a Mau Mau, I think." He shrugged. "Although, in the end, they were too stupid to think they could win against the Brits. *Ah*, but I digress, do I not? My father discovered years later—I do not know how, nor do I care—that his nephew had survived, that's you by the way. When I grew old enough, I figured that your father might have told you the location of the poison. My father knew it was in the cemetery at Durham Cathedral, but that was all. You see, his memory had grown dim."

"And so you followed me there last night?"

"I couldn't very well go digging up an entire graveyard now, could I? Even the Brits would have noticed if I had done that. Besides, you don't know how much joy I have taken in getting you to trust me. Making certain that I had plenty of antivenom for when I deceived you into thinking the snakes had left the falls."

Samuel turned to glare at him. "You son of a bitch!"

"My mother is of no concern to you." He shrugged. "But you are correct. I do not blame my father for having killed her." Up ahead was a wooded area ahead with two picnic tables for travelers wishing to take a break from this monotonous drive. "Pull over."

Samuel shook his head trying to put everything that had happened in place. "Your father killed your mother?"

"Seems we are a family of traitors, no?" He gestured with the pistol. "I said pull over." Samuel took his foot off of the gas. "Besides, I do not blame him. She was takataka."

As Samuel slowed the car, he spat: "From where I am sitting you also are nothing more than trash."

"*Ah*, but I am the trash holding the pistol, am I not? And, after I have our fathers' treasure, I will be very powerful trash, no?"

"Jenga, do you have any idea what horrors are in that box?"

Msaliti's eyes narrowed. "Not horrors for me Sammy. For me it is a lifetime of luxury. With my family connections supplying arms to the people you have made a lifetime betraying, I expect nothing more than the best from now on." He glanced through the windshield. "Up ahead… pull over there."

Samuel thought of refusing when he noticed what Jenga had not, a speeding car behind them recklessly passing a car to pull in dangerously close to their own. Samuel knew the face of the driver. *Two shocks in one day, but this one made sense. Matteson must have been following him all this time.* Pulling into the rest area, Samuel gambled that the agent would follow them into the roadside park and put an end to this. The threat of a world power acquiring the weapon was bad enough, but the idea that a reckless, sell-to-the-highest-bidder-gangster might get hold of the poison was a million times worse. He'd take his chances with the CIA.

Of course, Samuel had no doubt about what his cousin was planning for him once they got out of the car. Msaliti would take him into the woods and shoot him, and then return to the car and figure out a way to smuggle the box back into Africa. Hopefully, Matteson would do what Americans were known for, come in with guns blazing. He'd let the two of them shoot it out, and maybe even find a way to escape with the vials intact. He just needed to keep Jenga's attention long enough for Matteson to pull his car behind and draw his weapon.

"Jenga... Msaliti, whatever your real name is," Samuel said as he pulled up to the picnic tables, "it will not work the way you think. First, how do you think you are possibly going to smuggle that thing back home? You will never make it through security."

"You do not need to concern yourself with that. I have it all figured out, Sammy. I will find someone to take me across the channel to France and then work my way through Spain and then on to Portugal and Algeria and eventually back home."

Samuel shook his head. "You will never make it."

"You seem to underestimate me, Sammy. A man in my business survives by knowing certain people... people who can accomplish most anything." The jackal's grin had returned. "Now, turn off the engine and hand over the keys. Careful, I do not want to have to shoot you just yet, Sammy."

Samuel considered making a play for Msaliti's gun hand but anticipating just such a trick, Msaliti wisely pulled his right arm out of reach as he grabbed the keys with his left. "Now, get out of the car and show me this treasure that you have brought to me."

Samuel's jaw was like iron. "I will not. You keep speaking of this as a treasure. If even half of what my father told me is true, this is not something that you nor I will be able to handle. Jenga… Msaliti, if it is money you want, I have plenty. I will gladly pay you a king's ransom to let me dispose of this thing in the ocean."

"You can't possibly have what I can make from selling it to the highest bidder. I happen to know of a Saudi prince who would love to get his hands on such a weapon."

"You are forgetting about my inheritance. Uncle Osuroo is a wealthy man."

The smaller man nodded. "Yes, he is. But when he hears that his beloved Samuel fell off a tour boat and drowned, he will turn all his affection… and his land… over to the foreman who has become like a son to him, will he not?"

Samuel almost lunged for the man's throat, and would have if he hadn't seen Matteson walking stealthily to the passenger side of the car. He didn't appear to have a weapon, though… that wasn't good. Samuel kept the traitor's eyes focused on him. At some point, Msaliti would have to reach behind him and feel for the door handle. He wouldn't dare take his eyes off Samuel… that would be to the white man's advantage. *If the American was as good as Kwame had said he was, it should be all that Matteson needed to take this bastard out.*

"So, you think I will just hand it to you?" Samuel snapped. "You are a fool. You know nothing. Did your pig of a father not tell you? The box is booby-trapped. Anyone trying to open it without the proper key will be dead in seconds. It would almost be worth it to see you die out here in the middle of nowhere."

"You are lying!"

"You think you are smart." Matteson was inching his way closer. "Wasting all that time working for my uncle, waiting for me to return." Samuel's eyes danced as if in merriment. "I knew you were a little man, but now I see how little you really are. Are you so thick as to think that the man who had the intelligence to create this horrible thing would not have also had the foresight to protect it?"

"Give me the key!" Msaliti demanded.

"You son of a hyena, do you think I would be so dense as to carry such a thing with me? It is well-guarded and nowhere near here."

Msaliti had heard enough. "You will do as I say. Now, get out of the car!"

Samuel slowly did as commanded, and as he'd predicted, the traitorous bastard reached behind him with his left hand, never taking his eyes off his cousin. Just to be sure he had his attention, Samuel leaned into the car and glared threateningly at him. Msaliti had no more than half-way exited the car, when Zack slammed the open door onto his gun hand. Msaliti screamed in agony as the pistol fell harmlessly to the passenger side seat.

Zack thrust his left arm around Msaliti's pencil neck, lifting him to where Msaliti's toes barely touched the ground. "Looks like I got here in the nick of time, Sam. Mind telling me what this is all about?"

"He is not who I thought he was. He was going to kill me."

"To claim the poison and sell it, no doubt?"

Samuel didn't answer. Instead, he was trying to think of a way to turn the tables on both of them.

No one saw the Russian until it was too late.

"Gentlemen, if you will be so kind as to oblige me, I suggest you all take a seat at one of these fine tables someone has had the decency to place here for our services."

Zack knew that voice. *How the hell? Sergei!*

"Please, Mr. Matteson, that fellow in your grasp seems to be in a great deal of anguish. Won't you be so kind as to let him go?"

"Drop the act, Sergei, you don't care about this vermin any more than I do."

Sergei drew closer. "Perhaps not, but then I, for one, believe that we can all settle this in a civilized manner. Now, shall you all take a seat?"

With few other options, Zack turned and pushed Msaliti, now nursing his wrist with his other hand, toward the benches. For his part, Samuel sat on the bench on the opposite side of the table and kept silent. Only a few cars passed by, but the tables were a good ways from the road and Sergei held his pistol at such a strategic angle; no one paid any attention to what looked like a roadside picnic. "Now, gentlemen, it would seem that introductions are in order."

Zack spoke up. "Scum number one, meet scum number two. As for the big man behind me you've probably already figured out who he is."

"Indeed I have," said Sergei in the same courteous tone as before. He nodded to Samuel. "Mr. Kauxho-huena, I presume?" Samuel and Msaliti both lifted their eyes but neither uttered a word. "*Ah*, I quite agree, gentlemen. There is no sense in our making small talk. I really must be taking our little find to a safer place.

"Mr. Matteson and Mr. Kauxhouhena, I will be needing both your keys, if you don't mind."

"Stuff it, Sergei."

Sergei pointed the pistol toward Zack. "I presume that you know I mean business."

Zack's eyes betrayed his intentions and Sergei fired a warning shot into the dirt at Zack's feet. "The next one will be your kneecap, Mr. Matteson. Now, toss me the keys to your car." He glanced at Samuel. "You too." They both did as instructed. "Now, would one of you be so kind as to open the trunk of this vehicle here and place all the luggage into my car."

Samuel stiffened but Zack spoke first. "I'll do it." He stood and made his way to the driver's side of the Corsa and leaned in as if to press the trunk release, but instead grabbed Msaliti's pistol from off the passenger seat. But it was too late, Sergei fired several rounds but all found their way harmlessly into the chassis. It was the chance Samuel had been looking for. He leaped from the table and with his entire body bulldozed the Russian into the dirt, smashing his fist hard against the Russian's chin and knocking him unconscious. He glanced toward the Corsa where Zack was managing to crawl out, still clutching the pistol, but bleeding from his face and arms.

"You're shot," shouted Samuel.

Zack shook his head. "No, just shrapnel from the window. I'm okay."

As one, they both turned to where they had left Msaliti. He had disappeared.

"There!" Samuel shouted, pointing toward a small group of trees. "Grab him!" Zack took off into the woods, which was the chance Samuel had been hoping for. He hurriedly rifled through the unconscious Russian's pockets and took all three sets of keys. Rushing to the coupe, he brushed aside shards of broken glass and climbed behind the wheel.

"Nice try."

Samuel felt the barrel of the pistol pressed against his arm. "What? You're letting him get away? He is a notorious gun-runner; his name is…"

"Yeah, yeah, Msaliti Kauxhohuena. I know all about him." Zack nodded toward the back of the car. "You didn't think I'd leave you with that thing still in the trunk, did you?"

Samuel's shoulders slumped. "Fine, get in."

"Not in this bullet riddled thing I won't. We'd be pulled over by the first cop that saw us. Get the damn box and put it in my car and let's get out of here. He pocketed the gun as Samuel did as instructed and climbed behind the steering wheel of the Ford.

"Which way?"

"I don't care," answered Zack. "Just drive. And on the way you can explain to me just what you were planning to do with Satan's cocktail back there."

CHAPTER Forty-Nine

Samuel drove through the picturesque seaside town called Seahouses wondering what, if anything, had just changed. As far as he was concerned, he had just exchanged one problem for another. Now, instead of a traitorous, gun-running thug, he had a CIA agent for company—the very agent he had come here to avoid. Not only that, but he had been confronted by the Russian that Kwame and Matteson had warned him about. *Life can be very complicated,* he thought, as the image of his father popped into his head. *Baba, I'm going to need your help finishing this.*

Zack watched the Judas Owl carefully, the pistol within easy reach. "So, Msaliti, Gesi, and the rest of your uncle's family had no idea about you?"

Samuel shook his head. "Apparently, they did." He'd filled Matteson in on everything, well almost everything. Matteson didn't know that when he'd picked the Russian's pockets for the keys he'd also secreted the man's pistol as well.

"That Msaliti betrayed my uncle is, believe it or not, the worst part of this for me. My Uncle Osuroo is the kindest, gentlest man you would ever wish to know. That such a man almost acquired the box. It is unthinkable."

"Let me guess, you plan on dropping it into the sea?"

Samuel's hand fell to his side, where he could feel the small gun in his pocket "That would be my preference, yes. But I suspect you have other plans?"

Zack stared out the passenger window at some people walking past bright blue and yellow shops. He was quiet for a moment, allowing Samuel to slowly slip his hand inside the pocket. At last, Zack shook his head and said, "No, not really. Probably the best plan, under the circumstances."

Samuel noticed his own eyebrows arch in the rearview mirror. "Do you mean it?"

Shifting his weight, Zack reached inside his pocket for a small bag of candy. "Yeah, I mean it. What does Washington need with another weapon of mass destruction?"

Samuel pulled his hand out of his pocket. "Your superiors would approve?"

"My superiors don't know anything about this. I operate under my own rules sometimes, and I think this is one of those times. What they don't know won't hurt me."

"And the Russian?"

Zack grinned and rubbed his knuckles thinking about how he'd wished he'd been the one to hit Sergei — something he'd been longing to do since Ali Sabieh. "He sure as hell doesn't need to get hold of that stuff. He gave Kwame and me some sort of long story about a group of Russians searching for your father's box to destroy it, but to tell you the truth I never fully bought into it. There's more to Sergei than meets the eye. But with your magic elixir in the drink I don't think he and I will ever cross paths again."

"I have to admit, I didn't expect you to support me in this."

"Why not?"

Samuel reached up to scratch his neck. "The CIA doesn't have the best track record with us."

"Us?"

"Africans."

Zack rolled his eyes. "Not you, too? I've already had the lecture from Kwame. Don't blame me if we may not have been as attentive as you would have liked."

"Not as attentive? Are you familiar with America's track record in coming to our aid, Mr. Matteson? It is pitiful. Where was America when Rwanda turned into a hell on earth? Where was America when AIDS killed nearly a quarter of the people in some of our largest cities and towns? I do not see your soldiers taking on the scourge of terrorists in this country the way you do in those nations with rich oil fields."

"Okay," Zack countered, "but there's something else you don't see. What about the millions of Americans who contribute billions of dollars to things like hunger relief in Africa? What about the Peace Corps volunteers who've been coming over here for half a century to help people learn how to irrigate dry fields and rotate crops so that the land won't be used up? And what about the thousands of medical missions that American churches send over here? And as for soldiers, hey we tried in Somalia, remember?"

"Yes, and your President Bush ran at the first sign of trouble. President Clinton was no better, bombing aspirin factories to get the voters mind off of his sexual affair with a subordinate."

Zack looked away. He, too, thought America had blown a real chance to set things straight in Somalia where tens, perhaps hundreds of thousands had died from war and starvation. "Look," he finally said, "America has got its faults; hell, all countries do. But *I'm* the one that's here now. I'm the one who just saved your bacon, remember? Like it or not, buddy boy, I'm all you've got right now!"

Samuel stared stone-faced out the windshield as he drove. After a full minute he sighed. "You are right. You saved my life and if you are being truthful about allowing me to dispose of that damned thing in the boot then I owe you a debt of gratitude."

"Say that again."

"What?"

Zack grinned. "That part about me being right. I seldom get to hear that. Kwame would sooner choose thumbscrews than admitting I was right about something, and my usual partner, well… that's a whole other story."

Samuel wasn't sure how to take this American. Brash, cocky, arrogant as hell but there was something in the man's blue eyes… kindness perhaps?

Samuel had learned to read a person's eyes over the years; they were always a dead giveaway of an opponent's true intentions. Maybe Zack Matteson was one of the good guys after all.

"I don't run into very many Americans. In fact, you are the first in a long, long time. Most of my work has been in conjunction with the Europeans. They have been the ones fighting the blood-diamond trade and the slave camps."

Zack frowned. "Sure, because they didn't want the money going to the Chinese syndicates. All that money filters back to Beijing one way or the other. The Chinese want Africa in a big way, and they will keep taking it piece by piece until they have a strangle hold over the entire continent."

"While America does nothing."

Zack rolled his eyes. "Let's don't start that again. Listen, I'm sure that after this is over I could use someone like you in the future. I've heard a lot of interesting things about the Judas Owl. Maybe we can help one another."

"Me, work for America?"

"Why not? I could use a man such as you. Plus, the money would be good."

"I have plenty of money."

"Okay, so how about for the sake of helping rid the world of evil? Americans aren't the bad guys you seem to think we are."

Samuel turned and searched Zack's eyes. Matteson believed what he was saying. Samuel offered a shrug. "Perhaps if your country had shown an interest ten years ago, but I am retired now."

A knowing smile spread across Zack's face. "Sam, people like us… we never retire."

CHAPTER Fifty

Sergei's head throbbed, but he had known worse. He sat up, took stock of his condition, and then stood to dust himself off. *How long had he been unconscious?* He looked around for any sign of the other three, but they had disappeared along with Matteson's car. No doubt the gun-runner was hiding in the woods and Matteson and the son of Osmann Kauxhohuena were on their way to who knows where.

A coupe and two lorries passed, but no one paid him any attention. He checked his watch; he had been out for nearly an hour. Without keys, the two cars, still parked as if their occupants had stopped for a leisurely picnic, were useless to him.

"Chert!" he cursed aloud. *He had come so close, so very close.* His organization had searched for decades for the poison. Most had died during the process, yet the mission had remained for the select few who knew their founder's real intention. He happened to be one of them.

Okhotniki, the name which the founders had given themselves, were Leninists; holdovers from a time before Stalin. The war had nearly seen Russia obliterated by the Germans. The Americans and British had held them off by forcing the Nazis to stage a war on two fronts, giving the Stavka time to regroup and turn the tide of the war at home. But the West was soon at Russia's doorstep.

Russia's leaders had panicked. The West could not be allowed to roll their tanks into Poland and into the motherland as Germany had done.

Rumors had been that America was on the brink of harnessing a weapon of mass destruction. The founders of Okhotniki had no doubt that America would unleash it upon Japan first, but—or so the thinking was at the time—what would prevent them from striking Leningrad next? It was that type of thinking that set the stage for the cold war. By the time of Perestroika in the 1980s, a new strategy had taken hold amongst the Okhotniki.

Sergei rubbed his head and checked his suit for traces of blood against the white linen. "Okhotniki," he said aloud. "*Hunters* to the end." But was this the end? While he hunted for the same object that the founders had, his people had done so for an entirely different reason. He had seen enough of war... Afghanistan, Georgia, Moldova. He had gladly accepted the offer the Okhotniki made him before retiring as a colonel in the Russian army. Knowing what he did now about his predecessors, it was a good thing, too. They assassinated anyone who turned them down.

He had risen to serve as head of the secret organization as more and more of the founders died off. Weapons of mass destruction were nothing new these days, but this one had a potential that not even the evil Sturmbannführer Hans Kreps had known about. Later investigation of the village that Kreps had experimented on showed that the poison contained lingering properties which, after lying dormant for months, could remerge and keep on killing. In fact, it had done just that six years after Kreps had unleashed his demon.

An unprotected Russian investigative team had gone in search of the village to gather evidence of the nerve agent only to come in contact with the remnants of the poison. It hadn't killed them instantly this time. Whatever chemical changes nature had affected upon this devil's brew had caused it to slowly turn a man's internal organs into mush. Sergei shuddered even now. *To think that his predecessors had intended to synthesize this poison and add it to Russia's arsenal should the West attack was mind boggling. It would have been sheer madness. No country would have been immune. Nor would they now if Matteson and the African could not be stopped. Sure, the CIA man seemed to have good intentions, as did this man known by his enemies as the Judas Owl; but if the American was able to talk the Kenyan into giving him the poison then Matteson would only turn it over to bureaucrats at Langley. God knows what they would do with it!*

Sergei walked to the side of the road. The chances of his finding Matteson and the Judas Owl were slim at best; still, what else was there to do but try? He stuck his thumb out and climbed into the first lorry that pulled to the side of the road.

"Where to, mate?"

The perfect question.

If only he knew.

CHAPTER Fifty-One

Half a century. That was how long this abominable thing in Samuel's hands had been an unknown threat to the world. They had asked the captain to stop the small boat without explaining why. In a moment they would drop the metal box into the North Sea.

Zack and Samuel had fastened a large stone to the top of the box and then wrapped it with several layers of waterproof duct tape they'd purchased from a hardware store in Seahouses. If either man had known what Sergei did about the lasting effects of the poison, they might have taken even more precautions. But even now, they both privately wondered what the effects of the sea might be over time and what might happen if the vials inside the box ever broke open.

Samuel leaned over the stern of the fishing boat they had chartered and opened his hands. "For you, Baba." Then they both watched as the box long buried in Durham Cathedral's cemetery now sank to its forever grave. "It is finished," Samuel said, aware of the religious overtones.

He turned to Zack, whose jet-black hair was blowing in the sea-breeze. "Thank you," he said, a single tear channeling its way down his right cheek.

"In for a penny, in for a pound, I suppose."

"So, Mr. Matteson, what happens now?"

Zack looked across his shoulder at the tiny dots behind them. Out here, past the green-and-brown hues of the Farne Islands, all was strangely quiet. Even the sea birds overhead were strangely silent as if they sensed the solemnity of what had taken place. "Not really sure. I guess you go home and I go back to Camp Lemonnier."

The man known as the Judas Owl inhaled a deep breath and then slowly released it. Fifty years... now, at last, it was over. A lone tear fell slowly down his cheek.

"Hey, I can get in trouble for that!" They turned to see the captain of the vessel standing behind them.

"For what?" Zack said innocently, trying to figure out whether the man was truly as wizened as his face and hands looked or if years in the sun robbed him of his youth.

"Dumpin' that box into the sea, that's what." He frowned. "I assume it was someone's ashes. Ya' canna' do that out here. People 'ave to 'ave a permit for that sort of thing."

Samuel wiped the tear from his eye. "I apologize," he said. "You see, it was all that was left of my father. He was killed many years ago in a rebellion in my home country. He served the British Army during the War. He was even stationed for a time in Durham. This just seemed a fitting tribute to me."

The seaman looked down at the well-worn deck and cleared his throat. "Well, I suppose I can overlook it, bein' he was a patriot. My granddad died in the war, as well." *Younger than he looks,* noted Zack.

"We didn't know the rules about such things. We're sorry," lied Zack.

"Ach, I s'pose there's no harm," the captain said looking out to sea. "Ya' picked a good spot for it; the water is some 60 fathoms here."

Samuel nodded. The deeper the better.

The sun continued its dance from behind the clouds and then back again as the three men gazed silently out to sea, the captain giving the presumed mourners a moment for reflection.

"So," the captain finally said with a knowing grin, "I know you two said you aren't interested in fishing, but while we are out here, do you want to see something spectacular? I can tak' ya' to a place no one else goes where it seems the heavens and the sea jes' melt together as one."

Zack nodded to Samuel. "Up to you, Sam."

Samuel looked above where a solitary bird was flying circles overhead. He took another deep, cleansing breath before smiling. "Yes. Yes, that sounds perfect. Show us just such a place."

CHAPTER Fifty-Two

Seething and barely able to control his anger, Msaliti drove to the nearest petrol station where he purchased a map and filled the tank. It had been easy enough to thumb a ride from the first little old lady who'd happened to pass by… a lady whose body was now in the boot. Killing the old woman hadn't calmed his anger the way he had hoped, and even now, standing beside her ancient Ford, Msaliti's hands were shaking with rage.

How could this be? He had planned everything so carefully. He had spent years trying to find the Judas Owl, always careful never to reveal his cousin's identity to the terrorists and thugs to whom he and his brothers sold arms. Despite the barrage of questions he peppered his customers with each time the Owl had gotten the better of them, Msaliti had come no closer to finding him. It was by sheer coincidence that he had been able to discover that Samuel had once taught at the University of Nairobi. After searching his name on the internet for the umpteenth time, he saw a Samuel Kauxhohuena in an ancient listing of former professors. He had traveled to Nairobi and bribed a low-level records keeper to allow him to look at Samuel's file. The folder was worn and smelled of mold, but there was a listing of the next of kin at the bottom of his personnel record: Osuroo Bankole. Residence: Archer's Post.

As Jenga the experienced farmhand, it hadn't taken him long to fool the old man. In less time than he'd imagined, Jenga was able to work his way into Osuroo's good graces. He had reasoned that Samuel would eventually pay his uncle a visit, and when he did, he would charm his way into betraying the infamous betrayer himself. How often he had lain in bed late at night devising ways in which he could ingratiate himself to the Judas Owl. The snake had been nothing short of a stroke of genius. Carrying the antivenom to the waterfall that day had allowed him to save his cousin's life. Just as Msaliti had predicted, Samuel was putty in his hands from that moment on.

But now, to have it all come crushing down when he was so close, so damned close! He slammed his hand against the hood of the vehicle causing people filling their cars to stop and stare at him. *This was no good. He needed to calm down, and he needed to go somewhere and think. The weapon was lost, as was the fortune he would have made from selling it. What he needed to do now was find a quiet place and get hold of himself so that he could plan his next move. The money he would have made from the Nazi poison might be gone, but he knew where he could find more. No, not the tens of millions he had hoped for, but at least enough to take the sting out of all this.*

He would return to Archer's Post where he would take both his reward and his revenge.

****

The return flight from Manchester was the antithesis of what Samuel's flight into England had been. It was as if a giant stone had been lifted from his chest. *More like a boulder*, Samuel thought… *a boulder such as the one his father had hidden him behind so long ago.* A child's guilt can be a terrible thing to carry all one's life and it wasn't until the plane lifted off the tarmac that Samuel realized just how much guilt he'd suppressed over the years. There was nothing he could have done to stop his baba that day; his father had done what every good father would have done—protected his child.

For years, though, Samuel questioned why he had been spared. He'd often wondered if the universe had destined him to stand against the evil in his country. "Always stand against wrong," his father had told him. Hadn't he done that? For decades he had infiltrated blood-diamond gangs, terrorist cells, human-trafficking rings. But it had never seemed to be enough. There were always more groups, more criminals, more terrorists. Perhaps there would always be. But sitting in the window seat of the 757 and watching the British Isles disappear behind him, Samuel felt a strange sensation. It was one he had never felt before, not even when he'd come home to visit Uncle Osuroo and Archer's Post. It was a feeling of peace.

The poison was forever gone. His father's burden had been lifted. Staring out the window at the clouds below, Samuel was aware of just how it had been his burden too. Strangely, releasing the box into the deep had become the key to something new, something longed for, but something for which he'd never had the words to express.

Key?

Yes, there was one more task to be done: dispose of the key that had hung like a weight of shame and grief around his neck for years as a child, reminding him of the moment his father had placed it there. Even when as a teenager he'd had the courage to remove it, the key kept drawing him back. Just the very thought of it reminded him of his father's sacrifice during the war as well as what had happened behind the boulders. It wasn't until now that he realized just how much he'd hated the damned thing, not just for what it had the potential to unleash, but for the pain and grief it had caused his family.

The key had also been a link, the only physical one to his father and a time long past. As he peered out the window at the bushland surrounding Jomo Kenyatta International Airport, he realized he had a much more important link—the pledge his father had charged him with: *Always be brave and always stand against wrong.*

****

"I don't like it, Zack. This thing is far from over." Before calling Donna, Zack had phoned Kwame to tell him that he'd seen Samuel off at the airport. "Msaliti is not just going to walk away," Kwame said. "He will want money and he will most certainly want vengeance. You cost him a king's ransom by throwing that thing into the sea."

Zack laughed as he walked into the airport candy shop. "What's he going to do, track me down at Langley? I don't think so." Zack set two bags of jellybeans on the checkout counter and reached for a few loose pounds in his pocket. "Anyway, what harm can he possibly…" The realization of what Kwame was trying to tell him sunk in. "Oh, my God! You don't think he would do *that*, do you?"

"That's exactly what I'm thinking."

Zack threw down the money, snatched the bag of candy and dashed out of the store to the nearest ticketing booth. Whatever the next flight was to Nairobi, he was going to be on it.

****

Osuroo was frying bacon in small pieces to add to the spiced coconut stew. He had made a pot large enough to freeze some for when Samuel and Jenga arrived home next week. He sorely missed them both. He had gotten accustomed to having someone around the farm, and the past few months with Samuel home had felt nothing short of heaven on earth. He drained the bacon on a paper towel and crumbled the meat into the stew.

He glanced out the kitchen window as twilight fell across his beloved land. Even now he knew what Samuel did not, that his nephew would not stay. There would come a day when someone would come calling… the French, the Poles, who knew. And when they did, Samuel would answer the call. His nephew could no more help being who he was any more than the giraffe could help having a long neck or the lion its mane. One day he would go. But he would always come back. The land would not relinquish its call upon his heart. Archer's Post was every bit as much a part of Samuel as it was Osuroo.

The Samburu had a phrase for it. *Mipaka damu*. It was difficult to translate into English. Blood-bond didn't quite capture it. It had more to do the soul being tied to a physical place, and that no matter how far one roamed there was always a connection. Samuel had *mipaka damu*. Of that his uncle was certain.

As the old man cooked, he was unaware of the pair of eyes fixed on him from behind. The eyes watched him as he sliced the onions and added them to the stew, stirring them gently as if they needed coaxing to release their flavor and blend with the beans and the bacon.

"Salt, where is the salt?" he muttered as he searched the counter next to the ancient stove. Gemma had always restricted his salt intake but he had added it liberally all these years with no apparent ill effect. "Now, where could I have put it?" He turned toward the table where he had eaten his last meal and immediately clutched his chest. "My Lord! You gave me such a start. I wasn't expecting you back today!"

"I am sorry, Baba," apologized Samuel. "It was rude of me not to announce my presence." Samuel set his suitcase on the floor beside him and gave his uncle a hug.

"I didn't expect you to be back until next week." He held Samuel at an arms-length and then pulled him back again. "Samuel, you are a sight for sore eyes. I have missed you terribly." The men embraced a second and then a third time. "Sit down; you must be hungry. I will fry more bacon. Tonight we will have a feast. I am making one of your favorites."

"Not coconut stew?!"

Osuroo beamed from ear to ear. "And with bacon! Your auntie never let me put in bacon... or salt," he said remembering what he had been searching for.

"It is over there by the breadbox," said Samuel. "I hope you are not adding too much, Baba; you know it is not good for you."

Osuroo looked behind him to find the green-and-silver salt shaker that had once been his mother's. "I never know where I leave things," he said with a laugh. "Good thing they don't ask me to be in charge of the nursery at the church. No one would ever find their little ones."

"Sit, Samuel, sit. Tell me all about your trip. You and Jenga must have had a grand time... Jenga! Where is he? Don't tell me he's already gone to check on the farm in the dark." He shook his head. "That man will never rest."

Samuel took a deep breath. "No, Baba, Jenga is not here." He pulled out one of the kitchen chairs. "Come, let us both sit down. I have something to tell you."

CHAPTER Fifty-Three

While Samuel slept soundly in his old bedroom, Osuroo tossed and turned most of the night. Unable to rest, he quietly climbed out of bed so as not to wake Samuel and padded down the hall to the kitchen. It would not be daylight for at least another two hours. The old man wiped his eyes and stumbled to the cabinet where he kept the coffee. As quietly as he could, he turned on the stove and filled the ancient, blue-speckled kettle with water. Samuel had purchased him a modern coffee-maker, but as with so many things, Osuroo still preferred the old ways. Plus, he had told his nephew, coffee tasted like coffee when it was made the old-fashioned way.

He poured himself a cup, adding a single spoonful of honey, before sitting down next to the open window. In the distance he could hear the soft churring of a nightjar calling to its mate. Gemma used to wake early—though never quite this early—to start the breakfast. How many times had he told her that she should sleep in and not make so much of a fuss? He could still hear her telling him to hush. "I like this time of day," she would usually say. "It is so peaceful… that is until *your* feet hit the floor."

Like so many times before, Osuroo wished for Gemma to be with him now. He sighed. *Jenga? How could he have so misjudged him?* He had been lonely, that's how.

He never wanted to admit it, but growing old and being alone had taken a toll. Plus, the farm had fallen into disrepair. He had needed Jenga in so many ways, which was why he had fallen to the man's charms. *Nothing but lies!* He ran his fingers over the key on the table. The same key Samuel had brought out last night as part of his story… a story he had never shared before. *What a burden this must have been all these years.*

Osuroo closed his eyes and could still see the child from the past and how for years he never parted with this key to the very gates of hell. He had assumed it was merely a memento for Samuel, a reminder of his father. *If only he had pressed the matter, maybe he could have helped lighten the load his beloved child had carried.*

"What is that you are holding, old man?" A voice which had once been welcomed at this table now sent an icy chill down Osuroo's spine.

Osuroo turned. "Jenga!"

"From the look in your eyes, you already know that is not my name." The voice was familiar, but this was not the same man he had trusted so blindly. The wild expression was the same as the hyena when it had separated its prey from the rest of the herd. "You still haven't told me what that is? The key to the cellar, perhaps? The same cellar where you keep your important papers… the ones that will allow me access to your bank accounts and land after I kill you." The rage was replaced with another, one of glee. "You do not know how long I have waited for this, old man."

"You are nothing but *utapeli*; I see that now."

Msaliti laughed. "You call me scum, while you sit here on this land counting your fortunes, pretending to be a simple man, the ancestor of Samburu warriors." Msaliti pulled the pistol from his waistband. "You are nothing but a foolish old man."

"Killing me will do you no good; they will come after you."

"You delude yourself. After I burn your precious house down around you, they will not think to look at your neck, which I will have sliced just before doing the same to the Judas Owl."

Osuroo's eyes grew twice their normal size. "You dare call him that!" Osuroo stood, leaning against the chair for support. *If he was going to die, he would die like a man, standing up and facing his enemy.* "It is you, Jenga, who are the traitor. You clod of jackal-dung... *you* are the Judas!"

"You speak brave words, for one who is about to have his throat slit. Let us see just how brave you are." Msaliti slowly unsheathed the dagger he had brought with him.

"Those papers," Osuroo said, knowing that he was about to die but not willing to afford his foe any satisfaction, "they will do you no good, even if you escape being captured."

Msaliti's eyes danced. "Oh, but there you are wrong, old man. You of all people should know about Eliezer's Law. It comes from that precious Bible of yours. The Samburu adopted it centuries ago."

It fell on Osuroo like a ton of bricks. Eliezer's Law was the tradition amongst the Samburu that when a man died leaving no heirs, the inheritance fell upon the foreman of his land. Osuroo's eyes suddenly appeared as stone and his chin as granite. "I *have* an heir!"

"Not for long, old fool; not for long."

The sneer of his betrayer was the last thing Osuroo would see, that was his only regret. His muscles tensed to spring at his attacker even though he knew it would be futile. Suddenly, from out of the darkened hallway, a blur so fast that it caught both men by surprise flew at Msaliti sending him head-over-foot onto the tile floor. *Samuel had awakened and had heard everything!* Both gun and knife went sprawling across the floor. Msaliti tried to defend himself but he was no match for the sheer strength and rage of the bigger man. Soon, Samuel had Msaliti pinned on his back with both of his huge hands around the neck of this treacherous bastard.

Osuroo watched in horror as the scene unfolded in front of him. Jenga's eyes began to bulge as his arms flailed uselessly at his side. In a few seconds it would be over.

"Samuel!"

Osuroo said it again. "Samuel!"

Samuel glanced at him, his vow of never taking another life on the verge of being broken.

Osuroo uttered the one word Samuel had not expected; the only word that would break the spell of a lifetime of pent-up grief and rage.

"Gemma."

The expression on Samuel's face assured Osuroo that it was all he needed to say. Jenga's eyes no longer bulged as Samuel loosened his grip. "Get his weapons,"

Samuel said, able to breathe himself now. "Then call the police. We will turn this scum over to them."

"There will be no need for that." Startled, Osuroo and Samuel turned to the open kitchen door where a tall, spindly man who was more legs than anything else smiled at them. "I tried to get here in time to protect you, but I can see there was no need."

"Baba, this is Kwame," Samuel said, grateful for the intrusion. "He is a good man. I have worked with him many times."

Relieved that the second man was not a threat, Osuroo bent over to pick up the pistol. The sudden distraction caused Samuel to relax his grip too early, confident that the battle was over. Far from it! Msaliti sprang from the floor and snatched the pistol away from the old man's fingers. In one motion he turned and fired. Kwame fell as Msaliti aimed the pistol at Samuel, daring him to make a move. With his left hand he rubbed his throat.

"So now, old man. Watch how your precious Samuel dies." He grinned a hyena's grin. "When word reaches certain people that I have killed the Judas Owl, I will be rewarded nearly as much as I will by selling your property."

He aimed and two shots fired quickly... neither from his raised weapon. The foreman's head jerked forward with the impact of the first bullet. The second round proved unnecessary.

A white man stepped out of the shadows.

"Matteson!"

Zack rushed to Kwame's side. To his, and everyone's, surprise, Kwame was laughing. "You take the back door, I'll go through the front," he said, imitating Zack. "Next time, Matteson, *you* go through the back door."

The bullet had gone straight through Kwame's torso, missing all his vital organs. Osuroo telephone the Samburu medicine man; he was experienced at stabilizing a wounded man until they could get him to the hospital. The medicine man would earn Osuroo's finest bottle of Scotch tonight.

"You had me worried there for a minute," said Zack as Samuel knelt to press fresh kitchen towels against the open wounds.

"Elevate his legs above his heart so that he does not go into shock, Mr. Matteson." They turned as one to see a short, rather squat man in a white suit holding a Russian MP-443 straight at them. At this distance, Sergei could not miss. "Slide your firearm toward me, Mr. Matteson. You too, sir," he said politely to Osuroo. "Slide me that pistol… oh, and the knife, as well. Do not fear. I intend no harm to you or your nephew."

"What about us?" Zack spat.

"*Ahh*, yes… what about you? From the very beginning, you have caused me nothing but trouble. I suppose my predecessors would have simply shot you for interfering, but…" he paused and then shrugged.

"But what?" said Kwame, his eyes focused on Sergei's sidearm, one commonly used by Russian troops in the field.

"Have not too many people died in the pursuit of… what was it your father called it, Mr. Kauxhohuena? 'Hell's elixir,' wasn't it?"

Samuel stared in disbelief at the man in white suit. "How could you possibly know that?"

Zack rubbed his chin. "Don't bother, Sam. That guy's got connections you wouldn't believe."

Sergei smiled as he glanced at the kitchen table. "I assume this is the key that will open the cursed box?"

"It won't do you any good, Sergei," said Zack. "Samuel dropped it into the sea. You'll never find it."

Sergei nodded, but without the former smile. "I assumed as much." He stared at Samuel. "You are no Judas, Mr. Kauxhohuena. If anything, you are a savior. While Mr. Matteson may not believe me, I am grateful that the poison is gone. I just hope it remains that way for eternity." He turned his gaze to Zack. "Yet, you and Mr. Matteson both know where you released it; I'm not comfortable with that."

"I will tell no one," said Samuel. It was more a statement of conviction than an attempt to placate the Russian's fears.

"I believe you. But, Mr. Matteson here works for an organization that is less trustworthy." Still training the pistol on the small band, he reached with his other hand for the key and placed it in his pocket. "This is not as much assurance as I would have liked, but it will have to do." He grinned at Zack. "Not much to show for decades of searching, but I will have to take what I can get, *eh*?"

Zack returned the grin. He, too, was a hunter. And he would never allow anyone to go after the box in the North Sea. Especially not Sergei. As if reading his thoughts, Sergei cocked his head to one side. "I see that you trust me as much as I trust you, Mr. Matteson. I assure you… our secret is safe with me as long as it remains just that—*our* secret." He gestured toward Kwame. Take care of your friend."

"Till we meet again, Sergei." Zack's faux grin had melted into stone-cold determination.

"Let us both hope that never happens." With that, Sergei slipped through the darkness of the living room and out the front door into the night.

CHAPTER Fifty-Four

Seventeen Years Later

A hornbill flew lazily over a lone figure on the hill standing next to a freshly dug grave. Nearby, a lizard attempted to catch a fly but missed.

The view from here had always been the most magnificent at dusk, especially at that precise moment when the kapok trees turned black and the distant hills somehow seemed to stretch up to the very heavens themselves. Below, he watched as young giraffes folded their spindly legs under their bodies and rested their heads upon their backs, while the adults kept guard. In the distance he heard a hyena calling for its pack. The man sighed. He had no pack to call, no one to go home to, not since Osuroo had died. His grave was only meters away. Samuel had buried him here on the hill he had cherished so. Even at 94, Uncle Osuroo's death had left a crater-sized hole in Samuel's heart. He remembered the first time he'd felt that way—that night hiding amongst the boulders behind his burning house.

Samuel glanced at the fresh earth covering his own grave. Better that Matteson and the others thought him dead. He was too old now to continue the work of the Judas Owl. He needed to tend to his land, the land his uncle had left to him. It had fallen into disrepair after his uncle's death and while he had been away... again. At least he had been there for several weeks before Uncle Osuroo had died.

That's odd, he thought as he noticed a small envelope under a rock at the foot of the grave. He leaned down slowly and raised up even more slowly. It was just part of getting old. He slipped the envelope out of a plastic sleeve, tore it open, and read:

> *Don't worry, your secret is safe with me...*
> <u>*For now.*</u> *Z.M.*

How had Matteson known? How had anyone known? The Samburu weren't about to tell anyone who the old man was working the farm these days. Doubtful any of them even knew.

He stared at the note. Well, obviously someone did.

Matteson would honor his word, at least until something came up when he needed a favor. Samuel looked off into the distance. Of course he still had contacts, he still heard things, and he still could pass information on if there was a need. It would have to be something big, though, something mammoth. He shrugged. Like the adult giraffes in the valley below, Samuel knew that someone had to keep watch. There were always predators ready to pounce if given an opportunity.

He wondered, and not for the first time, just how much evil had been prevented by people like his father; people dedicated to the good, to the well-being of others. What was it his father had said that night, that horrible night behind the boulder? *Always be brave, and always stand against wrong.* Samuel gazed toward the hills in the distance, trying unsuccessfully to distinguish their crests from the darkening clouds above.

"I hope I have made you *both* proud, Baba," he said to the heavens, his eyes moist with the memory of the two men he'd had the good fortune to call by that name.

Samuel started down the hill as the sun set in the Kenyan sky. Somewhere behind him came the familiar but distant call of a solitary owl.

Acknowledgements

There are so many people who contributed in some fashion or another to this novel. My wife, Diane, for her love and support, my kids and grandkids, and of course my parish family as well. I owe so much to my editor, Peggy Shaw, for her corrections and her kind suggestions, and to my friends for their continued encouragement. Thank you also to Michele Burdell for a final readthrough. I would be remiss if I did not thank all the many Father Flenn fans these past few years. I trust that they will enjoy following along as Flenn's partner, Zack Matteson, has a couple of adventures of his own.

www.fatherflenn.com

Scott Arnold